Then came Earth.

It was a diamond floating among brilliant stones. An enormous blue, shimmering jewel, outstanding against the blackness of space. Mouth agape, his nose nearly pressed against the shuttle's main window, Hunter imagined he could see a white-hot halo surrounding the planet. There was no mistaking that one was in the presence of something great. This place *looked* like the center of the Galaxy.

"The first spaceship left it five thousand two hundred thirty-nine years ago," Erx told him. "And that was only to orbit. A lot has happened since then. The first outward expansion. Puffing the planets. Three empires rise, three empires fall. Countless wars, civil conflicts, rebellions . . . you name it. And that's just from the history we know about."

The hyper-shuttle swooped down into one of the portals and slowly came to a halt. The main hatch opened and Erx scrambled out; Berx followed close behind.

Now it was Hunter's turn. Yet, he hesitated. This could be a special moment, he thought. It would be wise to remember it.

Finally he touched his boot heel to Earth. A jolt of electricity ran through his body.

"What do you know about that," he murmured.

I've been here before. . . .

Also by Mack Maloney

STARHAWK

MACK MALONEY

ACE BOOKS, NEW YORK

STARHAWK

An Ace Book / published by arrangement with
the author

PRINTING HISTORY
Ace mass-market edition / June 2001

For information address: The Berkley Publishing Group,
a division of Penguin Putnam Inc.,
375 Hudson Street, New York, New York 10014.

The Penguin Putnam Inc. World Wide Web site address is
http://www.penguinputnam.com

Check out the ACE Science Fiction & Fantasy newsletter
and much more on the Internet at Club PPI!

ISBN: 0-441-00868-2

ACE®
Ace Books are published by The Berkley Publishing Group,
a division of Penguin Putnam Inc.,
375 Hudson Street, New York, New York 10014.
ACE and the "A" design
are trademarks belonging to Penguin Putnam Inc.

PRINTED IN THE UNITED STATES OF AMERICA

10 9 8 7 6 5 4 3 2 1

PART ONE

Out from Fools 6

It would take a long time for the *Xavius IV* to crash.

The L-Class space cruiser was almost a half mile in length and displaced more than a million tons Earth weight. It was built of electron steel and was capable of traveling in Supertime, so it was virtually indestructible in space.

But slamming into the hard surface of a planet was a different matter.

The gigantic spaceship was falling, quickly, toward an uncharted world. It was on fire and all of its critical control systems were either failing or already dead. Because the *Xavius IV* was a Starcrasher, there was no chance it would burn up on entry. But once inside the planet's atmosphere, the spaceship's descent velocity would become hypersonic. It would be moving so fast when it hit the ground, it could take up to twenty miles of plowing across the planet's surface before coming to a stop. And even if the vessel did survive more or less intact, its propulsion core would explode soon after it ground to a halt because that's what prop cores did when deprived of external power.

So this was a tight spot for the spaceship's two-man crew. Be killed in the sheer chaos of one million tons of electron steel slowly breaking up all around you. Or be annihilated twenty seconds later once the propulsion core realized it was starved of power.

Neither would provide a tidy demise.

The two pilots took their hands from the controls just long enough to touch gloves. It was not a handshake, but it would have to do. They hit the top of the atmosphere hard an instant later. Plunging through thick clouds, all one million tons vibrating furiously, they were moving so fast, a trail of massive sonic booms was following them down. The control panels in front of them were blinking madly; the ship's computer was crying out so many warnings, its synthetic voice became hoarse and garbled.

With one glance below, the pilots knew fate had picked the wrong planet for them to crash into. The world beneath them was made up of towering mountain ranges, broken up only by the occasional stretch of open space, small oceans that had dried up long ago. The stricken vessel was heading right toward a particularly nasty group of jagged peaks. With one last effort, the pilots turned hard to port, hoping to make some relatively flat desert beyond. The nose came up. They braced for impact. The sonic booms were so intense now, their ears began to bleed.

When they hit the ground a few seconds later, the impact was so powerful, a small electrical storm crackled to life above their tail. The huge ship bounced once, then began its long skid. One mile, two miles, three . . . Hundreds of attachment modules were being torn away from its fuselage. Tons of dirt and rocks were flying in its wake. Still the spaceship did not slow down.

Four miles. Five. Six . . .

The spaceship's exterior skin quickly became a mess of shredded secondary metal and severed power lines. The flight compartment canopy finally shattered. Millions of white-hot glass shards filled the cockpit, tearing away at the pilots' spacesuits.

Seven miles, eight miles . . .

They went right through a small mountain. With the glass shield gone, the debris poured into the flight compartment unimpeded. They hit another mountain. Flames burst from the main control panel.

Nine miles, ten . . .

The pilots could barely breathe now, they were being choked by all the smoke in the cockpit. Then the ship hit another large mountain and its needle nose began to crumple. Once it tore into the planet's crust in earnest, the ship began slowing down. In a great storm of dust and debris, it finally ground to a bombastic halt, two miles later.

Both pilots were barely conscious by this time. Dazed and bleeding, they were also hopelessly trapped. The cascade of dirt and crushed control columns had pinned them to their seats. They could not move their arms or legs. Unbuckling themselves would be impossible.

Not that it made any difference. A dozen computer voices were screaming throughout the wreck now, adding to the cacophony of hissing, crackling, and the sound of many things burning at once. But above it all, one artificial voice was very clear. It said the spaceship's propulsion core was going to blow up in exactly twenty-two seconds. . . .

A stream of sparks began raining down on the pilots. The cockpit ceiling started to glow, dissolving the partially crushed cabin roof not two feet above their heads. The smoke became thicker. They could hear flames coming through the tubes. The ship would go through one last convulsion before it blew up for good. Both pilots just slumped back in their seats and waited for the end.

That's when a piece of the cabin ceiling fell in on them . . .

The pilot named Erx never saw the hands that grabbed him by the shoulders and lifted him out of the dirt and debris. He was pulled through a hole in the ceiling and out of the spaceship completely. He could not see beyond his helmet visor. Blood was flowing into his eyes, blurring his vision. He felt himself being pushed into the back of a small, hovering aircraft. Then the hands finally let him go.

"Ten seconds to core detonation," the computer voice announced nervously.

"Go on without me!" came the human voice from below. "Go, I say!"

Erx almost smiled. It was his fellow pilot, Berx, crying out. They were going to be blown up in a few seconds—himself, Berx and this valiant, doomed rescuer. Still, Erx

appreciated his partner's last show of valor. He and Berx had
flown in space together for nearly a hundred years. Never
did he think it would end so soon.

"Five seconds to core detonation. . . ."

The next thing Erx knew, Berx was falling on top of him.
His colleague's head landed so hard onto his stomach, it
knocked what little air he had in his lungs right out of him.

And then suddenly, they were moving.

Very fast.

Three seconds to detonation . . . two . . . one. . . .

Erx felt the *Xavius IV*'s propulsion core blow up. The first
nano second of the shock wave ran through him like a billion
little knives. A prop core disintegration created something
akin to a tiny black hole, which then exploded with the fury
of a small sun. There was no way they could outrun the force
of such a blast.

But apparently their rescuer was going to try.

They began twisting and turning so wildly through the sky,
Erx heard himself screaming. Berx was screaming, too. The
violent maneuvers had them crashing up against the sides of
the small crawl space, bones close to breaking. Even above
their own shrieking, the grunts and gasps of the unseen pilot
were all too clear in the very confined area. These were not
very reassuring sounds to hear.

More twisting. More turning. Both Erx and Berx were
powerful men, bulked up from thousands of hours in space.
But the g-forces against their unprotected chests now were
excruciating. Suddenly they were tossed upside down, their
faces slammed against the small airship's canopy. They could
see the enormous prop core fireball coming right up at them.
It was so close Erx felt its heat on his battered face. It looked
both terrifying and beautiful, this thing that was about to
consume him.

But still they climbed. More twisting. More turning. The
heat on Erx's face began to peel his skin.

But then the hot sting of the prop core explosion began to
fade. The glow in the surrounding skies dissipated as well.
Some magical distance had been attained.

But was it possible? Had they actually outrun a prop core
fireball?

If so, neither man dared believe his life had been spared for very long. The terror now was in the manner their rescuer was flying. Even out of harm's way, he was climbing at blistering speeds, then diving away wildly, only to twist back up and scream skyward again. Irony was a cruel mistress, Erx thought, the blood still running into his eyes. To survive an enormous crash, only to be killed when his rescue craft goes out of control? Where was the cosmic justice in that?

But then suddenly, they came to a complete stop. Once again, Erx and Berx were slammed hard against the back of the pilot's seat. Their arms and legs became bent in almost impossible positions. Neither man could breathe.

All became quiet for a moment. Then the canopy popped open and a rush of atmosphere flooded in. They could hear their rescuer climb out, his boots landing with a thud on solid ground. He mumbled something about load distribution and shifting the center of gravity. Berx was somehow able to untangle his arms and legs by now. He lifted himself out of the cockpit and dropped to the ground below. Painfully, Erx did the same thing.

He landed in a heap on top of Berx, and again they fought to get disentangled. Finally they got to their feet. They found themselves atop a high plateau. Below them, many miles away, their spaceship was exploding in the last of its death throes. A thick column of black smoke was rising high into the pinkish sky. The electrical storm they had created was still raging above the wreck as well.

Their rescuer was standing in front of them, surprised that they had made it out of his craft on their own. Unlike Erx and Berx, who were both squat and rugged, this man was tall, lean, muscular. He was wearing a uniform that vaguely resembled those issued to Space Navy fighter pilots, except it was jet black and very worn around the edges. The man took off his crash helmet to reveal a handsome face bearing several days' growth of beard and a mop of shaggy hair.

"Are you two all right?" he asked them.

Both men checked their vital organs. Everything still seemed in place.

"If we can stand and talk and breathe, then we are all right," Berx said, taking the man's hand and shaking it vigorously. "We owe our lives to you, good sir!"

Their rescuer shrugged. "I couldn't just let you die out there," he said. "I mean, I knew it would be close, but my aircraft here is pretty responsive and, . . ."

But suddenly Erx and Berx weren't listening to him. Instead, they were getting their first good look at the aircraft they'd been rescued in.

"What . . . *what is this thing?*" Erx spit out.

The two spacemen were stunned. Nearly every spacecraft in the Galaxy was built along the same triangular design. This vehicle was not. It was *very* different. It had a cylindrical fuselage about fifty feet long and it bore a wing, a design element not seen in the Galaxy for thousands of years. It also had a tail, a bubble-top glass canopy—and wheels, something else not seen in the Galaxy for several millennia.

"How did you ever come upon this machine?" Erx asked his rescuer.

The man just shrugged again. "I built it," he said simply.

"But the design? It's so *alien.* . . . Where did it come from?"

The man shifted a bit uncomfortably. "I made it up," he said. "I guess . . ."

That seemed like such a strange reply, Erx and Berx turned their attention back to him. This man looked *different* to them, though they weren't sure why. Erx did the quick introductions, then asked him: "And you, sir? Your name is . . . ?"

The man shifted uncomfortably again. Miles away, the *Xavius IV* exploded once more.

"My name is Hawk Hunter," he finally said, adding: "Or at least I think it is. . . ."

2

The dwelling was built into the side of a mountain.

It looked like a castle. Two high towers. A rampart. Stone walls forming one barrier about five hundred feet out, a deep, dry moat providing a second ring of protection closer in. The drawbridge was made from the cargo hatch of a long-ago crashed spaceship. It lowered automatically now as Hunter's sleek aircraft approached.

Inside the walls was a courtyard, a small house at its center. Plain and square, it was made from pieces of skillfully melded debris. The house had many windows of different shapes and sizes, all of them filled with bits of superglass. There was a hole in the roof through which to see the heavens. A place to park the aircraft was close by.

The view from the dwelling was spectacular, if desolate. A vast desert stretched for many miles to the south. Towering mountains dominated the horizons east and west. Only a few trees dotted the barren landscape; they were stunted and windswept. There was very little water in evidence here. No vegetation. No animal life. Two suns hung in the sky, a large dull red ball and a smaller yellow disk. They were the only stars for three hundred light-years around, and indeed this was their only planet. Hopelessly isolated, this place was known as Fools 6 because so many hapless space travelers had met their end here.

Even for a Fringe planet, it was way, way out.

The interior of Hunter's dwelling was not spacious. Three floors with a main room, it was built mostly of stone and superwood, much of which was salvaged as well.

A huge fireplace had been cut into the east wall. A large fire was blazing away inside it. Suspended above the flames, a pot of synthetic stew was bubbling away. Erx and Berx collapsed into two chairs placed near the fireplace. They painfully pulled off their space helmets.

"I can't believe that just happened to us," Erx said, accepting a cloth from Hunter to wipe the blood from his face and hands. "One hundred and thirteen years flying the Galaxy, I can't recall having so much as a panel light go out. . . ."

"Nor can I," Berx agreed. "The closest we've come was near Anteaus, when we lost the inertia booster. That was forty-five years ago."

Erx moaned loudly: "I believe my heart is beating itself right out of my chest."

Hunter passed them both an enormous bowl of stew.

"This will fix you up," he said. "Or at least I think it will. The truth is, you are the first dinner guests I've ever had, so I'm not so sure if it's any good or not. . . ."

Both Erx and Berx gave their bowls a sniff. Erx grimaced.

"I believe we were thinking more of a *liquid* solution to the problem," he said.

Hunter pondered this a moment. "Do you mean like wine?" he asked.

Erx and Berx both smiled. They looked good for their ages, 146 and 151 respectively. Both were low to the ground, stout but unquestionably powerful. Both had shiny bald heads and were sporting huge, drooping mustaches. Battles scars on their hands and faces marked them as onetime front-line soldiers. Their uniforms—what was left of them—were dark blue with gold collar badges shaped like a double-X. These men were senior military officers and well-known throughout the Galaxy. They possessed friendly dispositions, though. And neither was opposed to drinking on duty.

"You have some spirits?" Erx asked, his features brightening, instantly perking up. "Way out here?"

Hunter disappeared into a storage room, returning with three mugs and a flask.

"I salvaged it from a wreck on the other side of the mountain," he explained. "I think they call this 'slow-ship wine.' "

Erx and Berx smacked their lips in unison. They were no strangers to slow-ship wine. A sweet liquor of dubious ingredients, it was known for its calming, opiate quality.

Hunter poured each man a healthy dose. The visitors began to drink—but then stopped in midgulp. They had forgotten their manners.

"Our apologies," Erx said as he made a quick toast in Hunter's direction. "To you, sir—and to your bravery. We owe you our souls!"

Hunter sheepishly raised his own mug. "It was more by chance than bravery," he replied. "It was hard to miss your rather spectacular entry."

"Courage and luck go hand in hand," Berx said—he was the more boisterous of the two, his mustache was longer, and he was slightly taller. "We're fortunate you were in the right place at the right time—so let that be our toast."

They all drank heartily.

"There will probably be a reward in this for you," Erx said, wiping his mouth with his sleeve. "I believe a bag of aluminum coins may soon be yours, Mister Hunter."

Hunter was baffled. *Aluminum coins?* This was not a familiar term.

"What would I do with a bag of aluminum coins?" he asked, looking around the house. "Unless—well, I could melt them down and . . ."

"Melt them down?" Erx cried. "Good sir, aluminum coins are currency—you can go just about anywhere in the Galaxy on their value."

"You *do* know that," Berx asked him. "Don't you?"

Hunter just shook his head. These men would probably be shocked by how much he *didn't* know.

He quickly changed the subject. "What happened to your ship?" he asked them. "Do you know?"

Both men shrugged and after some more sniffing, began nibbling at their stew.

"We haven't the faintest idea," Erx said between mouthfuls. "One moment we were cruising along, the next thing we know, we're losing power, we're losing speed, we're losing our propulsion core."

"We popped out of Supertime," Berx said. "And headed for the first place we saw. This place. Apparently we are not the first to choose it as an option to blowing up in space."

Erx drained his mug and nudged it toward the flask. Hunter poured both men another full mug.

"And what about you, Mister Hunter?" Berx asked. "How long have you been marooned here?"

Hunter hesitated again. Many times he'd wondered just what he would do when this moment came. When he would finally meet another human being and be asked *the question*.

"I don't think 'marooned' is the right word," he finally told them. "The truth is, I'm not really sure what I'm doing here."

Both men stopped eating for a moment.

"What do you mean by that, sir?" Berx asked.

Hunter just shook his head again. "It sounds strange, I know, but I *didn't* crash here. At least I don't think I did. It seems as if one day, I was *just here*. Standing on the side of this mountain, wearing this uniform, with not a clue as to where I came from."

Erx and Berx just stared back at him. This was an unfamiliar concept to them. Everyone in the Galaxy knew where they came from.

"Well, *obviously* you were part of the crew of this shipwreck nearby—and suffered amnesia as a result," Erx said.

"I don't think that's possible," Hunter said. "That wreck happened way before my time."

As proof, he pointed to the wall next to the fireplace. It was lined with electron torches, small, tubelike device capable of assembling or disassembling just about any form of matter in nature. Trillions of them could be found throughout the Galaxy.

Berx took one of the torches from the wall and examined

it. "It is an old design," he confirmed. "Three hundred years, at least."

"I built my aircraft with those tools," Hunter told them "Melding parts I took from the crashed ship and putting them together from a sketch I made one night. Believe me, I've been over every inch of that wreck and it is in an advanced state of decay. It was certainly here long before me."

Berx retrieved a small handheld device from his belt. This was known as a quadtrol. It could do just about anything, from reading a planet's atmosphere, to scanning of piece of machinery for defective parts, to doing a complete physical examination of a human being. Erx passed the device across Hunter's forehead and began reading results.

"There's no indication that you've suffered any trauma," he announced. "Strangely enough, you're in perfect health. And it says here that you are thirty-three years old, Earth time."

Erx leaned forward a little. "And you really have no memories of childhood? Parents? Siblings?" he asked. "No evidence of your past?"

Hunter just shook his head. "All I have are these," he said.

He reached into his left breast pocket and came out with a small piece of fabric. It had a strange design on it, a series of red stripes with a square blue block in one corner containing a field of stars.

"Foreign to me," Erx said, examining it.

"Me as well," Berx agreed.

Hunter unwrapped the cloth to reveal a small piece of wrinkled material inside. On this was the faded image of a woman's face, but not much more could be told from it.

"I found these two things in my pocket the day I realized I was here," Hunter said, carefully folding everything back up and returning the small bundle from where it came. "Along with the fact that the name 'Hawk Hunter' was written inside my boots, they are my only clues—if they are clues at all. I have constantly racked my brain, trying to remember how it is that I got here—but it seems to be impossible to recall."

He took a long drink of wine.

"I mean, I'm not without a brain," he said softly. "I know

how to speak, how to breathe, how to take care of myself. I figured out how to use the electron tools. I know how to fly—"

"That might be the strangest thing of all," Erx interrupted. "Even the Master Pilots on Earth cannot fly like you. The best fighter pilots in the Space Forces would be amazed by your ability—as well as envious."

Hunter poured them more wine.

"The name 'Earth' sounds familiar," he said. "This is your home planet?"

"It's *everyone's* home planet," Berx said. "It is our mother world, the place from which every person in the Galaxy is descended."

Hunter looked across at them. "Even me?" he asked.

The two spacemen nodded.

Hunter thought about this for a moment, then said: "I was able to get into the logs of that shipwreck as well. About half of them were undamaged. About half of them I could understand. I know the crashed ship was part of the 'Fourth Empire.' Do you know where that is?"

Erx and Berx laughed. "The Fourth Empire is every-where," Erx told him. "It is *the* Galaxy. This Galaxy. This planet, its stars, everything around it. Even you, my friend. You are part of the Fourth Empire."

Hunter almost seemed proud. "Well, at least it's good to know I *belong* here. . . ."

"You are happier than some upon hearing that news," Berx said under his breath.

"And as our greatest astronomers are certain that in the entire universe our galaxy is the only one that's inhabited," Erx went on, "the possibility that you are *not* from here is, well, *im*possible. Therefore your home world *must* be Earth. So there—one part of your mystery is solved."

More wine was poured. Erx intentionally spilled some of it into his stew. So did Berx.

"Could I be from a different time, then?" Hunter wondered aloud. "From somewhere in the past? Or even the future?"

Erx and Berx screwed up their faces in identical frowns.

"Well, actually, we're not into time," Berx said, his voice dripping. "No one is anymore, not really."

"He means the term itself is outmoded," Erx explained. "Ancient words like 'weeks' and 'months' are still used in charting travel through space as a passage of time. But like other archaic words we all use, they are merely convenient and part of tradition. Something for the quadtrols to recognize. At least that's my understanding of it."

"Of course, theoretically, we are always moving in time," Berx said, finally feeling the wine taking effect. "That's the principle behind the propulsion cores in our starships. Or at least I believe that's how they work."

He turned to Erx for help, but not much was forthcoming. "I think the propulsion core creates some kind of exception in the fabric of time that allows us to enter the faster dimension and move great distances quickly. Is that it?"

Berx just shrugged. "I think so."

"You really don't know?" Hunter asked them.

Both men shook their heads.

"No, not really," Erx admitted. Clearly this was a source of embarrassment for them.

"It all has to do with the Big Generator," Berx said. "You've never heard of that either, I suppose?"

Hunter just shook his head no.

"Well, it's a very complicated thing," Erx began sputtering. "But because of it, our ships fly and our weapons work, every planet can be sustained, and we can travel to the farthest reaches of the Galaxy in just weeks. But the truth is, we are not privy to the great secrets that it holds—or even where it is located."

Hunter thought a moment. "Are you saying this Big Generator has an effect on just about everything you do . . . yet you don't know how it works?"

Erx and Berx stared back at him for a long moment. Then they drained their mugs and in unison said: *"Bingo . ."*

3

They ate their stew and drank their fill of wine.

Then once Erx and Berx had recovered somewhat, the three of them climbed up the mountain behind Hunter's dwelling.

It was about three thousand feet high, but he'd carved a trail along its slope one day, ensuring a steady but easy climb. Still, this would be the longest distance Erx and Berx had walked in many decades. True, they were interstellar explorers. But the vast majority of their Galactic travel had been done on the seat of their pants.

No surprise, then that they were out of breath and sweating heavily by the time they neared the summit.

"My God," Erx said, slumping next to a conveniently shady rock. "Does this planet have *any* oxygen at all?"

Berx checked his quadtrol. "All of the vital readings are very low and there is an atmosphere leak of more than ten percent."

"Do you know when was the last time this planet was 'puffed,' Mister Hunter?"

"I don't know what puffing means," Hunter replied simply.

"Every planet in the Galaxy has been puffed at one time or another," Berx explained. "The Ancient Engineers used to call it 'terra-forming,' I think. It means the planet's biosphere has been altered to fit human habitation."

"Why do you think you can walk around out here without an oxygen tank to breathe from, my friend?" Erx asked. "Or a spacesuit to protect you from the rays?"

Hunter just shrugged. It was a good question.

"I guess I never thought about it before," he said.

Erx wiped his forehead of perspiration. "I envy your lack of knowledge," he said wearily. "Sometimes I think I know too much."

On the other side of the mountain was a vast salt plain. It stretched, nearly unbroken, to the far horizon. About twenty miles to the east were the remains of an enormous starship. It was sticking out of the ground at a seventy-degree angle. Its monstrous tail went up at least a mile into the sky, so high, clouds were forming around its top.

There was no real mystery how the massive vessel had wound up in this position. When it came down here, the vast salt plain had been a small ocean, and Hunter's mountain quite possibly, no more than the tip of an island. The starship had hit the water at hypersonic speed—and kept on going. Driving itself deep into the soft sea bottom, it stopped only when it reached a depth of a half mile or so.

Had the impact contributed to the quick retreat of the ocean's waters? It was a good guess. But why hadn't the ship's prop core blown up? Mostly likely the crew had been able to shut it down before they even entered the atmosphere.

Or then again, maybe something else had happened. . . .

Erx held his quadtrol out in front of him now and began reading information from its readout screen.

"Mister Hunter is right," he announced. "This wreck has been here at least three hundred years. It's a regal S-Class design. Old Empire markings . . ."

He paused a moment. "My God, its name is the *Jupiterus XVI*. . . ."

"*Jupiterus?*" Berx said. "Are you sure?"

Erx showed him the quadtrol's readout. They looked back at the massive ship with new, if troubled interest.

"That's no ordinary spacecraft," Erx said urgently to Berx. "It's a Kaon Bombardment ship."

Kaons? Hunter had never heard the term.

"What was this ship's function?" he asked them.

Erx and Berx exchanged a worried glance.

"I'm afraid that's a state secret," Erx said. "As officers in the Empire's military forces, we can't really tell you more than that. Suffice to say, it was a weapons system of incredible power. Then and now."

"I should have figured that," Hunter said, looking out at the ship now. "Not only did I build my aircraft's body from parts reassembled from that wreck, I built its power plants from the salvage as well. Interesting . . ."

He checked the sky. It was getting dark, and a stiff breeze was blowing up. In less than an hour, it would be a howling gale. Then the rains would come and the sands would blow. The combination could cut a man to pieces in minutes. Fools 6 was not a place to be traveled at night.

"Time to head back," he announced. "I hope you've seen enough."

The two spacemen assured him they had. But as Hunter moved away back down the trail, Erx grabbed Berx and asked him in an urgent whisper: "Is it possible that he reassembled some of the Kaon Bombardment system components to power his craft? Could that be why his aircraft flies the way it does?"

Berx nervously ran a hand over his bald dome.

"It's a good question," he replied. "But I'm not sure we want to know the answer."

4

The rescue ship arrived two days later.

It had picked up the SOS signal sent out by Erx and Berx right before their ship went in. As the closest military vessel of any size to Fools 6, this vessel had diverted from its course and appeared soon after the red giant's morning sunrise.

The ship's captain was a highly decorated star commander named Zap Multx. He was a ninety-seven-year veteran of the Fourth Empire's Space Navy. He was a huge, imposing man nearly twice the size of either Erx or Berx. His head was shaved in the style of the time, and he sported a very long, thin goatee. His vessel was the *BonoVox*, an M-Class battle cruiser. It was a massive warship, two miles long and 3.5 million tons earthweight. Like all Empire starships, it was shaped like a gigantic wedge. A small city of glass-bubble control decks dominated its upper shell, hundreds of weapons systems studded its immense fuselage below.

The *BonoVox* also was a troop carrier. More than twenty-two thousand Space Marines were quartered in its lower decks. Essentially these soldiers were Multx's private army. They were highly trained, highly motivated, battle-hardened special operations troops.

And at the moment, they were in a hurry.

• • •

Berx and Erx were sitting in Multx's opulent commander's cabin. They had beamed up to the starship shortly after it appeared above Fools 6.

Multx knew the two explorers well; their paths had crossed many times over the past century. Nevertheless, he made it clear to them that he was in a rush.

"If I hadn't heard it was you two stuck way out here, I would have never changed my course," Multx told them now. "I'm falling behind schedule as it is."

"Important matters somewhere else?" Erx had asked him.

"Only the Selesian System War," Multx replied with a sniff. "I am relieving Loy Staxx and his army. His men are, well, fatigued . . . or at least that's what I've been told."

Erx and Berx could read between the lines. Multx and his men were relieving a space corps that couldn't do the job.

"It must be tough going out there," Berx said, trying to feed Multx's gigantic ego and meeting with some success. "Sileasia is not a pretty neighborhood."

"It's nothing we can't handle," Multx replied with confidence. "Nine planets have been cleared, but three remain full of pirates, bandits, and assorted misfits. Still, it seems to be a mopping-up operation. I can't understand why Staxx's corps could not handle it."

"You will have no problems, that's for sure," Erx told him.

"We rarely do," Multx replied with a wave of his hand.

"So we may hitch a ride with you then?" Berx asked him.

"Certainly. It will give you a chance to see my men in action. We will be returning to the Pluto Cloud after that. I can deposit you somewhere in that region, I trust?"

"So close to Earth?" Erx asked excitedly. "Gladly."

They took the next few minutes briefing Multx on their crash landing, their near-miraculous escape, and the many skills of their mysterious rescuer.

Multx was intrigued.

"This man Hunter you go on about," he said. "How could he possibly learn to fly so well he was able to escape a prop core explosion? If he is the only living being on this planet, where did he take his training? Learn his technique?"

Erx licked his lips. He was still buzzing from two days of drinking Hunter's slow-ship wine.

"We have no idea—and neither does he," the spaceman replied. "He's a different sort, that's for sure."

"Yet he's been nothing but helpful toward us," Berx interjected. "We have been his guests for two days here and it's been extremely hospitable as well as interesting. He knows every inch of this forlorn planet. He has many unusual devices made from his own designs."

"He's quite clever and bold—without being a smart-ass about it," Erx added.

"But are you certain he's even human?" Multx asked. "Perhaps he's one of those well-constructed robots from years past. You know how some of the good ones were? They actually *believed* they were human."

"He's definitely not a robot," Berx said. "I scanned him: He is flesh and blood."

"But where he came from *is* a puzzle," Erx went on. "As we said, he doesn't even know himself. Yet I feel it unlikely that he was the passenger of a crashed ship and just doesn't remember. Nor do I believe he was ever part of the Empire Forces—either Outward or In-Close."

"What makes you so sure of that?" Multx asked. "His flying ability seems on a level of our master pilots."

"Which is exactly why a pilot of his ability would not be flying around in a two-million-ton spaceship. More likely he would have been identified by Space Forces Command upon entering military service and assigned to a front-line starfighter unit. My God, he'd be a senior master pilot—the *master* of senior master pilots, even."

"And the craft he flies," Berx went on. "It is the most unusual thing I've ever seen. It can go extremely fast, yet it defies all of our latest design functions. It actually has wings. And wheels."

"*Wheels?*" Multx asked. "What for?"

"That's how he keeps it from hitting the ground," Erx replied. "He does not park it in the hover mode. At least I don't think he does."

"But it is the speed of his craft," Berx reiterated. "He's told us that he usually flies it at one-one-hundredth throttle.

Yet the thing reaches incredible velocities very quickly."

Multx thought a moment.

"Perhaps in the excitement of being saved, you two have exaggerated these things in your mind," he told them. "It's a common problem in combat. We get many reports of people doing very heroic things, and—"

"We have seen him fly since, Zap," Berx said, gently interrupting. "He turns out his magnificent contraption twice a day. He performed maneuvers for us that were mind-blowing. And as I said, he did so at speeds that were simply remarkable."

"And that's while in-atmosphere," Erx added. "I can't imagine his skills in space."

"Well, his 'contraption' certainly can't be faster than our own space fighters," Multx asked them. "Right?"

Erx and Berx exchanged glances. It was considered impolite to criticize any of the Empire's military hardware, no matter how slight.

"That's hard to determine with the naked eye," Berx replied cautiously. "But I believe this man could fly anything. And do it well."

Multx mulled this over for a few moments. Finally he said: "Well, whoever he is, he'll be coming with us as well."

Berx and Erx were taken aback.

"Coming with us?" Erx asked. "Why would that be?"

Multx leaned back in his floating chair and spoke to the ceiling.

"If he's as good as you two say, denying his talents would not be in the best interests of the Empire. Every person in this Galaxy is a citizen of it. Every person may enjoy its fruits. But every person also must contribute for the good of all."

The starship commander was speaking the correct words . . . but Erx and Berx knew he had other things in mind. A starfighter pilot for his own personal Air Guard perhaps?

"You can't just snatch him up and carry him away," Berx said to Multx. "He seems very content here."

"Besides," Erx chimed in, "this man saved our lives. An act of goodwill on his part should not become a detriment to his future."

"Do you really think bringing him to Earth would be a detriment to his future?" Multx asked them suddenly.

To Earth?

Now the two explorers were simply confused. Even the highest officials of the Empire were lucky if they could get across the Pluto Cloud, never mind anywhere near the home planet. It was the same for military officers. Access to the motherworld was restricted to all but the extremely privileged. Why, then, had Multx spoken the holy word of Earth?

"What are you up to, you old fox!" Erx cried. "Clue us in. . . ."

Multx seemed to resist, but only for a moment. The three of them *did* have a history together. As young soldiers, they'd fought in sixteen major wars and dozens of smaller ones, all before Erx and Berx joined the Empire's exploratory corps. Multx knew the two men could be trusted and even helpful. Besides, it was considered bad luck these days to exclude friends from grandiose plans.

Multx snapped his fingers, and a small control panel materialized from nowhere. He pushed a series of buttons, and the walls of his quarters began to vibrate slightly. He had activated a hum beam. They were now immune to any form of physical intrusion or eavesdropping, either long-range or close by.

"My friends," Multx began, "being out on the Fringe for so long has dulled your brain cells. Think . . . we might have a pilot of extraordinary skill here. Someone who, if you speak the truth, might be better than any starfighter pilot we've seen in our long lifetimes."

"True," Erx and Berx spoke at once.

"Then what event upcoming on Earth might warrant this man's attendance?"

The explorers looked at each other and thought a moment. It came to them simultaneously.

"The Earth Race . . ." Erx whispered.

Multx smiled.

"Bingo," he said.

The Earth Race was an annual event that pitted the best pilots in the Empire against each other in a twenty-five-thousand-mile, obstacle-strewn, multidimensional contest.

Few things in the Galaxy generated so much excitement. The Emperor himself claimed to be a starfighter pilot in a previous life and thus had great affection for the competition. The hundreds of trillions of subjects within his domain did as well.

It was no exaggeration to say that the winner of the Earth Race would find the Empire at his feet. Untold riches were showered on the champion, including a permanent residence on Earth itself. By tradition, the winner also could have his pick of any assignment at any rank at any post in the Empire. Neither he nor his family would ever want for anything again; in fact, the largesse would be so vast, the winner's descendants would be well off for many generations to come.

But the rewards of the Earth Race did not stop with the winner himself. Those responsible for getting the right pilot in the right place at the right time in the right machine— they, too, were grandly compensated. For years, Multx had kept his eyes open, looking for a pilot of extraordinary skill. Throughout the many battles he'd fought, the thought of spotting a special flier in action was never very far from his mind. It was the same for all high officers of the Empire Forces—and the most ordinary of citizens, too. Being associated with the winner of the Earth Race could be the crowning achievement of a long lifetime.

"My God," Erx whispered now. "Our brains *have* been dulled! This should have been our first intuition as soon as we realized what Hunter could do."

He turned back to Multx. "What is your plan, Zap?" he asked in a very conspiratorial manner. "And can we be involved?"

"If this man is all you say he is, the answer is yes," Multx replied. "The race is but a few weeks away, so the stars are on our side. I have a close connection within the organizing committee. At the very least this person will observe our pilot. If he's that good, my friend will get him in."

"You can get him through the Pluto Cloud?" Berx asked.

"Not a problem," Multx replied.

"But we must be very cautious," Erx urged. "It has not been unknown for a new pilot to be snatched away by people higher in stature than us. My fear is word of Hunter's ability will travel fast, and some counsel to the Emperor will co-opt us. You know how nasty that Most Fortunate Earth crowd can be. They would vaporize their favorite relative if it meant getting close to the winner of the Earth Race."

"As would I," Multx said without missing a beat.

"And I," Berx said.

"That's why we must be wise, my brothers," Multx went on. "And keep all knowledge of Mister Hunter very low."

All three were silent for a moment.

"The fact that he is a man from nowhere can actually work in our favor, then," Erx finally said. "Even if someone hears whisper of his name, there will be no way of looking him up."

"Indeed," Multx said. "Now, we all know the race organizers love a bit of intrigue, so entering an unknown at the last minute will probably be to their liking. I will arrange with one of them to get Mister Hunter through the Pluto Cloud. But until then, we must keep this among ourselves. And Mister Hunter must stay obscure."

He regally cleared his throat.

"Now I cannot place myself on Earth to pursue this matter so early in the game," he went on, fingers to chin, stroking his goatee. "I have many things to do, and not doing them would be considered a dereliction of duty. You two, on the other hand, well . . ."

"What? We have nothing else to do?" Berx asked, insulted. "Is that what you're getting at?"

Erx interrupted again. "If it is, he's exactly right. It will take us months to get another ship. If he can arrange it, I'll happily go to Earth."

Erx again turned back to Multx.

"But we still have a problem," he said. "How do we justify taking this man Hunter from his home?"

Multx thought a moment. "Ah! I will arrest him on suspicion of being a spy. The way things are out here on the Fringe these days, just about anyone could be held on suspicion of espionage."

"I protest!" Berx cried. "This man is hardly a *spy*. There is nothing out here to spy on. . . ."

Multx relented on that point. He thought a few more moments.

"Well, how about this? According to you, he vandalized a ship of the Empire to build that vessel of his," the commander said. "That's certainly an offense that warrants arresting him and transporting him for further investigation."

This time it was Erx who erupted.

"His actions can hardly be called *vandalism*," he told Multx loudly. "My brother, from those dull pieces he created a flying machine of extraordinary ability. It's truly a work of art. You cannot put a man in irons because he created a masterpiece, no matter what the pretense."

"They'd skewer you on Earth, Zap," Berx agreed. "If spinning art was known to be his offense, then the wives of every one of your superior officers will demand that you ride the Ball for the rest of your career."

Multx shrugged and gave in again.

"Well, then this matter needs some constructive thinking," he said. "Which is something I don't have time for right now."

He released the room from its hum-beam shield. Erx and Berx knew it was time to go.

"We sail in one quarter and five," Multx told them. "I'm sure we can squeeze you two in someplace comfortable."

"And our friend below?" Erx asked.

Multx continued stroking his beard.

"I'll keep you informed of my plans," he said.

Hunter had never seen anything like the *BonoVox*.

The gigantic starship seemed twice the length of the hulk on the other side of the mountain, and at least half again its width. And unlike that shipwreck, this vessel was covered with weaponry. Towering gun spires, ascending arrays of missile launchers, forests of Z-beam tubes and space-torpedo ports. There were thousands of weapons-systems modules attached to its hull, with thousands of portholes running between them. It looked chaotic and perverse. But it had an undeniable strange beauty, too, all 3.5 million tons of it.

And here it was, right above his house, floating as if it were light as a feather.

Sitting near the southern corner of his roof, Hunter had been staring up at the enormous starship since it arrived earlier that morning. He knew nothing would be the same after this. Many days and nights he'd spent gazing up at the star-filled sky, wondering if there was civilization out there, somewhere, in the Cosmos. He'd had his doubts. True, this planet was littered with space wrecks. But they were all so old and decayed, they seemed ancient. And why had no one ever come here to salvage them? And why couldn't he see lights moving between the stars at night? Or any unnatural lights at all?

It was a strange yearning, this one he had. He could feel it either in his heart or his head, but it was always the same, a kind of frustrated anticipation. He was homesick—but he didn't know where home was. He could wind up living a long life, but what good was that, if this was not the place he was supposed to be? No, there might be a difference between loneliness and being alone, but the end result was the same: The soul cries. It wants to move on. East, west, up, down. It didn't matter. But to where? And how? Thinking too much about one thing was the surest way to go crazy, so in the end, it was just more logical for him to believe that everybody and everything in this universe were dead. And by some cruel twist of fate, he was put here, alone, with no explanation, the only one left in human creation. Doing his time in hell.

But now, in just two days, not one but two ships had come here. And suddenly everything had changed. The universe *was* alive. Or this little part of it was.

At least now I have some proof, at least one question has been answered. . . .

And he was happy—for a few moments, anyway. Because with life, one answer usually brought just another question. He was not alone; that was great. But would he ever be able to find someone, somewhere, who might be able to tell him who he was? And why he was here?

And did he really want to know?

These thoughts must have drifted into dreams, because when Hunter opened his eyes again, he found an enormous soldier standing in front of him. He towered over Hunter and was holding a huge weapon of some sort. The soldier was actually one of many; in fact, there were nearly a hundred soldiers crowding onto his roof. They had come out of nowhere. Literally.

They were all wearing dark gray combat uniforms and elaborate battle helmets. Through the tangle of space hats and ray guns, one soldier called for quiet and began reading from an ornamental scroll. The words were incomprehensible to Hunter; they were in an archaic Empire vernacular. He let the man finish, then turned to the nearest soldier.

"What did all that mean?" Hunter asked him.

The soldier replied: "Simple: You've been conscripted to the service of the Empire military forces."

"Conscripted?" Hunter asked. "Do you mean . . . ?"

"That's correct, comrade," the soldier said. "You've just been drafted."

5

The trip to the Sileasian System took two Earth days.

The *BonoVox* covered more than four thousand light-years in that time, most of it while cruising in Supertime, the mysterious seventh dimension also known as "the Ethers."

Under ideal conditions, a starship traveling in Supertime could traverse the Galaxy in less than a month. Indeed, some Empire ships could reach speeds of two light-years *a minute*. They did this without having to go through black holes, white holes, wormholes, or any other deep-space exotica. All that was required was a properly tuned, properly powered propulsion core.

Just how the Empire's starships were able to enter Supertime *was* a mystery—Erx and Berx were hardly alone in their lack of understanding of it. Something in the prop cores allowed the grand ships to cross into the seventh dimension and travel there with no more than the flip of a switch. But just how that miracle worked, and how the Big Generator was able to supply the massive amounts of power to make it happen, went beyond the faculties of most. The Imperial Family and the core of the Empire's military elite knew the secret of the prop-cores; at least, that was the common assumption. After that, it was all magic as far as the citizens of the Galaxy were concerned.

Not that they ever got a taste of it. Supertime belonged to the Empire's military class and their warships. It was their superhighway to the stars. Everyone else, from the space merchants to the space pirates, had to use craft powered by ion-ballast engines. On their best day, these cramped, noisy vessels could travel at barely one-hundredth the speed of a prop core model starship, and then only with frequent refueling stops.

And they couldn't crash through stars, either.

The Sileasian System was in a region of the Galaxy known as Slow Fringe 3, or sometimes, the Three-Arm.

This was the third arm of the Milky Way, counting clockwise from the Earth, and almost on the other side of the star system. It held comparatively few stars, just a few dozen million. Sileasia and its array of eleven planets was near the tip of the arm. It was a known haven for space pirates and bandits; their ilk had been terrorizing Slow Fringe 3 for more than a hundred years. In their bid to reclaim planets lost since the Third Empire's downfall many centuries before, the imperial forces had spent the past two Earth years clearing out the Sileasian System, one planet at a time.

It had not been the cleanest of campaigns. Shortly after the onset of hostilities, the various Sileasian lawbreakers had banded together to create a substantial opposition army nearly three million strong. They invaded nine of the eleven planets and held these worlds hostage against any Empire action. This made slow going for the Empire's soldiers, slogging it out, one world at a time, trying to kill as many of the enemy as possible while attempting to keep civilian casualties low. It hadn't always worked out that way. The death toll in two years of fighting already numbered in the billions.

Early on the third day, the *BonoVox* arrived off the seventh planet of Sileasia, a jungle world called Vines 67.

It was here that the Sileasian bandits had been waging a fierce guerrilla war against the Empire forces, specifically the two-million-man corps of Loy Staxx, a 141-year-old, highly decorated veteran of the Empire's Space Navy. Staxx had chosen to take Vines 67 one continent at a time, a substantial chore, as there were only three major bodies of water on the planet, and together they barely made up 30 percent of its area.

Recapturing Vines 67 was important, though. It was the middle planet of the three the bandits still controlled. The original plan was to subdue Vines 67 and then use it as a jumping-off point for campaigns against the two remaining opposition worlds. But even with a vast array of supporting forces drawn from the previously reclaimed planets, Staxx and his men had found the jungle war against the homegrown bandits a slow, draining, and costly affair. After nearly half a year of trying, they were being relieved.

Star Commander Zap Multx was here to finish the job.

Hunter had been put into a small compartment in a section of the *BonoVox* known as the Lowers.

This place had a hovering bunk, a food tube, and a supply of "brain rings" for amusement, though Hunter didn't have the slightest idea how to work the things.

He'd seen nothing else of the ship, having been beamed directly to this windowless billet after being "drafted." Erx and Berx sent him a new set of clothes, including a plain gray spacesuit and a pair of boots. In an accompanying holo-message, they told him what Multx had told them: that Hunter had to be "processed" at a military facility planet "nearer to Earth." The *BonoVox* had to make another stop first.

All that was fine with Hunter. It wasn't what he imagined military life would be, but he had no complaints about his accommodations. His bunk was soft, and the food tube offered a bewildering array of fare. And while he felt bad about leaving his flying machine behind, he didn't miss life on Fools 6 at all. After spending so much time kicking around one of the Galaxy's most dead-end planets, anything was an improvement.

Still, there was no getting around the fact that he was confined to a jail cell of sorts. The door to his compartment was sealed, and there was no unlocking mechanism on the inside. Why? He had a sense that he was being kept under wraps for some reason. As Erx and Berx explained it to him in their message, whenever the huge starship was about to enter a combat situation, all nonessential personnel had to be locked down in their berths, lest they see any of the Empire's many secret weapons in action.

"But how can any individual be 'nonessential?' " Hunter had asked their holo-images, knowing full well they couldn't respond. "I thought we were all supposed to be part of the same thing. . . ."

The most spectacular part of the flight was when the *BonoVox* actually went *through* a star.

How was this possible? As with just about everything else related to travel in Supertime, no one on board was really sure. The explorers' holo-message to him included one of the starship's flight engineers explaining it this way: "Much of what appears to be present in the other known dimensions does not appear to be present in the seventh dimension. Therefore, why would we have a problem going through something that is not there?"

At the incredible speed of Supertime, going through stars that weren't there was easier than going around them; starcrashing was simply a function of efficient transport. But the event was hardly routine. Whenever the massive vessel crashed a star, everything and everybody aboard the ship would glow with an intense golden aura. This luminescence lasted for just 0.0002501 second—the amount of time it took the ship to pass through the star's other-dimensional position in space. Then everything went back to normal again. It was superquick, but there was never any doubt whenever it happened. Even before the golden haze faded away, applause and cheering could be heard throughout the ship anytime the *BonoVox* made a crash.

It was early in the third day of the voyage when Klaxons began blaring throughout the massive starship.

The noise woke up Hunter immediately. He instinctively went to his compartment's door. It was still sealed. But on the other side he could hear the unmistakable sound of many people moving at once. Boots thudding along the passageway. Voices shouting through the pipes. The dark music of weapons and equipment clanging together.

Hunter had heard such sounds before. . . .

He found himself wishing the door would open and allow him to see what was going on outside. An instant later, that's exactly that happened. One moment the door was there, the next it wasn't. It hadn't slid open; rather it had disappeared, and then reappeared in the door slot.

That was strange enough. But in the same brief instant, Hunter thought he saw the very faint image of a person standing right next to him. A hand passed through the space where the door had been. A voice whispered: *You must see this.* . . .

Then the door just wasn't there anymore.

And just as he thought, the hallway outside was filled with soldiers. They were members of Multx's 23rd Special Operations Corps. Each trooper looked enormous. Their complex dark gray battle suits added about a foot to their height and at least a hundred pounds to their bulk. Each soldier was a self-contained war machine. His suit had plug-ins for various weapons. Each carried a large, tubular ray gun slung from his back, as well as a holster carrying two or three small blaster pistols. Life-support tubes ran up from each man's breastplate into the oversized bubble-top battle helmet. Two tiny dishes on top of this helmet provided for communications.

The soldiers trooped past Hunter, paying him no attention, eyes forward, chins up.

They were real warriors, he thought. Determined, Brave. Smart . . .

He had served with men like this before. . . .

The line of troopers finally disappeared through a hatch at the end of the passageway. The Klaxons were blaring at full peak now. Hunter could hear the sound of more footsteps moving on the decks above and below him. He had no doubt what was happening here. These soldiers were marching off to war.

He began walking down the empty passageway. The line of troopers had gone through a hatch to the right. Hunter's instincts told him to keep walking straight. He reached a large doorway, opened the hatch, and stepped through.

He found himself on a glassed-in balcony; it looked out on an immense chamber deep within the ship. What he saw here was unfathomable at first. There were thousands of troopers floating within this chamber. Each one was dressed in the same elaborate battle gear. There were also hundreds of small spacecraft hovering in rows near the top of the vast hall. These craft were long, glassy, and tube-shaped. They had six gangling legs hanging off of them, and a huge bubble nose. For some reason, they were known as "bugs."

Though it seemed very chaotic at first, Hunter soon came to realize the soldiers were floating up to these craft and climbing aboard. They were all moving very fast, yet no one was bumping into each other, or even coming close. As soon as a small troop shuttle was filled with soldiers, it would shoot off through a huge portal in the chamber wall, passing through an invisible membrane that protected those inside from the dangers of outer space. The whole affair was highly choreographed, highly drilled, well executed. The transports seem to hold about a hundred troops each. They were being spit out at a rate of about one every second.

Only after all of the transports had left the chamber did the Klaxons finally calm down. Hunter moved farther down the balcony and came upon a huge observation blister; it looked out onto the vastness of space beyond. From here Hunter could see the planet of Vines 67 below. It looked like a huge green ball dotted in a few places with patches of shimmering blue water.

The *BonoVox* was in a high orbit above the planet. The troop transports were lined up in columns just below the massive warship, obviously poised to invade this green world. Hunter looked to his left. Another starship was parked in an orbit nearby. To his right, another ship came into view. Then another. And another. He counted a dozen of the magnificent ships around the planet, and those were just the ones he could see.

This fleet was made up of Empire units occupying the already liberated planets in the Sileasian System. The ships were identical in design to the *BonoVox*, but they were all about a third smaller in size, leaving no doubt which vessel was the flagship here. They were spitting out hundreds of troop transports as well. Several thousand of the shuttles were lined up in huge phalanxes around the planet. Hunter guessed the invasion force totaled at least half a million men. Just getting them all together and in place was an astonishing feat of complexity and maneuver. They appeared ready to pounce at any moment.

Yet they were obviously waiting for something.

That's when another ship appeared. It was different from the rest. Though built in the Empire's standard triangular design, it wasn't as sleek as the other starships, nor did it bear the multitude of planet-blasting weapons the other vessels carried. This one had a huge red bubble just aft of its forward flight compartment. This odd ship was hanging close to the *BonoVox*'s starboard side. It was not spewing out troop carriers.

Hunter studied this ship closely. It had a ghostly air about it, yet to his eyes, it was a familiar one as well. Then it hit him. This starship was similar to the one sticking out of the ground back on Fools 6. What had Erx and Berx called it? A Kaon Bombardment ship?

Not a moment later, the red dome atop the strange ship began to glow. It became very bright very quickly. When it seemed it could get no more intense, a beam exploded from this cupola and traveled to the jungle planet below. It hit a spot just north of the equator, an area of exceptionally thick flora. Suddenly it seemed as if a quarter of the entire planet were bathed in crimson. The thousands of troop transports took this as their cue and began falling down toward the planet. Hunter could see explosions on the planet's surface. The glow from the neighboring ship intensified. He stared deep into the red dome and felt a chill go through him.

"Comrade? What are you doing here?"

Hunter spun around to find a huge individual standing right behind him. He was one of the *BonoVox*'s small army of on-board security troops. As Hunter tried to spit out an explanation, the security man raised a handheld device, pointed it at him, and pushed a button.

A moment later, Hunter found himself locked inside another compartment.

This one had bars he could see.

6

The *BonoVox* was in the throes of a saturnalia.

The entire ship was high on something. Food, wine, and other exotic intoxicants were available throughout the vessel, and anyone not on duty was permitted to indulge in any vice of their choice. This was no more true than inside Zap Multx's enormous stateroom. Here, the upper echelon of the *BonoVox*'s officer staff had gathered to revel and feast.

The starship had something to celebrate. The assault on Vines 67 had been an unqualified success. With the regular Empire Forces troops holding the flanks, Multx's highly trained soldiers had gone into the key bandit strongholds and quickly eliminated them, destroying all of the opposition's weaponry and razing their base camps. No prisoners were taken. The victory had been so complete, the bandit groups on the two remaining outlaw planets were already asking for cease-fire terms.

So Multx's 23rd Special Operations Corps had done in a few hours what Loy Staxx's men had been unable to do in nearly a year. As a result, Vines 67 was in the Empire's fold, and Multx's fortunes had gone up a notch. The key to the victory had been the proper coordination between Multx's hunter-killer battalions and the Kaon Bombardment ship. This was an option not afforded to Loy Staxx simply because he did not have the connections that Multx had. This alone spoke volumes about the inner workings of the Empire's military elite.

Multx's victory had been so swift and total, the *BonoVox* had already left the Sileasian System and was now streaking Inward. The star commander himself was said to be extremely pleased and had sent a very upbeat report back to Earth to herald his success.

So why then had he invited Erx and Berx to his victory party *without* the requisite bottle of wine as a gift?

That's what puzzled the two explorers now as they made their way forward from their billets in aft Uppers. They had watched the battle for Vines 67 unfold from the top-side observation deck; it was the perfect place to follow all aspects of the fighting. And even though they were veterans of similar actions in the past, they had never seen such ruthless efficiency in combat as displayed by Multx's corps this day. The speed by which his special operations soldiers had eliminated their opponents was frightening. To say victory had been expeditious was a vast understatement.

So why, then, no bottle of Venusian wine with their invite? The explorers could not fathom a reason for such a breach of festivity protocol, especially from an old friend such as Multx.

Even more inconvenient, Erx and Berx had to walk the entire length of the ship to reach the celebration's location, something that could take an hour or more. Usually the ship's command officers would send a transport beam back for those they didn't want to inconvenience. No such beam arrived for Erx and Berx.

About halfway to their destination, they passed a long line of troopers who had returned from Vines 67 just before the *BonoVox* began heading Inward. These men were in the same combat suits as they'd been wearing when they embarked on the lightning-quick campaign. But there was something different about them now. They were covered with dirt, mud, green soot, and no little blood. Their weapons appeared used and depleted. Even more telling, the men themselves looked drained. There was little evidence of the spirit the unit was known for prior to battle. These men looked grim, exhausted—

disillusioned, even. To an uninformed eye, the question was obvious: If the soldiers had just won the recent engagement, why did they look so downcast?

But Erx and Berx didn't have to ask.

They *knew why*. . . .

The explorers finally reached the front of the ship and were ushered into Multx's stateroom.

The place was packed with the high officers of the ship, several hundred in all. There was lots of wine, lots of vivid dress uniforms, lots of holo-girls. People eating, people drinking. High-pitched background music provided the sound track. The air smelled thick of bravado.

But all was not right. Standing alone in the far corner was Multx, the star commander himself. He looked awful. His face was drawn and pale. His normally razor-sharp eyes were bleary. His substantial shoulders were sagging.

Erx and Berx quickly got drinks and then approached him. One look told them all was not well. But before they could say a word, Multx spoke instead: "Do you know where your friend Mister Hunter is at this moment?"

The explorers looked at each other and shrugged.

"In his billet, I hope?" Erx replied uncertainly.

"Nay, he is in the lower brig," Multx said in a stern whisper. "For transgressions that carry the ultimate penalty, I might add."

"The *brig*?" Erx cried, a bit too loudly. "What has he done?"

Multx yanked them deeper into the corner. They did not have the protection of a hum beam now.

"He was caught in a highly restricted area of the ship during the operation against Vines 67," Multx said, again in a whisper. "He saw it all: from the battle formations before the attack, to the Kaon Bombardment ship in operation, to the beginnings of the invasion itself. He observed more than a half-dozen state secrets in process. Greater souls have been dispatched for less."

Erx and Berx were both alarmed and confused.

"But how was he able to leave his billet to do such

things?" Erx asked. "The plan was to keep him sealed in for the rest of the voyage."

Multx took a shallow breath. "We have no idea how he was able to get out. And neither does he. Or so he says."

A small crowd of officers drifted by them, trailed by a bevy of holo-girls. Multx allowed them to pass.

"What is Hunter's fate now?" Berx asked worriedly. "Certainly you can't execute him."

Multx wearily shook his head.

"It is only that my troops so handily won this engagement that I am able to go easy on him," he replied. "Few know of his indiscretion at this point. They are too busy with other things."

He waved his hand to indicate the roomful of inebriated officers.

"And I can maintain our facade," Multx went on. "But only if nothing else happens. I just hope Mister Hunter is smart enough to keep his lips sealed about what he saw."

"He *is* smart," Erx said quickly. "That much we know."

"And he will remain in confidence about this matter," Berx added. "We will guarantee it."

Multx wiped his brow with his uniform sleeve. He seemed pale.

"I don't want to regret taking him along with us," he said wearily. "But if our scheme to get him into the Earth Race goes awry, not only will the happy days we dream of not be forthcoming, we might have some answering to do to my superiors as well. . . ."

"All will be well, my brother," Erx tried to reassure him. "It's only by risk that our rewards might be great."

Multx gulped his drink and grumbled: "Let's pray that is so. Still, I think it's best that our feathered friend stay in the brig for the remainder of the journey Inward. Only then can we be sure he'll find no further trouble to get into."

It pained them to do so, but the explorers raised no objections to this. Though a jail cell was not much different from his original billet, Erx and Berx felt responsible for Hunter's plight. But it would be wise not to argue against Multx's decree.

Time to change the subject.

"We, too, watched the battle closely," Erx told him, trying to pump Multx back up again. "We could tell it went just as planned. Your troops were sterling in action. Your strategies, flawless."

Multx leaned back against the wall and rubbed his tired eyes.

"All true," he told them. "But this fight was not pretty, my brothers. Far from it."

Erx and Berx fell silent. What was the matter here? Where was the eternally confident Multx? The ever-boastful Multx? Multx the warrior? Multx the conqueror? The man known as the most-connected officer in the Space Navy? Certainly the incident with Hunter was not all that was weighing on him.

Finally Erx leaned forward and lowered his voice to a whisper.

"I must tell you, old friend," he said to Multx, "I've seen you looking better. Is something else troubling you?"

Berx jumped in: "You've just won a major engagement, Zap. So it did not go as 'cleanly' as you hoped—war is not supposed to be clean. We all know that. Why then so low?"

Multx hesitated for a moment. Rarely did anyone speak to him on such a personal level. But he knew his friends were right.

"I cannot answer why I feel this way," he finally revealed, looking down at his hands. "Because I do not know myself."

He paused to take a breath. It was almost painful to watch.

"I realize I have just eliminated a problem that has been plaguing the Empire for too long," he went on. "And did it quickly, too. Therefore I should be deliriously happy. Yet I am not, because I can't get rid of this notion that something bad is about to happen. To me. To this ship. To *all* of us."

"An intuition, you mean?"

"Something like that," Multx replied.

The star commander looked up at them, his face more ashen than before.

"And I cannot tell you, comrades, just what an unpleasant feeling it is. . . ."

7

Fly down to the dry sea today. . . .

Yes, that might be a good idea. See the south side of the
sky for one last time and then hurry back. The false sunset
looks blood red today, especially from fifty thousand feet.
Bury the throttles, lean back in the cockpit, open the canopy,
and stick his arms out. *Now you're really flying, man.* Helmet
off. Belts unbuckled. The beams from the crimson giant wash
over the face, warming whatever it was beneath the skin. Can
the embers of a dying star actually touch the soul? Can they
penetrate and open any memories stored there?

Through the scarlet cloud, turning this way and that. The
sky, spectacular. Throttles forward. Yes, everything is a blur.
But life is not just about being good, it's about being better.
Right on time, the face appears on the clouds ahead. The red
giant glows brighter. The clouds swirl. He sees her smile. He
hears her laugh.

You must see this.

Then . . .

Suddenly Hunter was awake.

The ship's Klaxons began blaring so loudly, he almost fell
from his bunk. What was going on? They were twice as

urgent as the day before. Was the ship about to fight another battle? So soon?

Now the lights inside his cell started flashing wildly. The thunder of boots running through the ship could be heard once again. Hunter was off his bunk and by the cell door in a flash. It did not dematerialize before his eyes this time. Rather it slid open cleanly. A security officer was standing on the other side. Behind him, soldiers were rushing up and down the long corridor. Some were dressed in battle gear, some not.

"What's happening?" Hunter yelled to the security man.

"Wake up, man!" the officer yelled back. "The ship is under attack! All prisoners are to report to the evacuation bay!"

Under attack?

"By who?" Hunter yelled at the security man, but the man was already gone, lost in the stream of troops.

Hunter tried to get his bearings. He wasn't even sure what part of the ship he was in. The chaos of the passageway was only getting worse. Lights flashing, the Klaxons at ear-splitting level. Soldiers pushing their way around each other, running in different directions.

Where the hell was the evacuation bay?

Hunter began moving with the stampede. He found his way to a balcony similar to the one from which he'd watched the attack on Vines 67. The vast war chamber lay in front of him once again. But something was wrong here. Soldiers seemed to be stumbling this way and that, floating, colliding, falling. Gone was the choreography, gone were the fluidity and well-drilled movement. At best there was controlled pandemonium inside the war chamber. At worst, panic.

Some of the troop transports were floating at the top of the chamber, but the soldiers in motion were ignoring them. Instead, the troops were igniting their rocket packs and hurling themselves directly through the huge protective membrane and into the wilds of outer space beyond.

What was happening here? Hunter didn't have a clue at first. Were these men abandoning ship?

Dozens of ship's security men were rushing by him now, but none of them gave a second look. Hunter moved down the passageway to the nearest observation bubble. Beyond the glass was an even more fantastic sight!

Far from jumping ship, the stream of troopers leaving the *BonoVox* were meeting a stream of other spacemen heading in the opposite direction. These unknowns were coming from a huge ship that had materialized off the *BonoVox's* starboard side, not two hundred yards away. This vessel was black, very sinister in appearance. While it was less sleek, less impressive than the *BonoVox,* it was bristling with small weapons and was dispensing armed spacemen as fast as the Empire ship could spit out soldiers to stop them.

Hundreds of soldiers began fighting within the small area between the ships. Some were shooting ray guns, others were engaged in vicious hand-to-hand combat. Space was suddenly filled with colors. The bright yellow of rocket packs. The deep red of ray gun blasts. Powerful beams from hundreds of weapons were streaking off in all directions. The sudden ferocity of the battle was simply mind-boggling. Those hit directly by a ray gun blast found themselves propelled at high speed off into deep space, a gaping hole in their spacesuits, and leaving only a trail of blood bubbles behind. Others were simply exploding whenever an enemy ray gun blast hit their own weapons' supply. A dark red mist was enveloping the fighting now. Hunter even thought he could hear men screaming as they fought and died out in the void.

Do something. . . .

Hunter felt a strange sensation rise up from the back of his neck. It was coming from deep within his brain. A voice seemed to be speaking to him, riding billions of receptors to the base of his skull. The voice sounded very much like his own. The *BonoVox* was in danger. That meant he was in danger as well.

Do something. . . .

The next thing Hunter knew, he was running.

Down the passageway, past the balcony, down a descent tube to the entrance to the vast war chamber itself. He jumped right through the force field protecting the main door. He found himself being lifted up to the chamber's ceiling.

He began tumbling out of control almost immediately.

Head over heels, arms over legs. He tried to focus his attention on the closest troop bug; it was about two hundred feet above him, and indeed it was the only flying machine anywhere nearby.

He put his head down and his arms at his side, thinking this was the thing to do. It did cause him to pick up a great amount of speed very quickly. But then he had no idea how to stop. He wound up slamming hard into the nose of the troop shuttle and bouncing off. Tumbling down about a hundred feet, he regained his balance and went shooting upward again. Another hard collision with the transport's nose. Another ricochet. Another plunge downward. Dazed and battered, Hunter twisted himself over and finally managed to "swim" up to the bug and climb inside.

One step in and he realized he was no longer floating. The shuttlecraft had its own gravity. His knees and elbows severely banged up from his collisions with the craft, he painfully made his way up to the flight compartment and squeezed himself behind the bug's control column.

The operations panel was a bewildering array of light switches and holographic buttons. Hunter had no idea what any of them did, so he just started pushing things. In seconds, the spacecraft began to shake and yaw.

He hastily studied the control panel's main 3-D screen. It seemed to offer a variety of options on what kind of controls he desired to fly the troop carrier. One icon presented a panel with the outlines of two hands. The fly-by-finger method—Hunter was not into that. Another offered a head ring, a band put around the head. Flying by brainwaves, he supposed. Again, not his thing.

He finally located an icon that most looked like the controls on his old flying machine. Basically a short stick for his right hand and a throttle bar for his left. He tapped this icon and instantly these controls appeared.

He quickly righted the spacecraft and then turned it around. He took it slowly and carefully at first, trying his best to avoid hitting any of the flying soldiers still rushing through the clear membrane to the battle beyond. When he saw a break in this stream, Hunter pushed the throttle bar ahead and suddenly found himself rocketing through the invisible portal and into space himself.

Now this was a strange situation for him. To the best of his knowledge, he'd never flown in space before. It didn't seem to be a problem, though. He was able to maneuver the awkward troop carrier through the swarm of battling spacemen, avoiding the never-ending streams of ray gun blasts coming at him from every direction. It was funny, though; Hunter wasn't even trying hard. He was turning this way and that, but it was almost as if the controls were moving themselves. Or was something deep inside him moving them? If so, they were working perfectly every time. Hunter felt like he was just along for the ride.

And he noticed something else: At first glance, it seemed as if the battle between the two starships was taking place as they were hanging motionless in space. The truth was, they were both flying in Supertime. The telltale sign was a slight blurring effect that surrounded everything and everyone, Hunter included.

Very strange. . . .

Hunter finally cleared the ferocious battle and turned hard to port. Now he had a clear view of the situation. The *BonoVox* on his left, the unknown attacker on his right. The space between them still ablaze with vicious combat.

Two words popped into his head now, and they didn't seem to be coming from anywhere deeper than the top of his skull.

Now what?

Directly below the *BonoVox*'s vast bubble-top control room was another chamber.

Just as big, with twice the amount of machinery and apparatus, by tradition this place was known as the ship's Oculus. Some believed the ancient name meant "the eyes." If so, it was apt. From here the ship projected thousands of sensor rays into every dimension of space for one thousand light-years in all directions. This was where the ship was steered, where its speed was determined. The glassy control deck above was simply a window into this place. A small army of technicians lorded over innumerable monitoring stations here. Among other things, they could detect anything moving—man-made or not—for more than a billion miles away.

Or at least that was how it was supposed to work.

No one had seen this attacker coming, for one simple reason: There wasn't supposed to be any enemy spacecraft in Supertime; only Empire spacecraft had the ability to cruise the Ethers. For all its magical machinery, whenever the *BonoVox* was in the seventh dimension, the Oculus was simply concerned with its navigation, and not scanning for enemy threats. That's how the attacking spaceship was able to appear right alongside the Empire vessel and begin spitting out spacemen before anyone in the Oculus even knew what was going on.

Even worse, this was no ordinary warship off their starboard bow. This was a Blackship, a vessel used by Fringe pirates to pillage unsuspecting planets and attack commerce vessels in flight. By definition, its occupants were ruthless and fierce, and known to show their victims no mercy. How had such a ship gained entry into Supertime? No one in the Oculus had a clue, simply because nothing like this had ever happened before.

A kind of controlled chaos was sweeping the Oculus now. The *BonoVox* had fought in countless engagements in its long history. But the starship's role in each of those battles was to provide purely offensive punch. The *BonoVox* attacked planets; it carried no defensive weapons of its own. So powerful was its vast arsenal that no weapon on board could be used against a target fewer than one hundred miles away. Using such a weapon would mean death to both the attacker and the target. The older class of Empire ships, those built more than three hundred years before, had carried self-protection systems. But as the techniques of using Supertime became more defined, and as the Empire strengthened its hold on the supertechnology, the need for such weaponry disappeared. The *BonoVox* carried no self-protection weapons because ship-to-ship duels were supposed to be a thing of the past.

But one was happening now—and it appeared the situation was growing more dire for the Empire vessel by the second. Reports flowing into the sensor center said that some enemy spacemen were close to reaching the hull of the *BonoVox,* intent on burning their way into the ship itself. The battle might soon be taking place *inside* the vessel. Fighting in the passageways? Battling enemy spacemen right on the control decks themselves? Absolutely no one on board the *BonoVox* was prepared for that.

But even among all this, something else very puzzling was happening out there. In addition to the sensors going crazy by continually detecting the marauding Blackship, the men in the Oculus saw that a third spacecraft had appeared on the scene. It was flying among the warring spacemen with considerable aplomb. It wasn't another Blackship. It was far too small for that.

So what was it?

Instantly the sensor arrays identified this third object as one of the *BonoVox*'s own troop transports.

It was empty except for its pilot.

His identity was unknown.

What happened next was witnessed by most of the officers inside the Oculus, as well as those in the ship's command center one deck up.

After hovering for a few moments on the edge of the midspace battle, the small troop carrier began accelerating very quickly. In seconds it was flying much faster than its previously known top speed. It roared over the top of the *BonoVox,* climbed steeply, and then went into a mindbending dive just above the bow of the Blackship. Just as quickly, a barrage of Z-beam blasts erupted from behind the enemy vessel's control deck—unlike the *BonoVox,* the Blackship carried loads of self-protection weapons. But even though the Z-beam streams were many, the troop carrier began dodging them with astonishing agility.

Then something even more remarkable happened. Empire troop shuttles were armed with only rudimentary ray guns. These were provided in the unlikely event that a bug was caught on the surface of a planet, alone, during an invasion and was forced to defend itself. The mysterious pilot was now firing these guns at the Blackship's flight deck—indeed, he was coming down in a screaming dive and directing his twin beams at the vessel's main control bubble. This seemed like madness! The shuttle's small ray guns were designed to kill troops, not do battle against miles-long spaceships. Yet the shuttle unloaded on the Blackship's command bubble and kept right on going, its guns full blast, making impacts all the way down the length of the attacking ship. Only after it delivered a concentrated barrage on the ship's propulsion section did it turn up and away and climb again, a storm of Z beams following in its wake.

All this was happening so quickly, the men inside the Oculus didn't realize that the Blackship's command bubble had caught fire. Two of its tail fins were alight as well. Yet the shuttle had looped over the top of the *BonoVox* again and now was going into a second mad dive. Once again the Blackship began firing at it. Once again the shuttle dodged the stream of Z beams. The bug began twisting and turning in seemingly impossible maneuvers, yet remarkably its nose guns kept firing on target and without a hint of hesitation.

Finally one of its blasts found a significant mark. A lucky beam made its way through the Blackship's hull and into the attacking ship's own version of an Oculus. This one beam destroyed the Blackship's entire sensor chamber. In one stroke, the vessel's abilities to see and hear were gone, and its electrical systems began to short out. A violent explosion rocked the Blackship right behind its control bubble. This in turn caused a string of explosions all the way back to the Blackship's hindquarters. The propulsion systems within began to disintegrate immediately, and the ship began losing speed. Suddenly there was a bright white flash, and then it was gone. The Blackship had been knocked out of Supertime.

But the drama was not over.

With their ship now gone, the several hundred spacemen it had dispensed to do battle against the *BonoVox* were suddenly all alone. They no longer had a ship to fight for. No one was around them now but the enemy.

Some of the attacking spacemen disengaged from hand-to-hand combat and flew back to the place where the Blackship had been. Others simply stopped fighting and hung motionless in space. It was clear they had no safe place to go.

So, one by one, the enemy spacemen began shooting each other. . . .

8

Hunter have never tasted Venusian wine before.

One sip though was enough to tell him that the slow-ship crap he'd been drinking back on Fools 6 tasted like bilge by comparison. This stuff felt like a cloud going down his throat. No bark. No bite. Yet the opiate effect was virtually the same.

"Refill, Mister Hunter?"

Before Hunter could reply, his goblet slowly refilled itself. He barely saw the hand of the invisible holo-servant pouring him another full measure while properly staying out of sight in some nearby dimension.

"Don't mind if I do," Hunter replied belatedly.

He was sitting in Multx's vast private billet, a compartment directly behind the flight deck of the *BonoVox*. Erx and Berx were on hand as well. Sitting nearby, each had already drained his second glass of wine and was looking for more. They seemed a bit reluctant to look Hunter in the eye.

Hunter had never met Multx before. Perched behind his huge floating desk, the star commander seemed a bit larger than life at first. He looked twice the size of a normal man, with monstrous hands and enormous shoulders. Polished head, properly greased goatee, resplendent in his Space Navy uniform, he certainly looked the part of a famous starship captain.

But Multx also appeared a bit haggard at the moment. And who could blame him? His premonition of dire things a-coming had proved frighteningly accurate. Fewer than a dozen hours ago, his ship had narrowly escaped being captured by the swarm of spacemen from the Blackship. Only by Hunter's quick action did the *BonoVox* survive. No one on board the Empire warship had ever seen anything remotely like the display Hunter had put on in dispatching the intruding vessel. Even the latest Empire starfighters would not take on a Blackship. Yet Hunter had done it in a lowly, barely armed shuttlecraft.

Even now, it didn't seem possible. . . .

Erx and Berx were trying to catch Multx's eye, hoping he would order their glasses to be refilled. But the star commander's attention was focused entirely on Hunter at the moment.

"Is it safe to say that you have a penchant for—how should I put it?—being where the action is, Mister Hunter?"

Hunter paused from taking another sip of wine.

"I'm not sure I know what you mean, sir," he finally replied.

Multx smiled wearily. "Well, just in the past few days, you rather dramatically rescued my two close friends here. Then you managed to get out of a very secure compartment to observe our most secret weapons in operation. Then . . . well, then you saved this ship from a catastrophe."

Hunter gulped some wine down in earnest then said: "I was just trying to help."

Multx thought about this for a moment, then snapped his fingers. A visual screen materialized out of nowhere.

"I see our ship physicians thoroughly examined you, Mr. Hunter," he said, reading from the screen. "Thankfully they confirmed that you are not a victim of amnesia or any other cranial trauma."

"That's good to know," Hunter replied. "I think—"

"But our records confirm that you are not listed as a citizen of the Empire," Multx went on. "Nor have you ever been a member of the Empire's military before."

"I believe that is true as well," Hunter said.

Multx dispatched the floating screen and turned back to Hunter. "I know you don't know where you came from," he said. "Unless something has come back to you in the past few days?"

Hunter just shook his head. "I've thought about it more times than I can count, and not just over the past few days. In fact, I never *stop* thinking about it. But other than my name and the fact that I apparently have some kind of flying ability—I simply cannot remember anything else."

"And it's the same reply as to where you learned to fly like that?"

Hunter just nodded. "It is."

Multx fiddled with his extra-long goatee hair for a moment.

"I am not a man without ego, Mister Hunter," he said. "Yet in this matter, I can only speak the truth. You saved this ship. You saved my crew. You saved my career. But again, this puzzles me: Whatever possessed you to do what you did? Only a fool would have taken on a Blackship with nothing more than a troop shuttle. Why did you do it?"

Hunter shrugged. He could feel the cloud wine taking effect.

"Something inside just *told* me to do it," he replied. "I started running; the next thing I knew I was in the shuttle and going outside. It was almost as if someone else were doing it—or that I was *watching* someone else do it. Beyond that . . ."

He let his voice trail off.

"Are you saying that 'instinct' played a role in this?" Multx asked him.

Suddenly Erx and Berx were paying attention again.

"Now, *that's* a word I have not heard spoken in at least a hundred years," Berx said.

"If 'instinct' is the right term, I guess that would be correct," Hunter replied. "Is that so unusual?"

Multx just shook his head. "You *really* are from someplace else," he mumbled.

"What he's trying to say is that 'instinct' is a very rare commodity these days," Erx explained to him. "Our social scientists claim it was bred out of the human race a long time ago. Even a touch of it should be considered a gift."

"You, however, seem to possess it in spades," Multx went on. "I have many soldiers under my command. I believe every one of them would gladly give his life if it meant saving one of his comrades or even an innocent civilian. But none of them would have done what you did today simply because . . . well, I just don't think it would have dawned on them to do it."

Hunter sipped from his goblet again. More clouds flowing down his gullet. He seemed to be getting both lighter and stronger by the moment.

"The Galaxy is actually a very small place, Mister Hunter," Multx went on. "And any word of heroics spreads very fast. My report on this incident has already been flashed to Space Command headquarters. Everything, including the fact that a Blackship somehow got into Supertime, is all regarded as top secret now. But I'm afraid it will be impossible to keep a lid on this thing forever. When word of what you did gets out, every one of my esteemed colleagues will inquire about your availability. I'm sure you would shoot right to the top of any admiral's personal Air Guard squadron."

"That would be quite a jump for someone who's just been drafted," Hunter told him

"Well, yes," Multx replied with a nervous grin. "But actually we think you have much more important things to do than that."

"I do? Like what?"

Multx smiled for the first time in a long time.

"I've made arrangements for you to continue on to Earth as soon as we reach the Pluto Cloud," he told Hunter. "I hope you don't mind. . . ."

Hunter nearly dropped his goblet. *Earth?* After what Erx and Berx had told him about the exclusivity of the mother planet? Why would he be going there?

"I don't understand," he finally replied.

Multx checked to make sure the room's hum beam was at full power. It was.

"Mister Hunter, you've never heard of the Earth Race, I suppose," he asked.

Hunter could only shake his head no.

Multx glanced over at his coconspirators. Both Erx and Berx were trying very hard *not* to make eye contact with him now.

"Well, do either of you want to tell him?" Multx asked them wryly. "Or should I?"

9

Its official name was the Inner-System Defense Array.

It was made up of nearly one million man-made moons set in various configurations on the edges of the solar system. Most were orbiting the same distance out as the planet Pluto, thus the unofficial title of "Pluto Cloud."

Each moon served as a military garrison and a security checkpoint. The swarm enveloped the solar system within a perfect bubble, demarcating the inner sanctum of Earth, its planets, and the sun. In the days before the Ancients, the Pluto Cloud would have been considered the wall around the castle, the trench before the cave. No one got through without the proper connections.

Luckily, Zap Multx had connections.

This was how Hunter found himself on a hyper-shuttlecraft heading toward the holy inner planets.

No sooner had the *BonoVox* arrived here, at the gates of the stellar kingdom, than he'd been summoned from his old billet to the shuttle bay. Once there, he, Erx, and Berx were quietly put aboard Multx's personal launch and sent on their way.

This region of space was literally jammed with starships. Most of them were military, but many cargo and scientific ships were on hand as well. One could hardly look in any direction without seeing several hundred spacecraft either docked or moving slowly about. All of them being scrutinized by security personnel. Yet the hyper-shuttle was allowed to pass through a gauntlet of robot guns and Z-beam platforms unencumbered.

Even the shuttle pilot was amazed. "I guess the magic word around here today is 'Multx,' " he said.

"Bingo," Erx and Berx agreed.

As luck would have it, an alignment of sorts was in the offing. The shuttle pilot was able to buzz all of the outer planets, a diversion that added only minutes to the length of their trip inward.

Pluto was burning bright green these days. The gas giants Neptune and Uranus were violet and cobalt blue. Jupiter and Saturn were like minisuns, fantastically multicolored, with hundreds of moons, most of them man-made, spinning around them. The asteroid belt had long ago been cleared away. Mars was now on its own, glowing like a neon-red sapphire, the warmth of the sun obvious on its face.

Then came Earth.

It was a diamond floating among brilliant stones. An enormous blue, shimmering jewel, outstanding against the blackness of space. Mouth agape, his nose nearly pressing against the shuttle's main window, Hunter imagined he could see a white-hot glaze surrounding the planet, almost like a halo. There was no mistaking that one was in the presence of something great here. This place *looked* like the center of the Galaxy.

"The first spaceship left it five thousand, two hundred thirty-nine years ago," Erx told him. "And that was only to orbit. A lot has happened since then. The first outward expansion. Puffing the planets. Three empires rise, three empires fall. Countless wars, civil conflicts, rebellions . . . you name it. And that's just from the history we know about."

Much of Earth's surface was now covered with huge triangular sections known as triads; they were what made the home planet shine. Some of these massive sections measured more than one hundred miles in length. They were made of a superhard material known as terranium. Similar to electron steel, terranium was also able to feed an earthy crust and was thus amenable to growing flora.

The triads had been built more than two millennia before by the mysterious people known as the Ancient Engineers. Just why they chose to lay down these huge sections was lost in the haze of time. An attempt to reclaim surface area lost due to rising ocean levels was one guess. The triads covered more than half the planet and were arranged so that Earth now supported just two enormous continents—one in the east, the other in the west.

What remained of the oceans was in between. Water drained off from the poles traveled along huge canals that separated the triads in some places. Besides feeding the terranium, these artificial waterways also provided landing areas for some of the Empire's largest starships. Another result of this massive engineering project was that every coastline on Earth was now uniform, every river and lake drawn perfectly straight.

The triads were connected by more than five thousand bridges. Some were thousands of miles long and linked the two continents at their closest points. But these spans were never used—at least not anymore. They, too, were ancient, but unlike the triads, no one was quite sure who built them. All that was known was they'd appeared after the triads had been put in place and before the rise of the Third Empire. In any case, they were considered sacred and therefore off-limits to all.

Earth's Moon still hung in the sky, bright as ever, a pearl orbiting a diamond. But it, too, was considered sacred and thus wisely avoided.

In fact, no one had set foot on the lunar satellite in more than three thousand years.

The hyper-shuttle spiraled down through Earth's atmosphere now, heading toward an enormous city on the northeastern edge of the western continent.

A layer of perfectly shaped clouds seemed to be hovering above the center of this metropolis. On closer inspection, however, Hunter realized these really weren't clouds at all.

They were floating cities.

"That's where the Specials live," Erx explained, sensing Hunter's curiosity. "The Emperor and his immediate family live on that one right there—the one that's so big, it's hard to miss. . . ."

The largest of the floating cities was about twenty miles below them. It looked like a huge castle in the sky. It had multiple spires, many glowing in very odd iridescent colors. Long, sloping passageways crisscrossed these spires like spiderwork. The airborne city was at least ten square miles in size. Other cities floating close to it were almost as large.

Because the floating cities were so big, and because they were more than a mile above Earth's surface, condensation tended to gather underneath them, forming . . . *clouds*. This created the illusion that the cities were floating on the cumulus.

Beneath the floating palaces was Big Bright City. It went on forever. Tens of millions of structures, from superskyscrapers to shacks, hovering roadways, air-car tubes, water canals, flags, banners, arenas, thousands of monuments to the Emperor, enormous, skyward-pointing power grids—and lights. Lights everywhere! Burning brightly, day and night. All colors, all shades, all tones. Everything bathed in a muted neon glow to ensure than no one ever went to sleep. The city was so large, it took up nearly one tenth of the entire upper western continent.

On its very eastern edge, right before its last triad met the sea, was Effkay-Jack. It was a sprawling spaceport facility, boasting hundreds of launch and receiving stations, huge housing units for the Empire's largest starships, its own weather control, and its own separate army. It was the largest spaceport in the Galaxy. On any given day more than fifty millior. people would pass through its portals.

The hyper-shuttle swooped down into one of them now and finally halted. Once the tiny vessel was recognized as the property of one of the most famous starship commanders in the Galaxy, it was surrounded by a small army of ground support personnel. One of them opened the main hatch, and Erx scrambled out; Berx followed close behind.

Now it was Hunter's turn.

Yet he hesitated. This could be a special moment, he thought. It would be wise to remember it.

Finally he touched his boot heel to Earth. A jolt of electricity ran right through his body.

"What do you know about that?" he murmured.

I've been here before. . . .

PART TWO

The Earth Race

10

When night fell, Big Bright City got even brighter.

Lights that had been blazing all day had their luminescence turned up a few more notches once the sun had finally set. The streets, the buildings, the airwalks were all absolutely clean and sparkling, thanks to a huge army of robots. Because every exposed piece of ground reflected the cool, green hue of terranium, the overall effect was that of a gleaming, emerald city.

Only the Very Fortunates lived in this magnificent place. More than two billion in all, and every last one of them had a reason for being here. They were either somehow related to the Specials—and there were several million of them alone—or worked for someone who was. But in a place where the ground that the Emperor's cloud city passed over was considered sacred—the "Holy Shadow," it was called—even the hired help had to be at least a Fortunate. No one below that class even dared step within the city's gates.

Unless you were in the high military, that is. Then you were treated almost like royalty, just a step down from the Specials themselves. There was no surprise in this. The Empire owed its existence to the military; its soldiers were considered celebrities, to be honored and respected, the higher the rank the better.

Anyone in a uniform who managed to get himself to Earth could find no better circumstance than walking among the people of Big Bright City—especially in the week before the Earth Race.

Once the first stars were in sight, thousands of narrow, extremely bright beams of white light went shooting up into the night sky. These were StarScrapers, the latest playthings of the Very Fortunates.

They were about the size of a quadtrol, handheld and tubular. They had unlimited power, thanks to the Big Generator. The device could shoot off into space, at Supertime speeds, and capture the light signature of a particular star. Because every star in the Galaxy was at least a little different from the next, each one produced its own unique blend of colors across the spectrum. These could be condensed and then be *dragged* back down to Earth, using the StarScraper's shaft of super white light as the medium. The Very Fortunates had chosen to call these captures "light songs." Most of them were incredibly vivid to the eye.

Once the light particles were drawn down to Earth by the StarScraper, they could be used in a number of different ways. Some of the Very Fortunates illuminated their dwellings with their own brand of starlight. Others bathed themselves in the glow for hours, swearing by its youth-giving properties. Some tapped into the star's audio frequencies to literally "hear the light" as well as see it. Some even would warm their cloud wine by starlight, claiming it increased the liquor's opiate properties.

And just like crashing through stars, people who used StarScrapers always had a certain glow about them.

Even when the Holy Shadow passed above their heads.

In contrast to the metropolis below, the floating city known as Special Number One had shut down for the night.

Its labyrinths of bright floating lights were dulled, casting eerie red and yellow shadows across the Imperial grounds. Anyone in the Royal Family who craved the nightlife had headed below a long time ago. The main gates were now sealed and a squadron of air-chevys began doing slow orbits around the hovering palace. It was customary for Special Number One to go dark in the week before the Earth Race. It was said that the Emperor took this downtime to recapture memories of his previous life as a starfighter pilot during the Third Empire—or so he claimed. Most believed the Emperor simply used the time to catch up on his sleep.

Nevertheless, with the activation of an impenetrable force field around the entire floating city, another day in the life of the High Specials was coming to an end.

Or so it seemed.

No sooner had the lights been lowered than a small air-chevy rose from the surface and approached the main gate of the floating city. After a quick surveillance scan by one of the Imperial sentries, the air car was allowed to pass through. It puttered its way through the maze of streets inside the palace walls, finally stopping at an nondescript building about half a mile from the Imperial House.

Two guards materialized; one opened the door of the air car. A man dressed in a long black cloak emerged and glided into the building. His air car then moved into the shadows.

The figure in black floated up the stairs and down a long corridor, finally reaching a huge oak door. He rapped on it twice and felt its lock spring open. He glided in. Two more Imperial guards were waiting for him.

"I'm here," the man simply told the guards. One disappeared behind another door, then reemerged. He motioned the man forward.

The dark figure lowered himself and walked into the room alone, closing the door behind him. Sitting on a couch next to a roaring fire was the person he'd come to meet. Long blond hair—at least today. Skin perfect. Eyes perfect. Mouth, nose, and cheeks, all perfect. It was Cyn-Nay, wife of O'Nay, First Empress and Queen of the Galaxy herself.

Or was it just the light?

The Empress waved the man in black toward a floating table containing a vast array of Venusian cloud wines. Then she activated a hum beam.

"You only ask to see me when something is wrong," she said to the man as he helped himself to a large mug of super'rose. He was a spy. One of the best in the Empire.

"I wouldn't be doing my job properly if that wasn't so," the man replied. "Secret as our talks have been."

"And you do realize that no one of any consequence can ever know that we speak?" she told him. "And that you should never approach me in any other setting than the one before us now?"

The spy nodded. "I do, my lady."

He sat down on the couch next to her. The Empress sipped her drink plaintively.

"So then? What is the problem?" she asked him, staring into the flames.

The spy shook his head.

"Well, that's just it," he began. "I'm not sure."

The Empress looked over at him. "Not sure?"

"It's just a feeling," the spy confessed. "But it's a deep one."

"Tell it to me, then," she said.

The spy took a deep gulp of wine. He would have to choose his words carefully.

"I think trouble is coming, my lady," he said soberly. "In fact, it may already be here."

The Empress thought about this for a moment. She used the spy only on the most secret of affairs. She had entrusted him to ferret out the truth for her, no matter where it might be hiding in the realm these days. Being able to do so was a rare talent. So when he spoke, she tended to believe him.

"And why do you feel this way?" she asked.

The spy leaned forward in his seat.

"You're aware of the attack on the *BonoVox*?"

She nodded. "Most unnerving. What have you heard lately? Has anyone got a theory on how a Blackship penetrated . . . what do you call it again?"

"Supertime, madam . . . and no, the word is solid on this: No one has any idea how it was able to break through the Ethers. There's a substantial internal investigation already ongoing. Ordered by your husband, I believe?"

She nodded brusquely.

"But how can they possibly investigate such a thing?" she asked. "It happened so far out. . . ."

The spy tasted his drink. "I am no expert on these things,

my lady," he began correctly. "But I believe there is a way, a formula of some kind, that can determine where and how much power from the Big Generator the Blackship used while in Supertime. Once this is discovered, they might be able to track these units of power back from the source to its recipient in the moments before the attack. Reconstructing the crime, so to speak. That can only lead to further revelations, I'm sure."

The Empress dabbed her eyes.

"What I find particularly disturbing about this whole affair was the fate of those marauders caught in space after their ship was destroyed. They chose to end their own lives rather than be captured? Is that so?"

"They shot at each other until the last man blinked out," the spy confirmed. "A very bizarre situation, all agree. Personally, I've never heard of such a thing."

"Wouldn't we have just held them in our jails had they been captured?"

The spy nodded. "And therein lies the strangeness. Our prisons are not places that further blacken men's souls. These people would have been interrogated, yes. Scanned. Brain scrubs, the works. But afterward, they would have been sent somewhere fairly comfortable and been fed and clothed. A vast improvement over life as a pirate, snorting ion-ballast crystals whenever your food tube runs low."

The Empress shivered noticeably. "Why kill themselves then?" she asked.

The spy just shook his head.

"Madam, no one I know has a clue," he said.

She shivered again. "This is not a good situation. . . ."

"True, but it is the reality of this Blackship appearing in Supertime, *that* is what's really bothering me," the spy said, "Not only is it baffling, it might prove catastrophic for all warships as well. We have always enjoyed complete invincibility within the Ethers. *Complete invincibility*. That's a tough thing to lose. I know for a fact that our top commanders are now considering sending starfighter escorts with all ships traveling in Supertime out on the Fringe. This has never been necessary before. But now, should something like this happen again—well, the captain of the next ship attacked might not be as lucky as Zap Multx."

The Empress nodded. "There was talk of giving the shuttle pilot who helped—does anyone even know his name?—some kind of commendation for his bravery. But Multx has managed to bury him somewhere. I can't say I blame him. It is not like a starship captain to want a lowly shuttle pilot to get medals for saving his ship."

"It's best that the *whole* affair be kept quiet—we don't need to be giving anyone any medals," the spy said. "As far Zap Multx, my sources tell me his streak of luck is about to end."

She sipped her drink. The fire waned a bit.

"But however the Blackship managed to get into the Ethers," she said, "wouldn't someone, somewhere in your network have heard something before the attack on the *BonoVox*? A loose set of lips out on the Fringe? A drunken braggart among the pirates? I mean, planning for such a monumental event could not have happened in a vacuum. Could it?"

The spy shook his head again. "Therein just lies more strangeness, my lady," he said. "Word of such a dramatic plot *would* have leaked out eventually and traveled around the Fringe very quickly. As you know, there are few secrets that last very long out there. Yet my best contacts tell me these particular pirates were absolute unknowns—they certainly weren't from the Sileasian System. No one knows what group they were from. No one knows where their bases are or even what sector they call home."

The Empress stared into the fireplace again. Another log appeared, sparking new life to the smoldering embers.

The spy went on: "And why in the world would they attack a ship like the *BonoVox*? Think of what havoc they could have caused among our trading and cargo ships. What plunder they could have secured!"

"What were their motives, then?" the Empress pressed him. "To capture a second ship capable of Supertime?"

The spy shrugged. "That's quite a goal for a first foray," he said. "Pirates are usually a disorganized lot, and long on dull minds. Some can barely operate the claptrap vessels they use now. Trying a ship-to-ship takeover, as your first sortie into the Ethers? I'm not sure even *our* best troops could pull that one off."

A brief silence fell. The fire was blazing again.

"So then," she finally said, "I'm sure the incident itself is already the whisper of the Fringe."

"It is," the spy confirmed.

"And the conventional thinking is?"

The spy paused before answering.

"That these pirates," he finally began, "if they were pirates, must have received the Supertime technology from someone . . . well, close to us, I'm sad to say."

The Empress was stunned. Her shoulders dropped dramatically.

"Are you suggesting . . . that someone in our *own* forces gave this sacred technology to them?"

The spy shook his head once again. "What other explanation could there be, my lady? Even if the pirates simply stumbled upon the technology—in a shipwreck, let's say—they still would have to implement it. And even then, they somehow would have to learn how to tap into the Big Generator. I don't know anybody who knows how to do that—not from scratch, anyway."

The Empress could barely move. "My God, where does that trail lead? Disloyalty in our ranks? That's exactly what led to the downfall of the Third Empire. And I suspect the first and second ones as well."

"Thus my fear of dark clouds on the horizon, my lady," the spy whispered. "When the storm hits, it might be some time before it is clear skies again."

A much deeper silence engulfed the room now. Even the fire fell quiet. The Empress's face had turned ashen. Her hands began to shake, and she could barely hold her glass. The very thought of *lèse-majesté* in the Empire's military was enough to make her chest tighten and her brow moisten with sweat. She hoped her facade would not fail her now.

Finally she broke the spell.

"You have always provided great advice and counsel for me," she said to the spy. "I pray this occasion is no different."

But the spy just slowly shook his head. "I wish it were not so, my lady," he said. "But I *have* no advice. Only that we must be vigilant—about many, many things."

He drained his drink and got up to go.

"If there was only a science to these things," he mused. "If only someone had come up with a way to predict events of the future. Five minutes from now. Five days. Five years. Five centuries . . ."

"No such science exists," the Empress said sadly. "Unless it is hiding in the heart of the poet. So we remain at a disadvantage, not knowing what the future will hold."

The spy laughed grimly. "Everything we can do—and yet the thing that we want the most, we don't have."

She finished her drink and watched her glass slowly disappear.

"Such as it is with life," she told the spy, "No matter how long some of us might live. . . ."

11

There were two major players in the Empire's military hierarchy.

The Space Forces (SF) were the element that projected the Empire's policies to the far reaches of the Galaxy. The Inner Defense Forces, more readily known as the Solar Guards (SG), were responsible for all security inside the Pluto Cloud.

Or at least that's how it was supposed to be.

It was one of the many ironies of the Fourth Empire that the Solar Guards could be found in just about every corner of the Galaxy, while many vessels of the Space Forces fleet spent their time cruising close to the Pluto Cloud, where the Empire's major repair, refurbishing, and training facilities were located.

The two services did not get along. Their top officers hardly spoke to one another, and when they did, they rarely agreed on anything. They used different types of equipment, flew different types of starships, and issued entirely different kinds of weapons to their soldiers. They even had different orders of rank and different styles of uniforms. The Space Forces wore blue with yellow trim, the Solar Guards wore black with red.

The Space Forces—comprised of the Navy, the Army, and the Air Service—were essentially mobile infantry and a means to get them where they wanted to go. The Solar Guards were more paramilitary, an army of policemen. They had spent much of the past three centuries cruising the Galaxy, working on countless investigations, some of them legitimate (such as tracking down tax outlaws), but many more done on a whim. As a result, the Solar Guards conducted their own wars and the Space Forces conducted theirs. The two services had never fought side by side against a common enemy.

The Space Forces liked to think of themselves as the senior, more professional service. Indeed, their roots went back more than a thousand years, a history that somehow survived the last two Dark Ages. The Solar Guards, on the other hand, were the upstarts, established just three hundred years before. While they boasted just half the number of men in arms as the Space Forces, their troops were considered more specialized, better trained, more ruthless. And, as keepers of the Inner Flame, they were also closer to the Imperial seat of power. Much time and effort were spent by the Space Forces to make sure their views and visions were not underrepresented before the Emperor. The top officers of the Solar Guards, however, excelled in wreaking havoc with any Space Forces initiatives.

The main conflict between the two rivals was philosophical. The Solar Guards believed the Empire's best path to success was to reclaim as many of the Galaxy's planets as possible, as quickly as possible, and bring them into the Empire's fold. The Space Forces were dedicated to the same goal, but they believed the best way to accomplish it was to go after the troublesome planets first—and bring the more peaceful, law-abiding planets back in gradually. So it was not a question of expansion, but how quickly that expansion would be carried out.

But what determined which worlds were troublesome? It was not a black-and-white issue. The Galaxy was divided into hundreds of millions of sectors, but for the most part, those systems in the center, called the Ball, were peaceful, loyal, and solid in their support for the Emperor. The worlds out on the fringe were more problematic. The farther one went from the center of the Galaxy, the more lawless and wild the planets became. Yet among these worlds were peaceful civilizations as well, many of them lost for more than a millennium and not even aware they were part of the Empire.

In bringing the rule of the Fourth Imperial Dynasty to the Galaxy, neither the Space Forces nor the Solar Guards could claim a spotless record. The Empire had more than ten trillion men under arms. Perfect performance was an unlikely possibility, to say the least, especially with the frightening superweapons the Empire possessed.

But the Spaces Forces, at least, recognized their errors and sometimes went to great lengths to correct them.

The Solar Guards didn't have time for such soul-searching.

There was a third service within the Empire forces.

This was the Expeditionary and Exploratory Force, known to all simply as the X-Forces.

The X-Forces were comparatively small. They had about a tenth the number of troops as the Space Forces, fewer than half that of the Solar Guards. The X-Forces mandate was to fly to the Outer Fringe and identify those planets lost since the last Dark Age and even beyond. In many ways they were the scouts before the cavalry.

While most of the big starships flown by the X-Forces carried their share of troops, they also lugged around many forms of humanitarian aid, plus scientists, physicians, and representatives of the Empire's diplomatic corps. Very often the first time the people of a reclaimed world even saw the Empire's banner it was painted on the side of an X-Forces vessel. Sometimes working in secret, sometimes not, the men and women of the Expeditionary and Exploratory Force were truly the professionals and went about their far-flung jobs accordingly.

As such, the X Forces had absolutely no political power anywhere in the Galaxy.

Which was why they were not invited to this very secret meeting.

Up the absolutely straight banks of the First Canal, about twenty-five miles north of the center of Big Bright City, was an area of preserved woodlands known by the archaic name Chesterwest.

An enclave of nature in the midst of the sprawl, the trees grew so thick in Chesterwest, some parts seemed perpetually bathed in twilight. One part, a place known as Sector Cello, was an especially isolated area, famous for its nearly impenetrable woodlands and countless places to hide. That's why the Space Forces and the Solar Guards had selected it as the best location to hold their very clandestine meeting.

It was close to midnight when the two shuttlecraft landed at the base of the Chesterwest mountain called Many Tears. There was a long-abandoned muster hall here. Constructed of blackwood and plastic, it was simply one big room, with no windows and just one door. Twelve men emerged from each shuttlecraft. They filed into the ancient muster building without exchanging a word, the sky above them dancing with the glow of StarScrapers being beamed up from downtown Big Bright City.

This meeting was very unauthorized. Unofficial contact between the SF and the SG without a representative from the Imperial Court on hand was considered a high crime of disloyalty. If the principals here had been caught gathering like this, they would all be executed, probably on the spot, most definitely without benefit of a trial.

Still, over the years there came times when the two opposing forces just had to talk, to settle some dispute, to smooth over some feathers. Usually the two parties sat at a table and had an orderly discussion. This time it was different.

This time it was very tense.

Zap Multx was there for the Spaces Forces; Loy Staxx was on hand as well. The most senior SF officer on hand, however, was an Army ten-star general, Skol Fyxx.

Like most SF commanders, Fyxx was a huge individual, square jaw, bald head, a few authentic body scars, and many tattoos. He was 199 years old. A veteran of countless wars, he was known throughout the Galaxy as a heroic commander and fierce strategic warrior.

On the other side there was SG First Commander Jak Dazz. Dazz was everything Fyxx was not. He was short, pudgy, free of any scars or tattoos. He was a raging ego-maniac, cunning and clever in battle, but with an absolute distaste for getting his own hands dirty.

As their men lined up behind them, Fyxx and Dazz now met in the center of the musty room. Fyxx was at least three feet taller than Dazz. Someone activated a humbeam; the room was now safe from eavesdropping from anywhere in the Galaxy.

"How long has it been, Skol?" Dazz asked, his voice thick with false charm.

"Not long enough," Fyxx replied.

Dazz looked at the line of SF officers behind his counterpart.

"Multx! You're looking . . . somewhat *recovered*," he said snidely. "When I heard about what happened to the *Vox*, I prayed that you were not among the casualties."

Multx looked like he'd just taken a sonic blast to the chest.

"I would have prayed in the same way for you, had it been your ship attacked. . . ."

Dazz laughed. His men laughed, too.

"Not much chance of that," Dazz said under his breath.

He fixed his gaze on Loy Staxx now, the man who had been forced to withdraw from the Sileasian campaign.

"And you, Staxx . . . I'm just glad to see you up and around," Dazz said. "I heard those punks on Vines 67 were a handful."

Staxx was a tall, proud man of color, 214 years old, with white hair and beard. As with Multx, he took Dazz's comment like a knife to the heart.

Fyxx took a step closer to Dazz, effectively towering over him.

"Let's cut the nonsense," Fyxx said with a growl. "You know why we're all here."

Dazz just smiled, took out an atomic cigar, and lit it up. He let the blue smoke fill the room. Then he crossed his arms against his chest and said: "Okay, this was your idea. So talk. . . ."

Fyxx could barely restrain himself. He could have crushed Dazz like a bug at that moment, but he knew only disaster would result from that. He tried to stay calm.

"Even though it is still a state secret, you seem to know a lot about what happened to the *BonoVox*," he began slowly. "Any ideas on how that Blackship managed to get into Supertime?"

Dazz just laughed again. His men did, too.

"Sure I do," he replied.

"Really?" Fyxx asked. "Enlighten us, then. . . ."

Dazz took a long puff of his cigar and blew the smoke just inches above Fyxx's head.

"Well, *obviously* those mooks got ahold of a prop core," Dazz said sarcastically. "And then figured out how to tap into the Big Generator."

More laughter from the Solar Guards.

"Is that so?" Fyxx spit back at him. "And where do you think these mooks got the prop core? Did they just find it? Or did someone give it to them?"

Dazz's features went hard very quickly. A darkness came over his face. "What are you suggesting, Fyxx?"

"I'm suggesting that it is just about impossible to come across a working prop core," Fyxx replied. "On the other hand, if someone gave them a spare and—"

Dazz's face turned bright crimson.

"Are you insane?" he shouted up at Fyxx. "Are you implying that we gave these mooks a prop core and then hooked them up to the Big Gee?"

Multx spoke up. He was more furious than Fyxx.

"Who else could have done it, you little ass?" he shouted at Dazz.

Dazz took two steps toward the *BonoVox* commander.

"Look, just because you can't read a long-range sensor array, don't blame us!" he roared back at Multx.

Multx exploded. "How much did you sell it to them for, you midget turncoat?"

Dazz lunged at Multx. They didn't come to blows only because Fyxx was able to catch the smaller man in midair. Still, the knot of opposing soldiers got tighter. Hands went to weapons. Dazz's bodyguards were gigantic; all six were more than seven feet tall and packing serious ray gun heat. They began moving toward Fyxx.

That's when Fyxx raised his hand and effectively silenced Multx.

"Be warned to stay cool here," he said to all. "Everyone loses if things get out of hand."

He set Dazz back on the floor. The SG commander took a breath and readjusted his clothes, but he was still red in the face.

"Tell your boy here not to go around accusing us of treason," he told Fyxx, pointing at Multx. He took another breath. "Now look, we don't agree on much of anything. But you guys can't seriously think that we'd give prop core technology to a bunch of mooks on a Blackship. It would be disloyalty of the highest order, for God's sake! And believe me, we're not in the business of cutting our own throats."

Fyxx looked Dazz straight in the eye. The SG high commander was saying the right words, but was he telling the truth?

"On your Oath of Honor," Fyxx said to him slowly. "Do you swear you know nothing about this? And that no one under your command has been involved?"

"On my *father's* Oath of Honor they did not," Dazz replied caustically. "Can you make that same statement?"

"I can," Fyxx replied without hesitation. "I would know, just as you would know. . . ."

A silence now descended on the room. The air of tension changed. The two dozen men realized they might have an authentic mystery on their hands here. Everyone knew that prop core technology was the second-most-guarded secret in the Empire; only the inner workings of the Big Generator were more shrouded. If the Solar Guards didn't give the prop core technology to the crew of the Blackship, then where *did* they get it?

Fyxx let down his bold front for a moment. So did Dazz.

"Every working prop core in the Space Forces is accounted for," Fyxx told him. "We checked. Double-checked. And triple-checked. Spares, front lines, from the fringe to the Ball. We know where every one of them is."

Dazz relit his cigar. "And so do we," he said. "And I'm sure your poor relations in the X-Forces have done the same thing."

So they were stumped. Another silence came over the room. It lasted for more than a minute.

Fyxx finally spoke: "Okay, let's say we make a deal."

"Propose," Dazz said.

"If I hear anything more about this, I will let you know," Fyxx told the SG commander. "Will you do the same?"

Dazz thought a moment, then nodded. "Done . . ."

The two men almost shook hands. Another silence followed. Finally Fyxx gave the order for the hum beam to be turned off. The meeting was over.

Still wary, the two sides backed away from each other and began filing out of the building very slowly.

That's when Dazz stopped.

"By the way, Skol, who are you picking in the Earth Race?" he asked the SF commander. "I hear there's a couple of real freaks among the field."

Fyxx just sniffed at him. "I don't gamble," he said.

Dazz snickered. He was back to his reptilian self again.

"Well, the way things are going," he told Fyxx, "maybe you should start. . . ."

12

Across the main canal and a few miles to the south of Sector Cello was an area known as New Brew.

No less thick of trees and hedgerows than Cello, New Brew at least had some roads running through it, and it was higher in elevation. On one of these roads was a house about an eighth of a mile from the top of a cliff.

It was modest for a dwelling in this very exclusive area, so close to the largest, most important city in the Galaxy. The house was a simple ten-room affair—rustic, almost—with a large garden out back and a jungle of overgrown wisteria and regalia hiding it out front.

This place was cool and damp no matter how hot the engineers made the weather. The road running by the house was barely paved, the path leading up to its door was just dirt and small rocks. If the intention of the person who lived here was to be inconspicuous—hidden away, even—he had succeeded grandly.

It was raining now this dark night in Chesterwest, and the winds were blowing a little more than usual. The knock came on the door just before midnight. Sitting by the light of many candles, reading his old battle reports, Petz Calandrx rose unsteadily and went to answer the door.

He was a short, elderly man, 222 years old. He had long

white hair, no beard, a bright smile, and a tanned, leathery face, the signature of a veteran starfighter pilot. His house was filled with books, or what used to be called books. They were actually holographic re-creations of texts that had been all but lost after the Second Empire fell. Calandrx loved reading the classic poets of that epoch and considered himself a minor authority on the military history of the era as well—what little of it there was. Calandrx spent days on end reading his books, always by candlelight, soaking up everything he could, looking for the signs of what inevitably doomed that empire, then releasing some of it in an occasional burst of three-meter verse.

Few things could distract him from his avocation these days. A call for a favor from an old friend was one of them.

He opened the door and found three people standing on his stoop. All three were wearing the same nondescript garment, a hood and a long tunic with hoods pulled tight; they looked not unlike a trio of grim reapers. Each person was hiding his face.

Still, Calandrx could see a faint glow coming from beneath each hood. Indeed, there was a hazy aura surrounding all of the three figures. Calandrx smiled. Eudora's Fire, they used to call it. He hadn't seen it in many years.

He shook hands first with the person in the middle.

"It's good to see you," he told the visitor. "And good to touch the hand of someone who has just crashed a star."

Hawk Hunter pulled back his hood.

"It's good to be here, General Calandrx," he replied. "And to shake hands with a true hero."

Petz Calandrx was not just a poet and a scholar. He was also the winner of the 201st Earth Race, an event held ninety-seven years before.

He'd been a starship captain at the time, a position he'd held only a short time after moving up from starfighter duty. He'd been a minor hero in the realm before that, distinguishing himself in the fiercely contested Sygma Cloud wars. Calandrx had excelled in the "terrain-attack" role performed by the Empire's starfighter units. A squadron under his command once strafed an entire planet—Zigamus 3—nonstop for more than an Earth day. Continuously ordering up weapons from their holo-systems, he and his eighteen aircraft put enough pressure on enough enemy strongholds to allow a rescue force to sweep down to the planet and extract millions of innocent civilians soon to be caught in the middle of the fighting.

This action won Calandrx several medals—and also made him a prime candidate for Earth Race 201. He won it in record time. Showered with riches and acclaim, he became a huge celebrity throughout the Galaxy. For one Earth year, the name Calandrx was never far from the lips of the Empire's seventy-five quadrillion citizens. He became so famous, in fact, that Emperor O'Nay decreed that Calandrx could never again travel in space—this on the off-chance that he might be killed in flight and thus put a tragic ending on a career that burned brighter than the stars in the Ball.

That was almost a century ago, and here was Calandrx, an intelligent hermit and still a prisoner of his own celebrity. Not many things made him happy. But at this moment, he was beside himself with joy.

These three people had crashed so many stars lately, they seemed to be glowing brighter than his candles.

The three of them trooped in, Hunter first, Erx and Berx right behind him. Of course, Erx and Berx had known Calandrx for more than eighty years.

He brought them immediately to his library and beheld them in the candlelight for a few moments. Sure enough, combined, the three of them were glowing brighter than twelve of his best wick and wax. At this, Calandrx could barely contain his delight.

"My God, is that all you three have been doing? Crashing stars?"

"Sometimes it feels that way, old friend," Erx said, shedding his disguise, if in fact a hood and tunic was a disguise. Anyone up to mischief these days always seemed to pick this combination of garb, as a way of blending in. Yet to say so was almost a *cliché*.

"Crashing isn't what it used to be," Berx said with false

disinterest. "In fact, I've been finding it rather boring lately. . . ."

Calandrx shook his fist in Berx's face.

"If I hear one more word like that from you," Calandrx scolded him, "I'll knock you so hard into the fifth dimension, you'll have to wait till next Tuesday for your ass to arrive. Crashing stars is an honor not shared by the vast majority of our galactic brothers and sisters. It's a gift to be able do it. It must be appreciated as such."

Berx laughed in his face. So did Erx. Only really old friends could treat each other this way.

"Do you have any slow-ship, Petz?" Erx asked him, walking to the blazing fireplace to warm his hands. "Or have you graduated to that crap they sell on Neptune?"

Calandrx shuffled off to his liquor cabinet. It took up one entire wall of his reading room. Several rows were filled with slow-ship wine; others held some "Neptune crap."

"Come, sit," Calandrx bid them as he reached for his oldest bottle of slow. "Imagine my pleasure when I heard from Brother Multx and accepted his offer of intrigue."

"Imagine our surprise when we found out you were his contact with the race committee," Erx said. "I would have thought you were above such things, Petz. Gambling, subterfuge, and such?"

Calandrx was in the middle of filling their goblets with wine. He intentionally poured Erx but half a cup.

"Someday *you'll* be planetbound, Erx," Calandrx told him. "And then you'll know the curse of getting no closer to the stars than looking up at them at night. When that day comes, I want to know how you'll be amusing yourself."

Erx thought about this for a moment. "I think 'abusing' myself is the more likely consequence."

Berx nodded. "Bingo, that."

Calandrx waved them off and turned to Hunter.

"They could probably behead him for it," he began. "But Multx told me a bit about your skill in saving the *BonoVox*. You must have extraordinary pluck to face down a Blackship with a shuttlecraft. I've never heard of anything so deliciously mad."

"If you mean 'mad' as being insane, I'm beginning to

agree," Hunter said, tasting his slow-ship wine.

"Do you want to hear about our crash on Fools 6?" Berx asked Calandrx with a straight face. The old pilot simply waved him off again. He was intent on asking Hunter all the questions.

"They say your flying ability was rather mind-boggling," Calandrx said to him. "With a swiftness of maneuver not seen before. What are you hiding, my son? Were you trained by some anonymous master pilot? Someone who is no longer with us? Or perhaps you found a brain ring left over from the Third Empire. Containing long-lost starfighter techniques? Is that it?"

Hunter was used to hearing such questions now.

"Someday I hope I'll remember," he replied. "And when I do, I promise I'll sit here and tell you everything."

Calandrx smiled broadly. "Well said," he declared, tapping Hunter's kneecap with the butt of the wine bottle. "I will look forward to that day."

They toasted and drank and Calandrx refilled their glasses. This time Erx got a full measure.

"Now for the matter at hand," Calandry announced.

The three visitors pulled their chairs closer to Calandrx. There was no hum beam to rely on here.

"I have secured a position for you in the race," the old pilot revealed. "It's the thirteenth slot, the last one available, meaning you'll be on the pole. But you will be entered without any qualifying stints or prerace interrogation. Your presence will be known to only a very few people until the day of the race itself."

Hunter was stunned. This seemed to be everything that Multx could have wished for. He would not have to prequalify. He would not have to answer a million and one questions for race officials prior to the contest. It seemed too good to be true.

And, in a way, it was.

"By what bargain were you able to secure these advantages for us?" Erx asked. "We must be giving something away. . . ."

Calandrx shot him a stern glance. "He will fly in the race, won't he?"

"If you say so, brother," Erx replied.

"And that's the important thing, do you agree?"

Erx nodded uncertainly. "If you say so. . . ."

Then Berx leaned over to him and stage-whispered one word: "Maccus."

Erx thought about this for a moment, then shook his head. "Of course . . ."

But Hunter wasn't really paying attention. He tended to agree with Calandrx. He could have cared less *how* he was able to enter the race, just as long as he could compete.

But he did have one big question. He was surprised that no one had brought it up before now.

"So I am in the contest," he said. "But what will I be flying?"

Erx and Berx just looked at each other. They had just assumed Hunter would be driving a radically adapted starfighter, like most of the other racers, maccus or not.

But apparently Multx had had something else in mind when he hatched this scheme—and Calandrx was in on it.

"My brother Zap has sent me the craft in which you will ride," the old pilot said with a cackle.

Erx and Berx looked around them.

"It is here?" they asked at once.

"You have room for a starfighter in here?" Erx added.

"What's up in your attic?" Berx demanded with a laugh.

Calandrx just looked at them and shook his head. "What's up in *your* attic?" he asked Berx. "I told you two that you were spending way too much time out on the Fringe. It's making you dumber, not smarter."

"Who else said that to us recently?" Berx asked Erx.

Erx shrugged and sipped his wine.

"Beats me," he replied.

Calandrx just shook his head, then reached inside his jacket pocket and came out with a tiny green box. He held it up to the candlelight for all of them to see. It was glowing.

"Here is your vessel," he told Hunter dramatically.

Hunter looked at the little box for a few moments.

"Either this wine is very good, or you're holding a little box in you hand."

Calandrx's face wrinkled in a wide smile. "I believe them

when they say you are not from around here."

Erx and Berx sat forward a bit and studied the tiny box.

"My God, Petz, you're suddenly trafficking in the tools of espionage, too?" Erx said. "Spying, gambling? In the old days they'd call an intervention for you."

Calandrx waved him away again. But Hunter was still confused. What *was* the tiny green box?

"It's a 'twenty and six,' " Berx said to him. "And old spy trick—but a good one."

He picked up the box and held it before Hunter's eyes. His crashn' glow was causing it to pulse with an odd emerald hue.

"Brother Calandrx is correct," Berx declared. "Whatever you are going to fly is here. Inside this tiny box."

Hunter looked to Erx; in this group he stood out as a beacon of reason.

" 'Twenty and six' is an archaic term for the twenty-sixth dimension," Erx explained, taking the box from Berx. "Few people bother with any dimension beyond thirteen or fourteen these days, but this one has some fairly interesting properties."

"You can hide things there," Calandrx said simply. "And no one will ever find them. . . ."

"Have you looked at what's inside yet?" Erx asked the veteran space pilot.

"I couldn't bear to," he said. "Not before you came."

He looked around his expansive library.

"I don't think I can retrieve it in here," he said. 'This room is just a bit too small and there might be a problem if I can't get it to go back into the twenty-six again."

He stood up, drained his wine goblet, and announced, "So then, gentlemen—to the garden!"

Calandrx's garden was more like a small woods with a clearing in the middle.

It was a rather large piece of real estate on what was actually a very crowded part of the planet—another benefit of winning his Earth Race so long ago. The trees ran on either side of the expansive lawn. Living sculptures and glowing plant pots dotted the top of the finely trimmed terranium grass.

The four starmen staggered out to the side of an old weathered cottage that was tenuously attached to the main house.

"Here, the perfect place," Calandrx declared, placing the small green box down on the ground about fifty feet away from the rest of them. Above, the sky was dancing with color from all the StarScrapers in use down in central Big Bright City, twenty miles down the main canal.

Once the green box had been put in position, Calandrx activated an electron torch and sent a long, thin beam of red light crashing into it. A small storm of sparks came cascading from the box. A strange mist filled the air. Then there was a sharp crack, and then a distinctive odor filled their nostrils.

A moment later, the contents of the small box popped into their existence.

"My God," Calandrx said with a gasp. *"What is it?"*

Hunter was stunned. Long, thin, rugged. A wing. A canopy. Wheels . . .

It was his old flying machine.

Erx and Berx began laughing.

"Brother Multx!" Erx said, shaking his head. "Never at a loss for the dramatic!"

"That old mutt," Berx exclaimed. "Did he take it with us when we left Fools 6, or did he have someone go back to get it?"

There was no answer to that question now—and frankly Hunter couldn't have cared less about how Multx had been able to retrieve it. The important thing was this: His flying machine was here, and obviously it was what Hunter would pilot in the Earth Race.

Once he had regained his composure, Calandrx began shivering with delight.

"It's such a beautiful machine!" he declared, approaching the strange craft and passing his hand along the underside of the fuselage. "It's so *not like* the flying triangles everyone flies now. It's so *less* boring."

He began walking the length of the aircraft, fascinated by its unusual design, its wings, its overall sleekness. When he arrived back where he'd started from, he could not stop shaking his head.

"I've never seen such a machine as this, not while I was

awake, anyway," he said. "This thing is stunning. It looks like it *should be* flying, not like those cheese wedges the Empire insists on churning out."

Calandrx looked to the stars and began searching for the right words. "Your machine contains what no one else can see these days. There is a unique design here. A unique passion. This thing has . . . what is the word they used many years ago?"

" 'Kick-ass'?" Erx offered.

" 'Ballsy'?" Berx weighed in.

Calandrx was shaking his head. "No, you dullards!" he said. "The word was 'style,' I think. Yes, that's it. *Style*. This machine has style."

Now that Hunter had been immersed in all things Empire for the past few weeks, he had to agree that his flying machine certainly looked *different*.

He was still astonished that it was here at all, on Earth, right in front of him. Its familiar smell wafted through his nostrils. He always believed an invisible aura surrounded the aircraft—he could feel its vibrations now just like every time he was near it back on Fools 6.

"They will freak out when they see this thing pull up to the starting line," Calandrx said.

"Bingo that," Erx agreed.

"And you should see this thing fly!" Berx said.

Then, to Hunter's embarrassment, the explorers recounted for Calandrx aerial displays he'd put on for them during their brief stay on Fools 6. Though their retelling was tinged with hyperbole, Calandrx took in every word as if it were Bible truth. He was clearly delighted at this turn of events.

"The Earth Race hasn't been shaken up in a long while," he said, rubbing his hands together at the possibilities. "If this thing can fly half as good as my brothers here say it can, I think we are in for some very interesting times in about a week or so."

Hunter looked skyward, through the streams of Star-Scrapers, out into the rim of the Milky Way. He imagined he could see Fools 6 way out there. Less than a month ago, he was on that isolated planet, wondering if there was anybody else in the universe. Since then he'd witnessed one space battle, fought in another, been smuggled across the Pluto Cloud, and had set his foot on Earth—*again*.

How much more "interesting" could it get?

That's when Calandrx turned to him and said: "So how does this magnificent craft work?"

Hunter began to say something but then stopped. Calandrx just stared at him. Erx and Berx did, too.

"How does it work?" he heard himself mumble.

"Yes, my son," Calandrx said. "How does it fly? How is it propelled through air? Through space?"

But Hunter was finally stumped. He had to speak the truth: "I don't know," he said.

And finding out would not be easy.

It took Hunter and Calandrx three hours just to get the flying machine's power plant access door open.

The problem came from the transfer out of the twenty and six. Such interdimensional leaps weren't always perfect things; distortions could occur. In this case, the flying machine that came out of the twenty-sixth dimension was slightly smaller than the one that went in. Mere micrometers in difference, it was enough to nearly weld the access door fasteners to the body of the craft. Using the electron torch didn't help. If anything, it made the atoms in the fasteners expand even farther.

Finally they had to replicate a tool that looked like a knife with its leading edge flattened out. By inserting this edge into the cross-groove in the fastener and twisting it, the fasteners gradually loosened up. But it took a lot of work and a lot of time to do the twisting.

Erx and Berx had fallen asleep somewhere along the way. They eventually drifted into the sixth dimension, where a good night's sleep was always a guarantee.

But Hunter and Calandrx stayed awake and took turns twisting, and finally the seized covers came off. But while gaining access to the interior of the flying machine's power plant chamber answered one question, it brought about a few million more.

"What madness is this?" Calandrx asked upon getting his

first glimpse of what lay within Hunter's craft.

What he saw was a massive jumble of wires, hoses, fasteners, screws, all surrounding a long shaft of steel that seemed to have thousands of small, shiny blades attached to it. This shaft ran nearly the length of the flying machine. A multitude of other unidentifiable things did, too. For someone like Calandrx, who was used to seeing a starfighter's orderly and compact power plant, this *was* madness.

"The shaft spins," Hunter began explaining. "It sucks in the atmosphere, it mixes with the power source, and together they produce propulsion. More than enough to get the thing airborne."

But Calandrx was still baffled. "In theory I can see how it would work—this just seems like such a strange way of doing it."

He looked up at Hunter.

"How did you say you built this?"

Hunter began to give his standard answer. "I gathered parts I'd salvaged from a crashed ship that was—"

Calandrx interrupted him with the wave of his hand.

"I *know* all that," he said. "I mean, how did you *build* it? How did you come up with the concept? The design? The blueprint?"

Here comes the really strange part, Hunter thought.

"It was just after I found myself on Fools 6," he began. "I woke up one night. Got dressed. And started drawing."

"Drawing?"

"Yes, drawing—I took a piece of burned wood and made drawings on my floor, my walls, my chairs and table. Once I started, I couldn't stop. I don't know where it all came from. I don't know if it was set off by a dream, or whether one piece of my lost memory decided to come back. I just don't know.

"But I transcribed everything I put down that night. And from that plan, I built this. And believe me, I was astonished that it actually worked."

"So, it really *does* fly?"

"It did," Hunter replied. "And assuming nothing else was skewered in the transfer, it should still be able to."

Calandrx went back to studying the machine's guts.

"You were obviously more than just a pilot, wherever you're from," he told Hunter. "You must have built your own machines as well. I mean, how else can we explain the fact that you were not only able to come up with this concept, but to put it together, successfully, as well."

Hunter just shrugged good-naturedly.

"You know how those electron torches are," he said. "Sometimes all you have to do is *think* about what shape you want something to be—and the torch just takes over and does it, big or small."

Calandrx looked up at Hunter very queerly.

"That's not how electron torches work," he said bluntly.

Hunter stared back at him for a moment. "Are you sure?" he asked. This was news to him.

He began to explain, but Calandrx put up his hand.

"Later," he said. "My poor brain already has too much to absorb this night. Let us return to the mystery of this machine."

He stuck his head back into the propulsion area.

"This thing you call the power source," he yelled out. "Where is it exactly?"

Hunter crawled into the access door. It took some wiggling and waggling, but he was finally able to point out a line of small black boxes he'd installed about midway down the bladed shaft. All the boxes were connected to each other.

"This was the only thing I had to improvise," he explained. "After the machine came together I couldn't figure out how to supply the power to it. I searched for anything aboard the wreck that might be capable of producing self-generating power. Nothing fit the bill. Then I came upon these boxes—they were deep down in the wreck, meaning they were somewhere near the nose of the ship. There were several dozen of them in all; each one had a connection where they could be coupled together. Something told me if these boxes were connected in the right sequence, they might be able to provide power.

"The strange thing was, I hooked up the first five boxes I could salvage, and on the first try, I discovered that arrangement provided more than enough of the propulsive force I needed."

Calandrx's frame was small enough that he was able to reach where the boxes were. He examined the alignment with his quadtrol and was startled by what he found.

"My God," he said. "This shipwreck on your planet. Do you have any idea what *kind* of ship it was?"

Finally a question Hunter could give an easy answer to.

"Yes, it was a Kaon Bombardment ship," he stated clearly. "The *Jupiterus Five*."

Calandrx hit his head trying to get out from under the access door.

"A Kaon ship?"

"Yes . . . I think they are a type of—"

"Oh, I know what type of ship they are," Calandrx cut him off. Then he started stammering a bit. "But what you've done here . . . with these components . . ."

He stood up and wiped his hands. Erx and Berx were still sound asleep, their interdimensional images just faintly visible on two of the garden's hammocks.

"Those two . . ." Calandrx said, indicating the sleeping explorers. "Do they know about these inner workings? About those black boxes?"

Hunter didn't think so. "I've never gone into much technical detail with them. They do know that the wreck was a Kaon ship, though."

Calandrx nodded with new understanding. "I'm sure they do—and after finding that out, they were probably too smart to ask any more questions," he said. "No wonder that pair has managed to stay out of trouble for so long. They're *experts* in knowing when to play dumb."

Hunter was having trouble following Calandrx. He could tell the famous pilot's thoughts were running a million miles a second again.

"Does this thing have a hover mode?" he asked Hunter.

Hunter pointed to a set of openings in the craft's belly.

"I'm able to direct the propulsive force downward through these. That was something I added on after completing the entire thing."

Calandrx examined the movable nozzles and just shook his head.

"Ingenious," he said with a laugh. "*Strange* . . . but extremely ingenious."

He closed the access door and sealed it again. "This thing, do you think you can fly it now?"

"Now? Like right here and now?"

"Yes," Calandrx insisted. "Can you?"

Hunter shrugged.

"Sure. Why not?" he replied.

Ten minutes later Hunter had the machine turned on and hovering.

Calandrx had to block his ears, the strange power plant was so loud. And while the flying machine looked strange enough sitting on its wheels, seeing it floating somewhat motionless just a foot or so off the ground was very bizarre. Unlike the Empire's current crop of starfighters, which tended to stay very still in their hover mode, this craft looked like it was raring to go, bouncing up and down, as if the slightest provocation would be enough to make it rocket away.

He came up close to the hovering craft and had a conversation with Hunter.

"Have you ever opened this thing up to full throttle?" Calandrx asked.

Hunter just shook his head. "Never really needed to."

"Want to give it a try? Do you think your airframe will hold together?"

"It should," Hunter said. "It's all melded electron steel. But where should I go?"

"Around the world," Calandrx yelled back. "Right around the globe itself."

"Really? You want me to circumnavigate the *entire* planet?"

"Precisely," Calandrx replied. "It's a test of a theory as to how your machine works. If this thing is powered the way I think it is, we will all be rich in a matter of days. If we don't all go to jail, that is. Now just stay low, go as fast as you can for as far as you can—and don't stop until you get back here."

He held up a box of candles and a handful of ancient

wooden matches. The candles were about two feet long.

"I will light this," Calandrx told him, drawing one candle out. "And watch it burn down. Then I will light another, and another, if need be. We will measure the length of time you are gone by the how many candles we burn."

That was fine with Hunter. He was just happy to be sitting inside his old machine again. Already he was drinking it in— the panel lights glowing, the control stick in one hand, throttle in the other. He was becoming part of it again. He jammed his helmet over his ears; luckily it had come through the twenty-and-six transport with no change in size.

"Okay with me," he told Calandrx. "Full throttle?"

"Full throttle," the elderly pilot confirmed.

With that, Calandrx stepped away, and Hunter commanded the flying machine to rise about twenty-five feet above the garden. He looked down at Calandrx, who was holding up the candle in one hand and the matches the other. Hunter saluted him, pointed the aircraft's nose west, pushed his throttle full forward, and was off in a great blast of noise and power.

He was back, coming from the opposite direction, before Calandrx lit the first match.

13

Big Bright City
The day before the race

It might have been the cheapest room in the city.

It certainly was one of the smallest. Located atop a sixty-six-story building hard by the edge of the east canal, the compartment measured a mere twelve feet by twenty. It had a tiny balcony, a small lavatory, a floating cot, one slightly cracked window, and a food tube that had been installed sometime in the previous century.

Several air bridges went right over the top of the diminutive apartment building. That was one reason for the room's cheap rent. The fact that one of the ancient triad bridges ran close by further lowered its desirability. While the vast majority of people in the Galaxy were superstitious, Earthlings were the worst of the lot. No one wanted to be anywhere near a sacred span if they could help it. No one . . .

Which is why Zap Multx had to pay just six aluminum coins for the use of the small room. He wasn't here because of the economics, though. Money was hardly a problem for someone in his position. No, he was here because he wanted to lay low for a while. Just him, his thoughts, his blaster pistol, and a few bottles of slow-ship wine. That's what he thought he needed. So he'd leased the room a week ago, using an assumed name. And once the tense meeting up in Chesterwest had concluded, he beamed directly here, without even having to pass through the front door. It turned out to be a great place to hide.

Most people assumed he was on his way back out to the Fringe, to resume his quest of saving the Galaxy for the Empire. Actually the *BonoVox* was parked in the seventeenth dimension at a spot just outside the Pluto Cloud. The One-Seven was where SF warships needing extensive repairs were sent while waiting their turn before the electron torch. The *BonoVox* needed no such repairs. But considering what had happened during their last trip Inward, Multx thought this was the best place to stash his vessel, at least for the time being.

Still, after sitting here for a week now, alone and drunk, how he longed to be back aboard her and flying in space again! Heading out to the frontier, the farther out the better. The Fringe. *That's* where everything was happening. *That's* what made the blood in his veins flow. If he was an expert on just one thing, it was this: As busy and bustling and exciting as Big Bright City was, especially on the eve of the Earth Race, it still couldn't compare to the adrenaline rush one could get daily out there, so close to the edge.

And that's what Multx knew he would miss the most.

Despite the air bridges and the sacred span and the thousands of air-chevys darting above, below, and around him, Multx's little room still had a commendable view.

It looked out over the east canal and into the real downtown part of downtown Big Bright. For the past six days he had watched the great city prepare for the Earth Race. The skies above, the waters below, the streets and airways—busy, maddeningly so. What happens when they give a party in a city of two billion filthy rich people? Another two billion show up. All just close friends, mind you, but it made for a very crowded place.

From his hiding spot, Multx believed he'd seen every last one of those four billion pass by him in the past six days. He was literally surrounded by humanity, everyone having someplace to go and something to do. It was fascinating to watch, but this distraction did little to relieve the dull ache in his chest. Multx did not like this feeling. After more than one hundred years as a military officer, nearly half of that time commanding a huge starship, one would have thought he'd gained an immunity to such lowly things as apprehension and uneasiness. But apparently that was not the case. Not in the past week, anyway.

It was the waiting—that's what was killing him. Sitting alone, in his dress white uniform, knowing it was just a matter of time before they found him.

And what would happen after that?

He didn't want to think about it.

It was early afternoon, the sun was just beginning to warm his tiny balcony when he heard a familiar sizzling sound behind him.

He turned from the porch to find two Space Navy guards standing in the middle of his compartment. They were in dress uniforms, armed, but with their weapons still holstered, at least for the moment.

"Sorry to disturb you, Star Commander," one of them said. "But you're wanted at headquarters immediately."

"Not a problem," Multx replied with a sigh. "I've been expecting you."

He stood up, buttoned his tunic, and drained his glass of wine. Then he took in one last breath of the canal air. It tasted bittersweet.

"Okay, brothers," he said, "lead the way. . . ."

Flash!

An instant later, Multx was sitting in the Grand Briefing Office (GBO), a multiwindow room atop the soaring, octagon-shaped skyscraper known as CD District One.

This gigantic building served as headquarters for the Empire Space Forces. It was nearly five times as big as the SF's largest warship and was at the southern end of Big Bright City, just before the canal known by the archaic name M'cpoto. (No surprise, the Solar Guards' headquarters was more than four hundred miles away, due north, at the exact opposite end of the vast city; it sat on the banks of an equally ancient and perpetually fouled canal known as the Chuk.)

Sitting across the huge table from Multx now were six star admirals. Each was more than two hundred years old; each was wearing a uniform weighed down by dozens of medals, ribbons, and battle pins. These were Multx's direct superiors, the gods of his world. And even though they were all smiling, Multx knew none of them was happy.

After receiving nods from the other five, one officer activated a hum beam, sealing the GBO in.

"Welcome, Brother Zap," the first admiral began. "We are enriched by your presence here."

Multx bowed his head slightly. The flattery sounded sincere, but these guys were very good when it came to these things.

"I draw strength from my friends and the Earth beneath my feet," Multx replied correctly.

The quick formalities over, the smile left the first admiral's face. It was time to get down to business.

He spoke: "Zap, old friend, we called you here because we are very concerned about the events following your successful operation on Vines 67. Some time has passed now since the *BonoVox* was attacked. Have you any further thoughts on what happened?"

"I do not, sir," Multx replied, cursing himself for having to use those words. "As my report stated, we had no indications of any vessels near us. Then, quite suddenly, this Blackship was simply there, off our starboard side, dispensing its war parties."

A stark silence enveloped the room. Multx began to say something further, but stopped himself instead.

The first admiral spoke again: "The fact that they were trying to board you, and not destroy you outright, is telling, don't you agree?"

"I do, sir," Multx replied glumly. Whoever the mysterious spacemen were, they had quite nearly succeeded in their goal. Had that happened, the *BonoVox* would have been the first Space Forces starship ever captured by an enemy, and Multx's name would have gone down in history—as a new adjective for failure.

The second admiral spoke now.

"It is not only disturbing that the bandits chose to take one another's lives," he said. "It's proved inconvenient as well.

They left us no evidence as to who they were, or how they managed to get into Supertime, true?"

"Yes, sir—even the fractional analysis of the visual sensor readings did not help us at all," Multx reported. "We were not able to penetrate the enemy's spacesuits or even get a glimpse through one of the helmet visors just to get a look at the faces of these men."

"So they were masked intentionally?" the second admiral asked.

"No doubt part of their overall nefarious plan," Multx replied. "If their attack failed, then we were not to know who they were. And if they had succeeded . . . well, I'm sure their names would be on everyone's lips by now."

Another painful silence descended on the room. Multx looked past the six men, through the huge window beyond. A gigantic starship was lifting up from below, preparing to rocket away into deep space. Multx felt his heart do a flip. How he wished he was on that ship—any ship!—right now.

The third admiral now spoke to Multx.

"This man you picked up on Fools 6—his name is Hunter?"

"Yes, sir."

"He certainly seemed to be in the right place at the right time, correct?"

"To say the least, sir," Multx replied.

"Where is he these days?" the third admiral wanted to know.

Multx hesitated, but just for a moment.

"He's been conscripted into the Space Forces and is due to begin training, here on Earth, very shortly."

"What kind of training?"

" 'Advanced flight training,' I think we could say," Multx replied quickly. He didn't want to dwell on *this* subject. It was the only bright spot in what had been a very dreary week. "I have no doubt that he will be an asset to our forces someday—and possibly the one good thing to come out of this incident."

Another silence settled on the room. The six officers closed their briefing books on cue. Multx tried to steel himself. The worst part of this day was now at hand.

The first admiral smiled unevenly, then spoke again: "Well, now that all our preliminary business is over, we have an announcement to make. It is my pleasure to inform you, Star Commander Multx, that you and your crew will be given special citations for your role in this unusual action."

Multx again nodded with as much dignity as he could muster. But he knew a very large bomb was about to drop on his head.

"And, as a result of discussions we had prior to your arrival here," the top officer went on, "it has been decided that you and your crew will be reassigned as well. . . ."

Multx grimaced. *Here it comes*, he thought.

"Instead of returning to the Fringe," the second admiral announced, "we would like you to make a 'goodwill tour' of the inner Galaxy."

That was it. Multx felt all the energy drain right out of his body. Those were the exact words he'd dreaded hearing.

"We are being sent to the Ball, sir?" he asked weakly.

"Correct," the first admiral replied, trying his best to sound upbeat. "I think you'll agree the citizens at the center of the realm have to wait far too long between visits of our grand ships. The appearance of the famous *BonoVox* in their midst will do wonders for their morale, not to mention their loyalty. Indeed, after what you've been through, you and your crew have earned such an assignment."

The other officers nodded in agreement.

But it was all Multx could do to remain sitting upright in his chair. Being sent to the inner part of the Galaxy was the equivalent of an old racehorse being put out to pasture. The Ball was no place for any warship, never mind one that carried twenty-thousand highly trained special operations troops. The star systems there were dull, peaceful, ardently devoted to the Empire. There had not been a military action anywhere near the Galaxy's core since the rise of the Fourth Empire nearly five centuries before.

Still, Multx could understand his superiors' decision. That a Blackship had somehow been able to puncture the Ethers was very disturbing. Even more chilling was the possibility that the bandits had somehow tapped into the Big Generator itself. Such a thing would shake the Empire to its very foundations.

But of more immediate concern was the fact that twenty-two thousand troops and crew members of the *BonoVox* had witnessed the strange midspace battle and knew what the mysterious spacemen had been able to do. And though they had all been sworn to secrecy, there was no way the Space Forces' hierarchy could take the chance of twenty-two thousand pairs of loose lips returning to the Fringe. (Indeed, rumors of a strange battle were already making their way across the Galaxy.) Thus the decision to exile the *BonoVox* to the Ball, to float through the complacent seas of the core for an indefinite period of time, far away from any front-line forces to whom such a dark secret as this would actually mean something.

For Multx, though, the goodwill tour was a career-killer. In a perfect world, he and his starship should be *leading* the search for the origins of the mysterious Blackship crew, not running away from them. But that important assignment would go to someone else now, a close rival of his, no doubt. And should they be successful, the prestige and glory would belong solely to them.

Assigned to the Ball . . . Multx would have rather heard the words of his execution decree. For someone like him, this truly was a fate worse than death.

Thus the penalty of being in the *wrong* place at the *wrong* time.

14

*Big Bright City
Race day*

Erx and Berx were late.

A colossal traffic jam of people, people-moving machines, soldiers, robots, hovering air cars, you name it, filled the streets around the Big Bright City arena. The Earth Race was scheduled to begin in less than an hour. Anyone not already inside the vast stadium was scrambling mightily in these last few minutes, hoping to secure entry before the crucial moment of noon.

Erx and Berx had planned ahead of time to avoid this massive crush. Instead they were making their way through the labyrinth of alleys and courtyards that bordered the miles-long arena's west side. They had thought this would reveal a creative shortcut to the main gate, and indeed, the way was clear when they started out. But in the last alley they had traversed before reaching their goal, they stumbled upon the main service entrance for the thousands of robots serving the arena.

This was not good. The narrow alley was full of mechanical men moving this way and that, sent out to this hidden street to tune down until they were needed again. The problem was that when they weren't assigned a specific task, robots tended to be clumsy. This was especially true of the industrial models, which were barely two arms, two legs, a torso, and a square head. These robots were of the lowest service type imaginable. They could deliver a drink, light an atomic cigar, push a broom, and that was about it.

As more of then flowed into the alleyway, they were beginning to tune out, which meant they would shut down in a frozen position until being activated again. It was nearly impossible to move them once they were down; thus moving *around* them became a nightmare. Though close to it, Big Bright City was not a perfect place. Strange things were known to happen here, too.

"Only on Earth could a bunch of robots block off an entire thoroughfare on the most important day of the year!" Berx cried as they soon found themselves in a virtual forest of walking oil cans.

"I fear this bad luck will carry through to our wages on the race!" Erx agreed.

They were in sight of their destination; that's what made it so frustrating. But they had only themselves to blame. They had chosen to spend the previous night drinking and whoring with holo-girls—and a late start this morning had been the result. So they would be late for the most prestigious sporting event in the entire Galactic Empire and miss placing their wager.

Blast the luck, they would have liked to think, but truth was this: The last week had been such a blur it was lucky they'd made it this far.

The reason they'd been sent to Earth in the first place was to watch over Hunter, to shepherd him through the pre–Earth Race process. To make sure that no other starship commander put his hooks into him and thus negated Zap Multx's brilliant ploy.

But they hadn't seen Hunter all week. Once Calandrx got him accepted as a finalist for race day, he was immediately sequestered. As his sponsor for the race, Calandrx was designated Hunter's one and only handler. Thus Erx and Berx were stuck on Earth, in Big Bright City, with nothing to do.

Well, almost nothing . . .

Because since leaving Calandrx's house that next morning, their unexpected vacation had devolved into an endless string of prerace parties, holo-girls, and indescribable feasts—all at Multx's expense. Leaving their rented quarters too late on this day, the busiest morning in the Empire, had been just foolish.

There was less than a quarter mile from the main gate, but that distance might as well have been a light-year or two. The jam of robots had ceased moving a long time ago.

But then something of a small miracle happened. . . .

There was a commotion behind them. They turned to see a line of Earth Police making its way down the alley. Noted for recruiting the largest individuals in the Empire, the EP served as the Planet's premier security force. Few things stood in their way when they got the call to duty. No surprise, they had a solution to the blockade of 'bots.

The captain of the rank simply directed a levitation beam at the swarm of robots. Causing the tin cans to rise about ten feet off the ground, he created a tunnel of sorts for his policemen to walk through. When the column passed by, Erx and Berx simply pulled their helmet visors down and fell in behind the group. Before anyone noticed, they had marched the final block and a half to the stadium entrance and right through the main gate itself.

At that point the two Earth Policemen in front of them turned and realized what the explorers were up to. These gigantic creatures lifted Erx and Berx up off their feet and literally threw them out of the line. They landed hard into the crowd jammed around the gate, knocking over a dozen people at least.

But it didn't matter.

They were in.

Three hundred feet below

"Are you sure you want to do this?"

Hunter looked up from his control panel and thought about the question for a moment. This might have been the first time since leaving Fools 6 that someone had asked him what *he* wanted.

"Sure I want to do it," he replied. "Why not?"

Calandrx smiled. "I'm glad you're still sounding positive about it. That's a good sign."

"Think that if you want," Hunter said. "But to tell you the truth, I'd do just about anything to get out of here."

They were in the subsubbasement of the Earth Race arena, locked inside one of the tiny, concrete vessel bays that made up the holding area for the contest's participants. Hunter was sitting in his cockpit; Calandrx was lording over a bottle of slow-ship wine. One of thirteen compartments that ran off a circular hallway that held an air tube in its center, this had been their home for the past six days. It was cool, damp, musty—not the best conditions for Hunter's flying machine. It also seemed to be quite haunted. Even though they were sealed in, they were periodically assaulted by the most ghostly howling, outright screaming, and the sounds of a woman wailing, all of it coming from somewhere deep in the walls.

It was a *very* strange place, but they had no choice except to be here. True, the regulations for the Earth Race took up an entire nanodisk of memory, much of it written in the archaic language that few people on Earth even understood anymore. But some of the rules were clear. One said that all pilots had to remain unseen in the six days before the race (thus the Emperor's "symbolic" week off). Another said the racers had to be sequestered here, with their handlers, five stories below the earth, in the 'combs, while preparing for the competition. No surprise, Hunter's star-crashn' glow had faded quickly in this place.

No one had seen them since they'd been interned here. Hunter had spent the time listening to Calandrx's war stories and getting an education on the Empire's military history, all while checking, rechecking, and then triple-checking every one of his machine's critical flight systems. This had kept him busy; there were many adjustments to be made to his craft after the skewing it had experienced while jumping into and out of the twenty and six.

It also kept his mind off of who might be doing all of the howling and screaming and wailing.

"You always hear the good buzz about this contest," Calandrx was telling him now. "But I know guys who started

off stinking of boldness, yet by the time they launched, flew
the race and crossed the finish line. . . . well, let's just say
they were different people. That transdimensional stuff had
scrambled their brains a bit. I know it did mine."

Hunter went back to testing his control panel lights. "If
you really thought you could talk me out of this, I wish you'd
done it six days ago. Then we could have avoided this hole
in the ground altogether."

"To the contrary, my friend," Calandrx said with a sigh.
"If you decided not to run this race, my life would return to
its old boring ways. Reading my books, lighting my candles.
Everyone needs a change now and then."

Hunter looked about the dank compartment. "But is this
really the change you were looking for? I mean, this place
gives me the creeps."

"Yes, I think they do that on purpose," Calandrx said
knowingly. "At least they did back when I ran the race. It's
their way of introducing you to the madness to come."

Hunter reattached his light screen. "Well, judging from
what you've told me about this whole affair, I don't doubt
that a bit."

Over the past few days, Calandrx also had relayed everything he knew about the history of the Earth Race. It was
fascinating in an odd kind of way. During its first century,
the race was exactly what its name implied: a contest to find
out which of the Empire's starfighter pilots could fly around
the globe at the fastest speed possible without having his
aircraft disintegrate around him. In those early years, no
money was offered in the winner's prize, there was no promise of homes or promotions or assignments to the most de-
sirable posts in the Empire. The winner got an aluminum
medal, a blessing from the Emperor, and that was it.

By its second century, the citizens had decided this was
way too boring. The perks were increased, money was intro-
duced as part of the first prize, and the winner was declared
by the Emperor to be a Very Fortunate by law. The race
pilots also were allowed to modify their aircraft after the
discovery of a "nonrule" in the race's regulations in about
the year 7074. This created a sprint in technology among the

participants that led to some mind-boggling speeds and finish times.

Over the past century, the race had evolved even farther. The idea was still to go around the planet as fast as possible. But several decades before, the twist of the interdimensional obstacle course had been added. The twenty-five-thousand-mile race was still basically the same; it's just that now, along the way, the competing pilots had to fly certain legs of it inside the thirteenth dimension, a place appropriately nicknamed "Bad Dream."

The interdimensional portals for this were articulated in the form of huge blue screens that came up fast and at unpredictable locations along the race course. The racers knew only that there would be three screens in all. What happened to them after they punched through one and gained the one-three was totally unpredictable. Nothing was stable inside Bad Dream; it was a mirror dimension ruled entirely by antilogic. Painful memories usually prevailed, though. It was possible for race pilots to refight some long-forgotten battle or to relive parts of their lives while traveling within. Even parts of *previous* lives could be dredged up. Or so it appeared. Though what happened inside the thirteen was usually wiped from the pilot's memory as soon as he punched out, some racers carried bits of their experience out with them.

Calandrx certainly had. In one of his punch-ins, he'd been jolted back to his first ever combat mission, an action against the fierce Ajax Tri-System pirates that had left everyone in Calandrx's unit dead except himself. In the weird world of the thirteen, he'd had to dogfight the pirates all over again, in space, at what his brain considered faster-than-normal speed, all while his colleagues were dying around him in extremely slow motion. Thus their every cry had echoed through his headphones, and he'd heard every one of their last breaths again. And his three other punch-ins weren't much better. To this day Calandrx maintained the only reason he won the race was that his interdimensional forays were actually *milder* than those of his fellow pilots, giving him the microsecond advantage needed to streak across the finish line just ahead of the pack.

When it was over, Calandrx had said, he tended to remember only the skills he'd displayed in surviving the flight itself. But his message was clear: What went on inside the thirteen could do a real head number if the racer was not ready for it. Though he never said it aloud, Hunter shuddered to think that being assigned to this cold, dark, and weird place was a way of getting him prepared for what was about to come.

But that certainly appeared to be the case.

He climbed out of the cockpit now and began removing the fasteners that held his machine's nose cone in place.

Calandrx passed him a cup of slow-ship and they did a quick toast. "May I rephrase my last question?" he asked Hunter, draining his wine in one long gulp.

"Sure. Go ahead. . . ."

"You say you *want* to do this," Calandrx said with a drawl. "But can you tell me *why* you want to do it?"

Hunter pulled the nose off his craft and confronted the gaggle of electronic stuff inside.

"You mean other than the fact that if I didn't do the race, I'd probably be a fifth-level recruit, cleaning the beam tubes on an S-Class cruiser by now?"

"Yes, of course," Calandrx said. "There *always* is a reason behind the reason. . . ."

Hunter began sorting out the mess of wires in the nose cone.

"I just have a crazy notion, I suppose," he said. "When I was back on Fools 6, I used to tell myself that if I ever got off the damn place, I'd do everything I could to find out who I was and where I came from."

"A noble ambition," Calandrx said.

Hunter stopped work for a moment and wiped his hands on the sides of his work uniform. "Well, what better way to find out if someone out there knows you than to take part in the biggest event in the Galaxy? You've told me that the winner's name is on everyone's lips the next morning, correct? Right across the Empire?"

"Word true," Calandrx replied.

"Then it should come to the lips of someone who knows who I am—and why I got dumped on the last planet in the Galaxy you can hit before you fall off the edge."

Calandrx pulled his chin in thought. "Fascinating," he said with a whisper. "And if no one steps forward to greet you, then that would mean you *are* from someplace else. Which would make you very unique indeed. . . ."

He let his voice trail off for a moment. Hunter went back to his nose cone.

"This is shaping up not unlike some of the epics written about the great warriors of the First Empire," Calandrx went on, pouring them another drink, "fighting not just to fight, but to win a noble cause. Going into the unknown, the uncharted, not just for the thrill, but also to learn something, to bring something back. The unselfish approach to heroics. It's actually rather refreshing. Perhaps you are a reincarnation of one of these people of yore. Perhaps you were a great warrior in the First Empire, four thousand years ago, flying this very machine. Or something like it . . ."

Hunter laughed. "I doubt that. . . ."

"Why so?"

Hunter indicated the whole of his unusual aircraft. The walls began to scream again.

"Look at this thing," he said to Calandrx. "We know it can go fast. But does the design look *only* four thousand years old to you?"

Calandrx scanned the strange aircraft up and down one more time, then nodded slowly.

"You can bingo that, my brother," he finally said. "It sure doesn't."

With thirty minutes to go before race time, Calandrx was finally allowed to leave the subterranean holding bay.

He had to make two substantial wagers, one for himself, one for his very unlucky friend Zap Multx. As the final minutes ticked away, the rules allowed for the contestant's handlers to go free to do just such things. So he and Hunter made one last toast, and Calandrx promised him he'd be the first to greet him in the winner's circle. Then they shook hands, a hole opened in the side of the bay, and Calandrx began the long climb up to the surface.

In their six days together, he'd never told Hunter his theory on why he thought the flying machine was able to dash around the world in less time than it took to strike a match. They'd tried it just once in the garden that night. That's all Calandrx needed to be convinced that Hunter's aircraft was so speedy because of the black boxes he'd salvaged from the wreck of the *Jupiterius 5*. Just how Hunter knew to combine them to produce such vast amounts of propulsive power was still a mystery to both of them. Pure chance? A Galaxy-shaking revelation? A favor from God? There was no way to tell. Hunter had randomly connected the boxes from the Kaon Bombardment system, and the result was a velocity that seemed so fast it defied the definition of speed itself.

There was a rub, though: The technology in those boxes made up one of the most closely guarded secrets in the realm, something right up there with the miracle of Supertime. As an officer of the Empire, Calandrx could not even speak of it, simply because discussing state secrets was an offense punishable by prison or even death.

So instead he'd told Hunter, just as Erx and Berx had earlier, that in this world, some things were better off not being known or spoken about. There was no regulation that said the winning pilot *had* to reveal what he had under his hood, ever. Historically, many winners did not, adding an air of mystery to the proceedings that everyone just loved. Hunter could fly the race, win the race, and never have to tell anyone how he was able to do it. Already hip to the way the Empire protected its secrets, Hunter couldn't disagree with the logic. True, they were as thick as thieves. But that didn't mean anyone had to know about it.

And in his heart, Calandrx knew there was no real disloyalty in this act of disloyalty. Besides, he had ulterior motives that went deeper than his oath of honor or the politics of the bulging galactic empire. In his chest beat the heart of a poet. Of course, the Galaxy was lousy with poets, but Calandrx considered himself to be better than most. As such, his eyes were always open, looking for signs only a poet would recognize. The way a married woman smiles. The way the clouds formed over a sunset. The way the wind blows on the coldest, darkest night. Much about life could be told from these things and more. You just had to know how to look.

He had been walking through downtown downtown a few

months before. It was a gray winter day, but with just the faintest whiff of spring in the air. He found himself on a nondescript street that was so old, its roadway was still made of bricks. It was in the least populated part of downtown downtown, over by the docks. On this street there was a wall, and on that wall someone had written something in dull red paint.

Now, this was a strange thing because Calandrx had traveled the Galaxy for more than a century and in that time, he'd seen much graffiti. Some planets were absolutely covered with it. Some of it personal, some of it political; the farther one got away from Earth and out toward the Fringe, the more graphic and edgy the graffiti would become.

But never in all his years had he seen graffiti here on Earth. He didn't know why. Maybe because Earth was so damn clean and the people who lived here had it so damn easy, no one had ever come up with anything clever enough or poignant enough or obscene enough to scrawl on a wall.

But one person had. And the message was so simple, it was actually a work of art, of politics, possibly even a piece of great literature.

For on that wall, on the little barren street, in dull red paint, were written three words: *Something is coming. . . .*

What excitement ran through Calandrx when he saw that scrawl! He'd been waiting to read those very words ever since he'd won the Earth Race ninety-seven years ago—and maybe even before then. He knew history and he knew that empires not only rose and fell, they also changed in between. You just had to look for the signs. A Blackship in Supertime? A man from nowhere figures out one of the greatest secrets of the age . . . without even trying? Three words splashed on a wall on the most insignificant street in the heart of the Galaxy. Could this be the change in the wind he'd been yearning for it ever since the Emperor exiled him here on Earth?

At that moment, he thought so. Because just like his anonymous tagger, he believed something *was* coming. It was, in fact, inevitable. And if the pilot in him wasn't able to fly off this planet to go look for it, then the poet in him sure wanted to be here, on Earth, when that *something* finally arrived.

• • •

Its official name was the First Galactic Sporting Events Arena. To the Specials, it was the Holy Imperial Stadium of the Great O'Nay.

To the citizens of Earth, it was simply the circus.

It was an enormous structure, two miles long and a half mile across. The rows of seats went up nearly thirty stories. A small coral sea dominated the center; the track itself was layered with precious red-diamond Martian soil. Tens of thousands of flags flew from the arena's spires.

More than a million people could fit into this place, and on this warm sunny morning, every seat was taken. Several million more citizens were packed into the thousands of sports clubs and cloud holes surrounding the stadium. Trillions more were watching from all points across the Galaxy. The start of the Empire's most sacred of sporting events was fewer than thirty minutes away.

The sky above the circus was crowded as well. Thousands of air-chevys were circling the arena. Some were towing banners or laser messages; others were jockeying for coveted hovering spots. Farther up were the larger airships, military vessels of all sizes, from scout ships to huge V-Class battle cruisers. More than a dozen floating cities were in the vicinity as well.

Most of those on hand, both on the ground and hanging in the air above, were Very Fortunates, citizens with no real holy blood in them but who were close to the Imperial family nevertheless. That was the only way to secure a space in or above the circus on this, the biggest day of the year. Everyone here had *some* connection to the Specials.

Well, almost everyone . . .

Erx and Berx had no such pull. They had no seats, no confederates on the inside, not even a reserved place to stand. But this was not a problem. They were galactic explorers; they'd roamed the outer borders of the Fringe, fought in the interstellar wars, crashed a monstrously large spaceship and still come back for more. Negotiating a crowd of snobs was a piece of cake for them. After placing their bets, they'd slowly wormed their way through the throng, cajoling here, threatening there, until not ten minutes after their arrival, they'd secured a spot on the main track beam rail, close to the starting line itself.

This was the place to be. All the action was here, practically at their fingertips. The beam rail was thick with track handlers, bookies, soldiers, priests, angels, space technicians, viz-screen engineers, and robots. Hundreds of beautiful women, some real, some not, were circulating about as well.

Delighted with themselves and their location, Erx and Berx broke out flasks of slow-ship wine, did a quick toast, and began drinking heavily. They'd never been within a light-year of the Earth Race before, and both knew it was unlikely they would ever get this close again. It was important that they enjoy themselves. The weather was appropriately clear, the sky deep blue, with just a few clouds softening the warm glare of the sun. In a place where it was summer most of the time, these were still exceptional conditions. The metero engineers had done their jobs well.

Time passed quickly. The crowd grew, the sky above the arena became more crowded. Just a few minutes before noon, Number One, the largest of all the floating cities, drifted over the stadium. A hush went through the crowd as the arena was enveloped by the Holy Shadow. A huge, gleaming review stand, known as the *zadora*, had slowly begun to materialize about halfway down the first leg of the track and not a hundred yards from where Erx and Berx stood. As it completed its pop-in, the arena was suddenly flooded with Earth Police. More than twenty thousand of the huge cops began appearing all over the stadium, and especially in the area surrounding the *zadora*. The ethereal bass music booming throughout the stadium faded away. A very special moment was at hand.

Berx began gulping from his wine flask. "I'm not sure I'm high enough to handle this," he said.

Erx held his timepiece up to his bleary eyes; he could just barely read the numbers. "Well, drink up and get ready," he told Berx. "It's seven seconds to noon . . . five . . . four . . ."

Both men took this as their cue to turn their eyes away from the gleaming *zadora*. Others around them did the same. At the exact moment the last second ticked down to noon, the arena was rocked by a huge thunderclap. A collective gasp came from the million-plus spectators. Those who dared to look saw a bright emerald beam begin to illuminate the review stand. The beam intensified until it was all but impossible to look at it. Then came an incredibly bright flash of light.

An eyeblink later, a magnificent throne appeared on the top level of the *zadora*. Sitting on it was a man of undetermined age. He had a full white beard and very long white hair that fell past his shoulders. He was wearing a flowing emerald gown and had a gold-green miter on his head. In the center of the miter was the distorted image of a three-leaf green flower, the ancient symbol of the last three empires. This was O'Nay, supreme ruler of the Galaxy, Emperor of the Milky Way, the current god among men.

The circus erupted in cheers and applause, shaking the arena to its substantial foundation. Lights flashed, flags waved, the booming music came back on louder than before. Overcome with emotion, some people fainted. Others cheered through finger-size voice amplifiers that were all the rage this year. This went on and on . . . and on. One minute, two minutes, five minutes, more. O'Nay made no notice of the crowd. He sat, looking straight ahead, expressionless, possibly oblivious, to what was going on around him. Only when he raised his right hand slightly did the throaty roar finally begin to die away.

But not for long. Came the exact moment it reached its lowest ebb, there was another tremendous flash of light. This one was bright, eye-blinding yellow. It quickly faded to reveal that three more people had joined the Emperor on the reviewing stand. His wife, his son, and his gorgeous daughter were officially OTP—on the planet.

The stadium erupted again. More lights, more music, more vapors. Though not quite the magnitude as before, this new round of cheering took another five minutes to subside. When relative silence returned, the Emperor raised his right hand again and, without any means of outward amplification needed, spoke four words that all could hear: "Let the race begin. . . ."

The voices of the one million began building again, like

the low rumble of waves, a sea of anticipation. Erx and Berx opened another flask and drank another toast.

"To our good fortune," Berx proposed. "And the temporary bad luck of others."

"Bingo," Erx replied.

They drank the entire flask in no more than a dozen gulps.

The music began blaring ever louder. Number One had moved away, and the arena was awash in bright sunlight once again. Holo-girls drifted by them as if carried on the wind. The air smelled of power, money, and sex.

"Finally!" Erx exclaimed, turning Berx around and pointing him toward the far side of the arena. A gaggle of racers had floated onto the track and were making their way up to the starting line.

"It's showtime!" Berx yelled in response.

The first half-dozen racers were variants of the standard Empire Starfighter, the ubiquitous F-176A model, also called the Holy Fighter. It was a needle-nosed wedge, thirty-six feet long and twelve feet wide at the aft. This was the basic Empire design. Blended body, no wings, no tail.

Contestants could adorn their racers in any way they wished; many were predictably outlandish. One of these first racers was colored bright red with checkerboard squares of black and white decorating its aft section. Another racer was sun yellow with blistering orange flames trailing down its back. A third was glowing deep red from its needle nose to its nontail. Three others opted for variations on the always sinister *in toto* dull-black scheme.

Six more racers came onto the track. They were Starfighters, too, but not the standard F-176A model. These beauties were rebuilds of a Starfighter design from nearly three hundred years before, known as the F-32B. They were a bit larger, a bit bulkier, but they also sported elegant color schemes, more glowing than shine, and had distinctively large cockpits and antique ID scrolling. These half-dozen racers were regarded as the class of the race, the *élégance*. They received a thunderous cheer as they glided toward the starting area.

Then came the thirteenth entry.

It did not float out of the waiting area. It rolled, on three strange black things that looked more like toys than attachments to an Earth Race entrant. Few people in the million knew these things were called wheels. Their use had died out thousands of years ago.

This was, of course, Hawk Hunter's flying machine. It looked huge at fifty-five feet, its wings flapping as it bounced its way along the red-dirt track. Perhaps the strangest thing of all was that Hunter's canopy was not a tiny piece of squared-off superglass but a relatively large tear drop bubble. Unlike the other racers, the citizens could clearly see Hunter within his cockpit, pushing buttons, yanking levers. What's more, his craft was not painted in the living hues of the other dozen entrants. Rather it was sporting three simple colors: red on the nose, white on the wings, blue on the tail and body. Like the wheel, this color scheme had not been seen on Earth in thousands of years.

Dead silence fell upon the huge stadium when Hunter's aircraft appeared. The crowd was stunned by the sight of the odd-looking machine. At first they didn't know whether to cheer, applaud, or salute.

Then it began to sink in—and the laughter started.

If one million people cheering at once sounded like waves crashing on a shore, that many people laughing sounded more like thunder. Low-pitched, rumbling, building, building into a sonic roar that suddenly stopped . . . only to start up again a quick breath later.

The stadium was in hysterics now. It had been a closely guarded secret that a maccus had been entered in the race. This was another archaic term that could mean several things, including "unusual one," or "different from the rest." But there was another translation that was on everyone's mind and in everyone's throats now.

This was the definition of maccus as jester, loon.

A *clown* . . . with wings.

Nowhere was the laughter so intense than in the galleries surrounding the Imperial Seat. This area was thick with some of the most high-ranking officers in the Empire. Each one was spit-polished and medal-heavy, each one vying to get as close to the Imperial Family as possible. The sight of the strange participant sent gales through the gallery. *Whose unit was this thing from? Is it too late to bet against it?*

Down near the starting line, though, two men in the million were not laughing. Actually Erx and Berx were on the verge of tears. The aircraft that had looked so strange and sleek on Fools 6 just looked strange here. Strange and old. Both explorers had bet substantial purses on Hunter's machine; even more important, they'd been harboring dreams of basking in Hunter's reflected glory. But all this seemed very much in jeopardy now. Compared to the hovering Starfighters, Hunter's contraption looked ridiculous.

Erx and Berx knew that Calandrx, in pulling his own strings with the race organizers, had managed to get Hunter entered as the maccus. But they'd thought he and his strange craft would have been greeted as something new, different, extraordinary, even spellbinding. Never did they consider that their new friend would be greeted with such overwhelming ridicule and abuse. But that's exactly what was happening now.

"This is not good, my brother," Erx said as the derisive laughter swelled even farther. "Not good at all."

The thirteen racers nudged their way up to the neon starting beam. Hunter took the longest to get into position, needing more than a few adjustments of his nose wheel before getting exactly even with the other participants. This only served to throw the crowd into more fits of laughter. Taunting chants of maccus! filled the stadium. Erx and Berx sank even lower into their boots.

"Fear not, my brothers!" a voice boomed in their ears, strong and clear above the roar. *"Our time is finally at hand!"*

They swung around to see that Calandrx had come up behind them. Unlike them, he was all smiles. The explorers were mildly astonished to see the elderly pilot. How had he been able to find them in this enormous crowd?

"I knew you two would gravitate right to the center of the critical mass," he told them with a hearty slap to each of their backs. "And a fine location it is, too. Now we three brothers will be in a perfect position to see the extraordinary happen."

"How can you glow so?" Erx asked him, having to shout

above the sustained roar of the raucous crowd. "The entire Galaxy is laughing at our friend. The man who is carrying our wagers. We could all be very poor this time tomorrow. Your levity is baffling."

"And you two don't realize what you miss when you go to sleep," Calandrx replied tartly, taking the flask from Berx's hand and helping himself to some slow-ship wine.

"Please clarify," Berx told him. "Before that wine takes effect."

Calandrx grinned. All was right in *his* universe, at least for the moment.

"Did our friend out there ever tell you that when he flew for you on Fools 6, his throttle was opened to only one-eighth speed?"

Both Erx and Berx shook their heads no.

"And did you know that we conducted an experiment six days ago this night, after you fell asleep in my garden?"

"How could we know if neither you or Hawk told us?" Erx complained.

Calandrx shrugged.

"That's true—but sometimes good things must be held in confidence," he said. "Even from old friends."

He drained Berx's flask, then licked the spout with his tongue.

"But now all you have to do is prepare yourself, my brothers," he said. "For we are about to see a display guaranteed to put a lie to this rowdy behavior around us."

Erx and Berx just stared back at him.

"But what experiment are you talking about?" Erx pressed him.

Calandrx wiped his mouth on Berx's sleeve.

"I'm tempted to say—but my words would ruin it for your eyes." He handed Erx one of his ancient wooden matches. "Hold this. . . ."

Then he pointed out at Hunter, who was still trying to maneuver his way to his starting point. People were throwing expended food packs and empty wine flasks at him now.

"When he leaves, strike the match."

Before Erx could reply, the countdown commenced. Speaking slowly, sensually, the Emperor's stunning daughter,

Xara, began counting back from ten. Her sultry voice did the impossible. It quieted the crowd instantly.

When she spoke the word *zero,* it oozed off her lips. Then the starting beam blinked.

In one motion, the wheels on Hunter's flying machine lifted off the ground and he hit his throttle.

There was a bright flash—and before the twelve other racers even moved, Hunter was already gone, leaving only a thin trail of smoke behind him.

15

The real trouble started for Hunter right after he hit
the first transdimensional screen.

Up until that point, the flight had been just like his trip
around the planet a week before. His throttles were pushed
right to the max, as Calandrx had suggested. The sensation
was one of going extremely fast, but with zero blurring or
head trips. He could see everything on the ground in perfect
focus, clear and crisp—it was just dropping off behind him
very, very quickly.

But at the same time, it seemed to him like no time had
elapsed since he'd rocketed out of the stadium. In some ways
he was still back there, maybe just a billionth of a trillionth
of a micrometer past the starting beam. He was here, but he
was also still leaving there. It would seem impossible—and
yet there was a perfectly good explanation for it. For as Hunter would eventually come to find out, whenever he pushed
his machine's throttle to maximum power, he ceased traveling in regular time—and began traveling in an entirely different piece of time and space. That's why everything
seemed to be happening all at once. That's why he was going
so fast.

And that's why it was hard to gauge exactly how much
regular time had elapsed before he hit the first blue screen.

• • •

Once out of Big Bright City, the terranium earth below him had turned uniform, pastoral, even dazzling in some places. Lush forests, gently rolling hills covered with flora, the most incidental canals and lakes shimmering in aqua blue—indeed, everything seemed to be a shade of either yellow, green, or blue. As he made his way west, there were no clouds, and certainly no bad weather. Only once did he turn around to see if anyone was behind him, but there was no one in sight.

When the first screen appeared, it came up fast and unexpected, as advertised. He'd just passed over a very wide canal that seemed to cut the upper half of the western continent in two. Flying at about two miles high, one moment the sky ahead of him was clear; the next, it was replaced by a massive cloud of bluish mist with numerous lightning bolts running through it. Hunter hit the screen not a microsecond after seeing it. He was nearly blinded by the impact; it knocked him so far back in his seat, his crash helmet snapped off and slammed into the back of the canopy. His entire flying machine began shaking violently. All the things he'd tightened down before the race were coming loose again— he could *hear* them. For several terrifying seconds he could see nothing but the panicky blurs of his panel lights bouncing madly before his eyes.

He instinctively grabbed his control column with both hands and held it as rigid as possible. It took a while, but the vibrations finally died down and the aircraft bucked its way back to flying straight and true. His crash helmet bounced back down onto his lap and he hastily shoved it onto his head. Finally his vision cleared and he was able to see where he was.

At first it seemed like he was still flying over the heartland of the western continent—except now it was night. But something was very different here. The darkness was evenly scattered everywhere, and everything had a thin neon glow around it. This was *not* the Earth's surface he was seeing below him now; this was a ghostly image of where he'd just come from. Not so much a mirror dimension, but an X-ray of one. He could even see through things. Even his flying machine seemed to be only partially there.

Even stranger was the sensation that he was actually moving inside a tiny bubble. The Earth, the sky, the stars—it was as if he could reach out and touch them with his fingertips.

Very strange.

Very claustrophobic.

Welcome to the thirteenth dimension.

But it got even more bizarre. The interior of his cockpit had been transformed, too. Many of his control panel's readout screens were gone, to be replaced by stacks of weapon-targeting systems, gun triggers, and bomb-release levers. Hunter made the mistake of looking down at these things for more than a moment—it was purely on impulse. When he looked up again, he saw a huge ball of fire coming right at him.

He was somehow able to yank his craft to the left just before the *faux* meteorite streaked by him. The violent maneuver saved him, but also caused the flying machine to go out of control. Suddenly he was nose down, spinning uncontrollably. The machine began shaking all over again.

This might be called a stall, he thought.

The distorted image of the distorted surface of the Earth was racing up to meet him. Hunter tried to yank back on the control column, but it did no good. He was still spiraling down toward the ground at very high speed. He had to think quickly; he was getting dizzy and felt close to blacking out. His hand wavered over the throttle for a moment. Calandrx had told him not to touch the power levels once he was airborne, as all kinds of unpredictable things might result. But Hunter was falling even faster now, and his incredibly powerful propulsion system was hurling him earthward that much quicker.

That's when a strange thought hit him: *Was there really this much gravity here in Dreamland?*

Maybe.

But maybe not . . .

Hunter blinked his eyes once—and suddenly he was flying straight and level again. Control of his flying machine instantly returned to him. It had been some kind of an illusion, a mind trick of the type Calandrx had warned him about. He pulled up on the stick, just making sure it was real. Then he was looking up at the green-starred sky again.

That was a close one.

But now the surface of the Earth began to drop away even quicker than before. Hunter realized he was suddenly approaching space—or what looked like space. His instrument panel went mad. He could see numbers flashing by in Supertime speed just outside his cockpit glass. He was suddenly flying through a field of small gray moons—some were about five hundred feet across, some were smaller, all showing what appeared to be impact craters. But these moons were also swinging wildly, as if each one were dangling from some unseen string. Two were looming right up ahead of him now. Hunter had to ask himself a question: *Should I go under, over, or between the two moons?* But while he was considering his options, the two globes suddenly erupted in an explosion of red light. Hunter was startled. These things seemed to be headed right for him. But were they Z beams? *Real ones?*

He yanked the flying machine to the left just as the barrage went by him. In a flash he pulled on the control column and corkscrewed back up to his previous position. A second barrage was coming right at him. Another twist, another dive; the lethal-looking beams went right by his cockpit, so close he could feel their heat. Or so he imagined.

Hunter didn't even have to think about what to do next. His instinct took over. He snapped his fingers and suddenly a weapons control was locked in his fist. He turned the flying machine twenty degrees off center and squeezed the trigger. Two blinding beams of yellow light erupted from his nose cone—weapons that weren't really there. He squeezed again. Two more beams appeared. He squeezed *again*—now there were six beams of extremely bright Z rays flowing out of his nose.

Six . . .

It seemed to be the right number.

The beams smashed into the first moon; it went up in an orange flash and was gone. He flipped over. There was no need to fight the second moon; Hunter simply streaked around it—and then found himself back over the X-ray image of the Earth again.

Another close one . . .

He looked down at his hands and saw the weapons control quickly dematerialize. When he looked up again, he found himself heading toward a set of gigantic mechanical teeth.

They had to be more than a hundred miles away, yet in this distorted world, they were quickly filling his entire field of vision. There was a mighty gleam coming off their razor-sharp edges; each tang was at least a mile long. They were moving up and down so quickly, a surge of static electricity was exploding outward each time the gigantic jaws came together and opened again. It was a scene right out of a nightmare.

And it was no optical illusion. Hunter could tell these things were real—or as real as anything could be inside the thirteenth dimension. No amount of blinking was going to make them disappear. And no matter how fast he was going, Hunter knew if one of these things came down on top of him, he and his flying machine would be crushed into oblivion.

He was suddenly right on them. In a heartbeat, the giant incisors were directly in front of him, closing shut. Again, his instinct took over. He stood his machine up on its wing and before he could even think about it, he streaked through the narrow opening just as the teeth snapped closed.

A really close one . . .

But the bad dream was not over, for once on the other side, he found himself facing another set of monstrous jaws, these fewer than fifty miles away. He just barely made it through them when a third set appeared, even closer to him. Then a fourth. And a fifth.

This was getting serious. Hunter was just barely getting through the monstrous obstructions before they clamped shut; each time, they were a bit closer to chomping off the tail of his aircraft. This went on for what seemed like forever, each time making it through the gigantic mandibles, but with less and less time to spare.

Finally the set in front of him clamped shut—and stayed shut. Hunter had nowhere to go but up. He yanked back on the controls and soon was looking deep into the night emerald sky—if there really was a night sky in Dreamland. The stars were most definitely green, and there seemed to be many more of them. No matter—this was not the time for stargazing. Hunter continued pulling back on his controls and soon was upside down; then, an instant later, was looking at the distorted colors of the ground again.

And I think that's called a loop. . . .

He wound up in nearly the same place from where he'd started the maneuver. The teeth were still closed. Hunter squeezed his trigger, and the six weapons in his nose lit up again. They were so bright, they felt like they were burning away his eyes. His barrage hit the clenched jaw a nanosecond before his aircraft did. This was just enough time for them to blow a hole large enough for his machine to streak through. He twisted his way among the subatomic debris, then yanked the flying machine back to level again.

That was the end of the giant teeth.

But no sooner had he caught his breath than his instrument panel began blinking madly *again*. A viewing screen appeared out of nowhere—it smashed into Hunter's helmet after a clumsy pop-in from God-knows-what dimension. The screen was displaying two very strange icons; they were moving from the top to the bottom of the field. A warning buzzer went off in his ear. He looked up from the screen to see a pair of aircraft coming in the opposite direction, heading right at him. Their noses were lit up with Z beams.

Jessuzz, not again . . .

In a heartbeat Hunter twisted right, and felt the bottom fall out from underneath him again. He was spinning out of control once again, the ground racing up at him. He blinked once. Nothing. He blinked again. Still nothing.

The hell with this . . .

He pulled back mightily on his control column and pushed the aircraft hard left. Something deep inside his power plant growled in response, but he ignored it and quickly recovered flight.

Now he found himself on the tail of one of the aircraft. This contraption looked worse than his own. It, too, had wings, a tail, a large bubble-type canopy, and, Hunter would have bet, wheels as well. It was silver and had a large red-star emblem on its wings and tail.

Familiar . . .

He pushed his trigger. His nose cone erupted again, and the enemy aircraft vaporized into nothingness—only to be replaced by another. Hunter squeezed his trigger again. This aircraft exploded, too—and was replaced by another. And then another. And another.

This must have been some kind of nightmare back where I was from, he thought. No sooner had he dispatched one enemy aircraft than another would slot in and take its place, almost as if its pilot were anxious for his turn to get slaughtered. Again, this went on for what seemed like an eternity—until finally Hunter smacked himself in the forehead and blinked.

All signs of the enemy aircraft quickly disappeared.

He took in a long, deep breath. . . .

That's when another of the aircraft went right across his nose. Its cockpit was on fire, its pilot was struggling to get out. It seemed to hang motionless in front of him for a very long time. The pilot's skin was searing right off his face. He was looking right into Hunter's eyes, his mouth opened as if to scream. . . .

That's when Hunter swerved violently to the left to avoid the flaming wreckage . . . and punched out of thirteen.

He'd popped out over a vast stretch of aqua water.

There was no solid ground anywhere that he could see. No triads, bridges, or islands. This was not a lake or a wide canal he was crossing. This was something else. The Western Ocean. It looked cool, calm, pacific. If he looked hard enough, he could almost see right down to its bottom; the water was that clean.

The sun was coming over his shoulder now. He turned around and looked behind him. There wasn't another racer in sight.

He checked his instruments. All the weird weaponry had vanished, and his usual array of controls had reappeared. Everything seemed to be running fine. He was still moving incredibly fast, and just as before, it seemed more like the world was turning beneath him than he flying over it. He felt his body relax a little. Out of the corners of his eyes he could still see the people in the arena stands, cheering for him. Or at least he thought they were cheering for him.

When he looked forward again he saw another blue screen coming right at him.

Pow!

This impact was even more violent than the first. The flying machine began vibrating so fiercely, Hunter found himself reaching out for something—anything—to hold on to. Once again, he grabbed the control column, with two hands, and held on. It took nearly twice as long this time, but finally the aircraft settled down.

Once his eyeballs stopped shaking he saw that his cockpit was once more jam-packed with imaginary weapons. And he was back over the X-ray Earth again, all darkness and neon outlines, everything looking like it was there and not there, everything closing in on him just like before.

But there was something very different going on here as well.

A vid screen had appeared in front of him. It became one with his control panel, but strangely it seemed to be draped over his eyeballs as well.

This screen was flashing a message in large red letters: RESET GAME—NOW.

Next to these words was a three-dimensional icon that looked like an old-fashioned power switch. Hunter found his right hand reaching out to this switch and flipping it to ON.

Suddenly the screen became filled with bizarre shapes and colors. His flying machine began rocking violently again. Outside, he could see that the neon world below had suddenly become very real. And now the ground was rushing by him at incomprehensible speed. But something was drastically wrong here—his inner ear was telling him so. A wave of vertigo ran through him, and in an instant he knew why. The surface below him was actually turning quickly in reverse. Although everything in his cockpit indicated that he was moving forward at a very high rate of speed, he was actually hurtling backward.

Basic human instinct drove his hands to his controls—he

had to stop this. But no panel he touched or button he pushed had any effect. It was as if his whole being were caught in a rewind. Not a pleasant feeling.

This went on for what seemed like forever, which wasn't that far from the truth—until suddenly it just stopped. The ground below him ceased turning in the wrong direction, and his flying machine regained some semblance of normal forward flight. Hunter took a deep breath and squeezed his steering controls very tightly. He was bathed in sweat.

He caught his breath and looked out the cockpit to the surface below. It was night. He was over two very long roadways that were running parallel to each other. Thousands of wheeled vehicles were moving along these roads at relatively high rates of speed, half in one direction, half in the other. Most of the vehicles were traveling in one of four designated lanes. They all seemed to be in a great rush.

This place below him looked like the Earth, but certainly not the one he'd just come from. It was almost pastoral. He could see many trees and fields and valleys, and hundreds of tiny houses scattered off in every direction. The moon was hanging high overhead, like a huge orange ball, illuminating it all.

Hunter's flying machine was flying roughly five hundred feet above the long, ribbonlike roadways. Two huge green bridges were right below him; they spanned a fairly wide river, which by looking off to his left, Hunter could see emptying into a vast ocean. He checked his direction indicator and found he was now traveling due south.

"Okay, now what?" he heard himself say.

No sooner were the words out of his mouth than he looked down at his cockpit display to find it had changed dramatically once again. Most of the flight control indicators had vanished. They'd been replaced by a second large video screen with lines of alphanumeric information pulsating across it. Suddenly one line of information froze on the screen. It began flashing in large red letters: *The Princess is in peril. To successfully complete this segment, you must rescue her in the time allotted. . . .*

A small clock then appeared in the upper-right-hand corner on the video screen. It began flashing: *120 seconds*. Hunter felt his flying machine shudder a bit. Another message flashed onto the screen: *Failure to complete the task will result in termination*.

Hunter blinked once, and the game clock began ticking down. . . .

This is crazy, he thought. But he knew he had no choice but to do as instructed. It was the word "termination" that bothered him the most.

But how was he supposed to save "the Princess" when he didn't know who or where she was?

No sooner had that thought gone through his head than the video screen began flashing again. One of the vehicles moving on the busy road below was being highlighted in the center of the screen. It seemed to be going faster than the other vehicles, and it was weaving into and out of the designated traffic lanes.

No sooner had Hunter's forward viewing device attained a lock on this particular vehicle than a message began flashing in bright red letters across his eyeballs: *Hurry . . . she is in mortal danger*.

By this time the game clock had ticked down to 108 seconds.

Hunter had no idea what to do—he would have to improvise. He lowered his altitude to about 150 feet. When the designated vehicle took a sharp right-hand turn, leaving the main roadway by way of a smaller, curving one, Hunter turned his aircraft and followed it.

The vehicle drove onto a much thinner roadway; no other vehicles could be seen on it. The vehicle traveled at high speed for a half mile on this road until pulling onto a dirt path and driving toward a small lake that was nearly surrounded by overhanging trees.

When it stopped in a parking area near the water's edge, Hunter was waiting for it.

He'd jammed his flying machine into hover mode and was now hanging about 100 feet above the small lake. No sooner had he stopped moving than his video screen changed fields again. Now it was flashing a menu of sorts. The options read: *Bright blue light. Whirring FX. Yellow Beam. Flashing lights: red, white, amber.*

Hunter looked down at the vehicle. He saw that some kind of tussle was going on in the rear seat. There were only two people inside the vehicle, yet one seemed to be fighting with the other.

Hunter looked at the game clock ticking away on his video screen. It was now down to 89 seconds. 88 . . . 87 . . .

Purely on a guess, Hunter hit the *options-all* portion of the screen. The entire menu began flashing. An instant later his flying machine erupted in an explosion of sound and light. Just like that, he was emitting a bright flashing aura of red, white, and amber. A whirring sound filled his ears. A incredibly intense beam of yellow light shot out from the belly of his machine. It bathed the vehicle below him in an almost phosphorescent glow.

Now another option popped up on the menu screen. It read: *Initiate power outage*. Hunter hit the options panel— and every electrical light within ten miles of his location instantly blinked out.

Another option now appeared. It read: *False time shift available*. With a shrug of the shoulders, Hunter hit that as well.

That's when everything just stopped . . . except the clock in the corner of his video screen.

It was down to 54 seconds.

Now Hunter saw the side door on the vehicle open and a young girl jump out. She began running frantically away from the vehicle, looking over her shoulder at the bombastic display being caused by his flying machine as it hovered above the lake. Hunter could not see her face—all he could tell was that she was wearing a skirt and white shoes, and her top was partially torn away. She had long hair and it whipped behind her, back and forth the faster she ran.

He checked the game clock. It was now down to 41 seconds and counting.

"Am I doing this right?" he wondered aloud.

There was no way to tell.

He kept the bright yellow beam pointed on the parked vehicle. He could see the remaining figure inside, frozen in fear by the bright light and the noise his flying machine was making.

Hunter looked up again. The girl was now running down the single-lane roadway. His time was down to 29 seconds. Strictly on intuition, he hit the *False time shift* option again, and everything began moving once more. The wind was back in the trees, the ripples were back on the water.

That's when he saw another vehicle approaching the small lake from the direction of the major roadway. It had whirling bright blue lights on its roof and was emitting a strange whooping sound. The girl ran into the middle of the roadway and waved her arms, causing this vehicle to stop. Two men in uniforms jumped out and went to her aid. That's when Hunter's video screen began flashing: *Princess saved! Good work!*

Hunter looked at the ticking clock. It was now down to 11 seconds. He quickly yanked the flying machine out of its hover mode. He had to get out of this crazy place. He pushed his throttles forward, and an instant later, he was streaking along at treetop level. He began looking for a blue screen through which to escape. But once he got back over the major roadway, he found not one but dozens of blue screens. They were erected alongside the roadway, and they had words and numbers bathed in a reflective glow displayed all over them.

Which one do I go through? he thought.

The game clock was ticking down. Nine seconds. Eight seconds . . . Seven . . . Six.

That's when Hunter saw a much larger screen about three miles off to his left. It was at one end of a huge area where several hundred of the ground vehicles were parked. Strange shapes and colors were flashing across this screen. But as soon as Hunter pointed the nose of his aircraft toward it, it turned the unmistakable color of misty blue. This had to be it: his way out.

He pushed his throttle full forward and, with less than 0.01 second remaining on the game clock, slammed the flying machine right into the blue screen.

Or at least he thought it was a blue screen.

Suddenly he was moving forward at a speed faster than his senses could comprehend. The surface below him was flashing by in one long, blue blur—it was the reverse of the sensation earlier when he'd found himself streaking backward.

Fast forward.

That was it. He was stuck in fast forward.

Now came a violent crashing sound. His eyelids snapped shut and stayed that way. Hunter tried to open them, but they would not cooperate. This was not good. How could he blink if his eyelids refused to yield? He reached out for the controls and gave the stick one mighty yank backward. His machine shook from one end to the other. He felt like he was spinning out of control. His power plant let out one long scream.

But then came a flash of light so intense, he could feel its warmth on his retinas even though his eyes remained closed.

Then, just like that, everything settled down. He opened his eyes and took another long, deep breath.

He was back over land again.

Passing below were great cities, golden deserts, lush forests. He rocketed over a vast plain, which was dotted with high, snow-topped mountains not unlike those back on Fools 6. Hunter could see the eastern ocean ahead of him. Beyond that lay Big Bright City and the finish line. He had not slowed one iota. Still, it felt like he was just leaving the starting line.

He turned around to check his six-o'clock position. No one was behind him.

When he looked forward again, he saw the third screen coming.

He hit it *really* hard. Again, his machine was shaking down to its rivets. Passing from one dimension to another was not so good for his chassis. He lost control of his aircraft for a third time, but quickly did the two-hand trick, and as soon as his eyeballs stopping juggling, he was able to get the aircraft back under control.

He looked around him, expecting to be over the X-ray world again, but this was not the case. He was no longer streaking above the distorted image of the Earth. He was in space. *Outer space.* The real one, this time. Endless blackness with trillions of twinkling stars, some bright, some dim, the Earth nowhere in sight. Hunter looked at his hands. They were shaking. He looked at his instruments. There were no weird weapons this time. His original equipment returned and everything seemed to be working, even though his flying machine was definitely not adapted for space travel.

At least he didn't think it was.

He tried to get his bearings. The vastness before him was dizzying. He still had the sensation of unfathomable speed, but this piece of space was so immense, it was like he was not moving at all.

So what was going on?

Why was he here?

His reply came an instant later.

They appeared as two faint lights at first. Way, way off, coming out of a star formation that looked somewhat familiar. The two specks grew larger very quickly. Hunter could tell this was not some kind of transdimensional optical illusion. These weren't fake meteorites, or death moons, or crappy versions of his own aircraft. These two objects were *real*—and they, too, were traveling at a tremendous speed.

And, of course, they were heading right for him.

In the big thirteenth dimension, everything just seemed to come his way.

In the hairbreadth of time it took him to make a quick turn to the right, the two objects were nearly on him. Moving incredibly fast. One seemed to be following the other—or maybe chasing it. Neither made a turn toward him, thank God. Hunter yanked his flying machine left again and banked to a roughly intersecting course. Would he able to see the two objects as they streaked by . . . or would they be just a blur?

As it turned out, they were a little bit of both.

The first object was gigantic . . . and familiar. It passed within a mile of him. Hunter got a damn good look . . . and felt his jaw hit the top of his helmet brace.

It was the Blackship—the *same* Blackship he'd shot out of Supertime during the attack on the *BonoVox*. There was no doubt that this was the same vessel. Its control bubble was shattered and smoking, its tail section was still on fire. What's more, a string of dead bodies seemed to be trailing behind it, like expired puppets on a thousand-mile-long piece of invisible string.

What the hell is going on here?

But even more incredible was the spacecraft hard on the crippled Blackship's tail.

Everything that flew in the Empire came from one basic design: the triangular wedge. But this thing chasing the ghostly Blackship was not like that. This craft was completely different.

It was round.

A perfect circle.

Saucer-shaped.

16

Back at the Circus

Erx had barely struck the match when suddenly there was a commotion off to his right.

A flash of light. A cloud of dust. A mighty gasp from the crowd.

"By the one true God!" Berx exclaimed.

It didn't seem possible, but Hunter's racer had reappeared at the starting line. A thin trail of smoke indicated it had arrived from the east—yet the faint contrail he'd left upon departure was still visible in the west. His flying machine had disappeared not two seconds before. Now it was back again.

Erx and Berx had never seen anything like it. It didn't make sense.

"Can we be disqualified for . . . *sorcery*?" Erx asked, still holding the burning match in hand.

"If this is not real, they'll have our heads!" Berx bemoaned.

"It is not sorcery nor illusion, my brothers," Calandrx told them. "Now, I'm not sure exactly *what* it is—but it doesn't matter. Hunter has won. It will be verified that his flying machine traveled the course and mastered the obstacles."

"And that means . . ." Erx began to say. He was still a bit

dumbstruck. The match had not even burned down to his fingertips yet.

"That we are all very wealthy?" Berx finished for him.

"Wealthy?" Calandrx asked. "Yes, we are wealthy! We are wealthy in heart, in spirit! In goodwill . . . but, you see, we had those things already."

He thrust his arms skyward and let out a howl. It was possible that he was even happier now than back when he'd won his own Earth Race.

"We are wealthy because we've been allowed to live in such an *interesting* time!" he bellowed. "The only difference is, now we've got some coin to go along with it!"

It was just about this time that the million-plus crowd began to realize what had happened. The maccus has won the race? they asked. Yes, the maccus has won the race! And at such a tremendous speed, it seemed as if it had never left the arena at all.

As this information made its way through the stadium, the combined energy of one million people about to cheer at once began building like a thunderstorm.

"We must make haste!" Calandrx told Erx and Berx now. "Our brother will soon be at the center of the Galaxy. He will soon be trafficking with the Specials themselves! It is our duty to usher him through to this newfound celebrity!"

"Bingo that!" Erx and Berx replied as one.

It took just a few seconds for a team of officials to complete their postrace scan of Hunter's aircraft.

The six men had run their quadtrols up one side of the flying machine and down the other. Then they did a kind of group shrug and made the official hand signal to each other. Six thumbs went straight up. Hunter had indeed run the race. He had bested the obstacles and was the first to cross finish line. That's all that was required.

His time for the twenty-five-thousand-mile course, however, was an astonishing 2.7511 seconds. This handily beat the old record—by more than an hour.

By the time Erx, Berx, and Calandrx finally got through to the winner's circle, a gaggle of race officials, military officers, and Very Fortunates were crowded around Hunter's aircraft. They were all craning their necks, pushing in on one another, trying to get a look at the Galaxy's new hero.

The three friends forced their way through the gawkers and helped Hunter climb from his cockpit. Another huge cheer went up. Erx and Berx grabbed Hunter so tightly, he nearly lost his breath. Calandrx began kissing the top of his helmet.

"You did it, brother!" Erx was screaming. "You did it for all of us!"

The roar of the crowd became deafening. Excitement and no little chaos filled the air. No one could really hear or say anything, the noise was that loud.

But this did not stop Calandrx from trying to ask a very important question.

"What do you remember, my brother?" he yelled in Hunter's ear. "What did you see inside the thirteenth dimension?"

Hunter tried to block out all of the noise and think a moment.

Not here. Not now, a voice inside him said.

Finally he yelled back to Calandrx: "Let's talk about it later!"

It took two squads of Earth Police to hustle Hunter and his friends over to the award ceremony.

It all happened very quickly. One moment Hunter was being mobbed in the winner's circle; the next he was standing at the foot of the *zadora,* looking up at the quartet of Imperial thrones, his flying machine hovering a few feet behind him.

He couldn't tell if it was intentional or not, but a ray of the midday sun was streaming through an opening in the arena wall in such a way that it was blinding him. He tried to make out the faces of the Imperial Family twenty-five steps away from him, but their features were hazy at best.

Erx and Berx were standing at attention on either side of him. However, Calandrx was not there. Loath to steal any of Hunter's thunder, he'd left to cash in their wagers. Surrounding the bottom of the *zadora* was a huge coterie of Empire military officers and their various forms of female companionship. They were all staring in at Hunter, almost as if they were studying him. At the same moment, his picture was being beamed to the tens of thousands of viz-screens floating around the arena. Transmissions were being sent across the Galaxy as well. Trillions were watching him at this moment.

And all this made Hunter acutely aware of just one thing: He was the oddest-dressed person in sight. He was wearing the old uniform he'd found himself in back on Fools 6—and just by style alone it certainly marked him as being not of this place. From his crash helmet to his combat boots—he could almost see the thousands of billions of people around the Empire staring at him in bewilderment.

If someone out there *did* know him, he certainly wouldn't be hard to recognize now.

On a whispered prompt from Erx, Hunter went to one knee and bowed. The Emperor must have made some sort of gesture, as the crowd erupted once again with cheering, chanting, screams of delight. A bag of aluminum coins had materialized on the step in front of him; two more appeared before Erx and Berx. The crowd roared again. The echoing bassy music began pumping through the stadium once more.

Then the Emperor raised his hand again and the crowd calmed down very quickly. Hunter heard a voice speaking slowly, quietly, but the words made no sense to him. They had a complex rhythmic cadence to them and featured a number of syllables that were repeated over and over again.

Although he could not see his lips moving, Hunter assumed that this was the Emperor himself speaking—and that the dialect was the archaic language few people on Earth understood anymore. The proclamation went on and on—so long, Hunter's mind began to wander. He thought back to what he had just done. The ultraspeedy takeoff. Hitting the screens. Battling the obstacles. Seeing the Blackship. And its pursuer.

It all seemed like such a blur now.

He lifted his head slightly and squinted. Finally he was able to see the entire top of the *zadora* and the four people sitting there. And as the last ray of the sun moved away, his eyes fell not upon the Emperor, who looked almost transparent, or the Empress and the Prince, who both seemed bored—but upon the Emperor's incredibly beautiful daughter. Of the four, only she was looking back down at him.

Oh, my God . . .

Suddenly the crowd was cheering again. The Emperor had finished his invocation—if indeed it had been he speaking all along. The ceremony was drawing to a close.

Hunter glanced around at Erx and Berx, who were still standing ramrod straight right behind him. He gave them a look as if to say: What now?

That's when he heard a voice whisper in his ear: *The race might be over . . . but the games have just begun . . .*

Flash!

The next thing Hunter knew, he was sitting at a corner table inside a huge, low-lit room. It was a club of some sort, with at least a thousand people crowded in. Music was blaring. There was much laughing, drinking, carousing. Erx and Berx were sitting next to him. They were just as stunned as he.

"My God, where are we now?" Berx exclaimed.

Erx took a quick look around. "Could this be . . . the *Vegasus*?" he asked excitedly.

Berx began looking about the room. "If that is so, then we've suddenly come up a lot in this world."

Hunter was still shuddering from the sudden transport.

"The *Vegasus*?" he managed to ask.

"An entertainment craft run by the Very Fortunates," Berx explained to him. "It's so exclusive that only the most connected of the upper class ever get on board."

Erx scanned the room with his quadtrol. It confirmed that they were indeed aboard the *Vegasus*.

"And at a such a good table, too!" he added. "Calandrx will be furious he missed out on this. . . ."

Hunter wasn't so sure. This just didn't seem to be the elderly pilot's scene.

Word was moving quickly through the enormous flying nightclub that the winner of the Earth Race was in the house. Bottles of 'cloud wine began arriving on their table at a rate of one a second.

But how did they get here? And why?

Hunter looked to his left to discover that the answer was

sitting right next to him. He was a young man, maybe ten years less than Hunter. He was wearing a shiny black military uniform, not Space Forces or Solar Guards or Double X Corps. This uniform appeared to belong to a branch of the military all its own. The person had popped in so quietly during their first few moments in the nightclub, they did not realize until now that he was sitting with them.

This person was looking back at them, grinning widely. It was Erx who recognized him first.

"By the Lord," he said with a gasp, "you honor us with your presence, sir."

Hunter looked over at Erx and then back at the man sitting next to him. Then it hit him. It was the Emperor's son, the Prince. His name was S'Keem.

Hunter began babbling some flowering greeting—apparently a requirement when suddenly in the presence of a Special. But the Prince simply waved away his clumsy attempt.

"It is I who should be praising you," he told Hunter. "What you just did in the race was *awesome*. . . ."

Hunter mumbled a words of thanks, and that's when he realized that their table was actually surrounded by huge armed guards wearing an approximation of the Prince's unusual uniform. Apparently S'Keem never went anywhere without his private army.

Hunter looked over at Berx as if to say, *What should I do?* Berx made a quick motion to his lips. *Talk to him—quick!* was what he was trying to say.

Hunter turned back to the Prince. His face was handsome if still boyish. There was, however, a deviant twinkle in his eye.

"I'm very glad you enjoyed the race," Hunter began stuttering. He was not good in situations like this. How he wished Calandrx were here now!

"Enjoyed it?" the Prince replied, grabbing one of the dozens of bottles of 'cloud wine on the table. "There has never been anything like it ever before in the history of the race. Do you realize that the other contestants are now just crossing the finish line?"

To prove his point, the Prince snapped his fingers and a huge viz-screen appeared. Sure enough, they were instantly looking at the arena somewhere below. It showed the other twelve racers rocketing across the finish line, a series of wild streaks and the sound of electron beams being broken heralding their return. Some of the racers were smoking heavily. Others had had their elaborate color schemes distorted by the trio of transdimensional leaps.

The trouble was, few people were on hand to see them arrive. By the time the last racer crossed the finish line, the vast majority of the huge crowd had already left the building. In fact, in the background they could clearly see a brigade of robots beginning the postrace cleanup.

The Prince shook his head.

"Now, that's sad, isn't it?" he said with a cruel grin. The viz-screen vanished, and he turned back to Hunter. "I guess they just didn't know what they were up against."

Hunter shrugged, but in a very polite way.

The Prince finished off one bottle of wine and quickly opened another.

"What would your reply be if I asked you how you were able to win this race with a time of barely two seconds?" he asked Hunter directly.

Erx, Berx, and Hunter went straight up in their seats. They could almost hear Calandrx in their ears urging them: *Don't say a thing!*

Yet Hunter could only wonder: *What was the penalty for lying to the son of the man who ruled the Galaxy?*

But before he could find out, the Prince drained his second bottle of wine—once again, no goblet, straight from the bottle—then reached for another.

"I realize that all winners strive to keep their secrets secret," he said, slurring his words a bit now. "That has to be the history of this thing, I suppose."

He grabbed another bottle of free wine, popped it open, and began guzzling it. Hunter sensed that some of the Imperial bodyguards were getting wary.

"But there's no sense denying it," the Prince went on, his voice getting louder, more rowdy. "At this moment, *you* are probably the most celebrated person on Earth—that's a feeling I know well. Your notoriety, spreading throughout the entire Galaxy at great speed. You're soon to be a hero, my friend; another sensation I have experienced."

He took another massive gulp of 'cloud.

"It's that 'prime domicile' in Big Bright City that really makes me envy you," he went on, the words coming a bit more difficult now. "I'm stuck *way* up in the sky! Can you imagine how *boring* that is?"

He drank some more; his slurring got worse.

"And soon you will be able to pick your rank and any assignment, anywhere in the Empire." The Prince shook his head. "Soon many riches will be yours."

Hunter just stared back at the kid. He'd never seen anyone get so drunk so quickly.

"Now, I know I can't compete with all the booty my father's realm can throw at you," the Prince went on, struggling to pronounce every last syllable. "God knows I've had that shoved down my throat all my life."

He slugged the bottle again.

"But besides bringing you up here, I have my own token of appreciation to give you," he said, adding: "And some things are better than a nice home or money."

With that he made a gesture to one of his many bodyguards. Through the haze of the celebration now, Hunter saw this man glide over and have a whispered conversation with the Prince. The man then handed a small yellow device to the royal son, gave Hunter a friendly wink, and disappeared back into the crowd.

The Prince examined the lemon-size device for several moments. He was very interested in the series of numbers blinking in the tiny window at the top the gadget.

"Excellent! This is an Echo-323," he proclaimed. A murmur went through everyone within earshot. Even Berx stopped consuming his mug of wine to listen in.

"Really, my Prince? A three-two-three? I thought they were impossible to acquire. . . ."

The Prince waved the device in front of Berx's face and pointed to the numbers.

"Have you forgotten that I am a man of many powers?" he asked Berx somewhat sternly.

But Berx was ignoring him. He was captivated by the device he held in his hand.

"Someone in here *really* likes you," he said to Hunter.

The Prince took another huge gulp of wine, then turned back to Hunter himself.

"Have you ever seen an Echo-323?" he asked him with an Imperial air.

"How?" was all Hunter could reply. He had no idea what any of them were talking about.

The Prince finished his bottle, broke open another, and then pushed Hunter farther along the seat. This opened up a space big enough for another body. Then the Prince hit a button on the small device. The next thing Hunter knew, a beautiful female . . . *projection* was sitting next to him.

Hunter stared at her, mouth agape, a bit of sweat forming on his sunburned brow.

"Echo . . . this is Mr. Hunter," the Prince said with a drunken laugh. "Mr. Hunter, this is Echo. . . ."

Hunter went to shake her hand, but his appendages were slow in responding. Or at least some of them were. He couldn't stop staring at her—and she was staring right back. Finally she took his hand in hers, and for an instant he thought he'd be able to pass his fingers right through it. But nothing could have been farther from the case. Her hand felt warm, soft . . . friendly.

"Hello, *Mister* Hunter," she said with a sly smile.

Hunter had only heard of holo-girls; he'd yet to see one in the flesh, or at least he didn't think he had. (There was no way to really tell, of course.) But this one before him was perfect. Face and shape. Perfect. Her hair, blond and flowing. Perfect. Her voice, sweet, melodic. *Perfect.* Her eyes, blue and sparkling.

Perfect.

"Watch this," the Prince said. He pushed something on the device. Echo's breasts began to grow. And grow. And grow. She was giggling, almost embarrassed. Just as it became clear that her top was about to burst, the Prince pushed something else. Her breasts began to shrink, almost until they were non-existent. Echo giggled again.

The Prince gulped more wine, then pushed something else. Echo's hair turned from blond to red. Another push, her tight silver top became a simple white blouse. Push. Her skin-tight pants became a skin-tight skirt. *Push*. Her purple boots disappeared to reveal two very beautiful bare legs and feet.

Hunter was speechless.

This sure ain't Fools 6, he thought.

The Prince went to push another button—but one of his entourage leaned over and froze his hand in place.

"Better to give it to 'im, sire," the man half growled. "He's the one who won the race. It's *his* gift, not yours. . . ."

But the Prince shoved the man's hand away.

"I have to see if this thing is working properly, don't I?" he bellowed at the bodyguard. "Our friend here is new at this. He might run into complications. You don't want his first experience to be a bad one, do you?"

The hulking bodyguard replied: "My orders are to not let you ever "

But the Prince cut him off with an icy, drunken stare.

"And I'm countermanding those orders," he said. The tone in his voice indicated this was not the first time he'd barked those words.

Once again he turned back to Hunter.

"You don't mind, old boy, do you?" he asked.

Hunter didn't know what to say. He still had a hold of Echo's hand, and he really didn't want to let go. "Mind what exactly?"

"That I take her out a bit, for a bit of a test ride," the Prince stuttered.

"You're unbelievable, sire!" another bodyguard said, disgusted. "No self-control at all . . ."

But the Prince was now ignoring his entire entourage.

It was up to Echo to break the impasse.

"You should let him run his test," she finally cooed to Hunter. "It doesn't take very long."

The Prince let out a yelp of victory. Then he put his arms around Echo, pushed the device's main control button—and they both disappeared.

"What happened?" Hunter asked, astonished. "Where did they go?"

Erx pushed a mug of wine toward him. "Just wait a few seconds," he said.

Sure enough, there was a quick yellow flash . . . and the

Prince and the Echo 323 were back. Not ten seconds had passed.

Echo looked the same, but the Prince's appearance had changed completely. There was now more hair on his head, about a half inch of additional growth, and on his face as well. He was noticeably thinner, and his eyes were bleary. But he looked extremely content and calm. Very, very calm. Like a man who'd just spent a month or so on a deserted island somewhere with a very beautiful female. Which was exactly what had happened. Sort of . . .

"They went into the thirty-fourth dimension," Erx explained. "Or is it the thirty-fifth? Either way, the Echo-323 is programmed to bring you to some paradise setting—wherever it is, it's all projected anyway. She'll morph any way you want her. Echoes have a large memory. That means you can just go . . . go far away, for a bunch of time. Days, weeks, however long you can stand it—then be back here before I take another sip of my drink."

"What I miss?" the Prince squealed in delight.

But before anyone could reply, the club was suddenly filled with a blinding white light. The crowd was stunned. There were a few muffled screams and squeaks.

The bright light slowly condensed into a very powerful yellow beam that became focused on a spot about three feet away from Hunter's table. The light began twirling, turning, forming a tunnel of sorts. Just barely visible near the source of the beam Hunter could see a translucent face. It was radiating a very warm, soothing light. The face seemed to be at the end of this very long tunnel.

The Prince shielded his eyes and finally got a good look at what was happening. "Oh, shit—it's my father. . . ."

Flash!

The Prince disappeared.

Echo took one look at the situation, kissed Hunter on the cheek, pushed her own button, and then *flash!* She disappeared.

Most of the crowd scurried away. Erx and Berx were frozen in place, though. So was Hunter.

The light finally dimmed a bit, enough for the figure at the end of the tunnel to be seen.

It was indeed the Emperor.

Or at least it looked like him.

He lifted his hand and pointed down at the table.

Flash!

Hunter disappeared.

The next thing he knew, Hunter was standing in the middle of a desert.

Or at least it looked like a desert. It was flat for the most part, though there were some mountains directly to the east. It was dry and hot, too. But the "sand" beneath his feet felt more like tiny glass globules than authentic silica. This gave everything the same shimmering effect that Earth was famous for.

Floating two feet off the ground next to Hunter was the Emperor—or at least some approximation of him. He was dressed in a flowing, all-white gown with a golden aura surrounding it. His face was a complete blank. His arms were raised out on front of him, as if he were sleepwalking. The wind was blowing, yet his hair and clothes were not moving at all. In fact, Hunter could see right through him, clear to the other side.

What's up with this? Hunter thought. Like many things in the Fourth Empire's Galaxy, it seemed as if the great O'Nay was there, yet at the same time, not really there at all.

Suddenly a viz-screen appeared out of nowhere. It nearly split Hunter's forehead in two. He had really bad luck with these things. They always seemed to want to hurt him no matter where they popped in.

The man on the viz-screen looked as weird as the ghost hovering next to him. He had long white hair, a blank face, and that "Special" look in his eyes. He wasn't an exact twin of the Emperor, but he was close.

An Emperor wannabe?

The man in the viz-screen spoke to Hunter: "As the victor of the Earth Race, you will be allowed to cast eyes upon the holiest of holy things in the Empire. This is the Emperor's wish."

"You do all his talking for him?" Hunter asked innocently.

The man in the viz-screen seemed insulted. "The Emperor

does not talk *directly* to his subjects," he told Hunter, his voice dripping with arrogance. "Especially in the form you see before you."

"There's more than one of him?" Hunter asked, looking up at the motionless apparition.

"The Emperor has three modes," the man in the viz-screen replied. "This one is his 'sacred spirit.' He's calling to you now."

Sure enough, the ghost was pointing to something over Hunter's shoulder. He turned to see that they were actually standing near a group of plain white structures built astride a huge, flat, dry lakebed. The buildings looked absolutely ancient.

Flash!

Suddenly they were standing at the front entrance of the largest building. A faded sign next to the door read: Domain 51.

Flash!

Now they were inside the building itself, looking down at the entrance to a huge amphitheater contained within. There were dozens of soldiers in stark black uniforms standing at rigid attention around this sizable portal. The only means of illumination that Hunter could see was by candles; there were hundreds of them everywhere. Their flickering cast odd shadows on the Z-gun turrets built into the walls of this place.

Flash!

Hunter was now inside the chamber itself. It, too, was lit only by candlelight. In the middle of the chamber was a huge black monolith. It was about a hundred feet high and the same measurement square. It stood alone. A huge seamless, impenetrable presence.

Hunter didn't have to ask what this was. He knew already.

It was the Big Generator.

It was guarded by another small army of black-uniformed soldiers. They were standing at attention in small groups scattered around the inner chamber. They did not seem to notice that Hunter and the Emperor's ghost were there.

The chamber had a definite religious air to it. There was no sound. Hunter could see no means of access to the huge black box. There were no dials or switches or panel lights on the thing. No cables or wires running into or out of it. No controls, at least anywhere nearby.

The viz-screen appeared again. This time Hunter was able to duck before it brained him. The same guy, with the same blank expression, began talking to him again.

"From the Big Generator everything is possible in our Galaxy," he said without a nanoiota of emotion. "It is a gift from on high. The power it generates goes everywhere and encompasses the realm. It runs our spaceships. It runs our planets. It runs everything on our planets. From the dimmest panel bulb on the most distant world to the prop core of our largest M-Class Starcrasher. All of the energy comes from here."

"Fascinating," Hunter said. It was hard not to be impressed. "How does it work?"

The man in the viz-screen suddenly looked nonplussed.

"What do you mean?" he asked.

Hunter shrugged. Could he have been any clearer?

"I mean, 'How does it work?' " he asked again.

The man in the viz-screen started stammering. "Well . . . that's a closely guarded secret . . . the most closely guarded secret in the Empire. . . ."

But Hunter persisted because he really wanted to know.

"Do you mean *how* it works is a secret?" he asked. "Or the fact that no one *knows* how it works?"

Even the Emperor's ghost turned slightly red on that one. The man in the viz-screen started to say something.

But before he could answer—

Flash!

Hunter now found himself standing inside a huge apartment.

It was empty of furniture except for one couch and a floating bed. There were windows everywhere, and judging from the harsh glare flooding in on him, it was easy to guess that he was atop a building somewhere deep in downtown Big Bright City.

His new home.

But before he could take one step or have one more thought, there came a stern pounding on the apartment's front door. Hunter quickly walked down the hallway and activated the security screen next to the main entrance.

He saw a small army of Imperial Guards looking in on him.

Damn . . .

Could these be the Emperor's bodyguards coming for him? Maybe to arrest him on a charge of insolence or blasphemy?

No . . . these guys were wearing different uniforms than the ones he'd just seen out in the desert. They were carrying bigger guns as well.

He slid the door open.

"Can I help you?"

The six monstrous soldiers didn't say a word. Instead, they stepped aside to reveal that someone was with them.

It was a woman.

A very beautiful woman.

She was dressed all in black. Black jacket. Black miniskirt, black stockings. Black boots. Her low-cut black top showed a hint of substantial breasts. Her hair was blond and flowing over her shoulders. Even with the heavy makeup, her face was stunning.

Hunter heard himself say: "Wow . . ."

His first thought, of course, was that Erx and Berx had arranged for another Echo 323 to be delivered to him. They were such great guys!

But then it dawned on him—holo-girls had no need for a royal escort. Could someone this beautiful be the real thing?

She smiled. "I'm sorry, Mister Hunter. Am I disturbing you?"

Hunter fumbled for a reply. "That would be impossible, I think," he finally said.

She smiled again. Her coterie of guards popped out.

That's when Hunter realized just who this was. He recognized her from the race earlier that day.

It was the Empress. The wife of O'Nay. Alone. Standing at his apartment door.

"Well, are you going to invite me in?" she asked him.

Hunter stumbled back a foot or two. She wiggled by him, allowing the door to close behind her.

She walked into the apartment, took a look around, and

smiled. "Nice place—though I should say you need some more furniture—and it could use a woman's touch. Even a holo-girl might help out here."

"I still don't know how to work those things. . . ." Hunter said, regretting each word as it floated from his mouth.

But she just smiled again. She was stunning, if several years older than he.

"You must be the only man left in the Galaxy who doesn't," she said.

She took a seat on the couch; he did too. Five words kept spinning around in his head. *What is* she *doing* here?

"I hear you were off with both my husband and my son today," she said. "Did my son behave himself?"

"I can't imagine he ever misbehaves," Hunter answered as politely as he could.

She laughed. "No need to be nice about it. It still happens on a daily basis."

Hunter looked around his place helplessly. "I'm sorry . . . I don't have anything to offer you . . . that is, I'm not sure if you even—"

She reached over and touched him on the knee. He felt a jolt of something go right through him.

"Relax, Mister Hunter," she told him. "An Empress can have a sip of wine every once in a while."

She gently snapped her fingers, and a bottle of wine was suddenly in her hand. Another snap, two goblets appeared. But this was not a bottle of extravagant 'cloud wine she was holding. It was slow-ship.

Hunter just looked up at her and laughed. "You'll never convince me that you actually drink that stuff."

"Should I take that as a challenge?" she asked him.

Hunter began stuttering some reply. Jessuz, what was going on here? One moment he's at a party in the sky, the next he's inside a mountain somewhere—and now he was sitting next to the Empress of the Galaxy.

This sure ain't *Fools 6,* he thought.

"My husband took you to that awful place in the desert, I suppose?" she asked, pouring him some wine.

"We went to the desert, yes. . . ."

She rolled her eyes. "With all those guards. And the security. And that Big Generator thing?"

Hunter nodded. "That was the tour."

She sighed dramatically and handed him his wine. "But I insisted he bring you someplace *interesting*."

"Well, it *was* interesting, especially . . ." Hunter began to say.

She tapped his knee again, gently interrupting him. *"Please!"* she said. "There's interesting . . . then there's really *interesting*. . . ."

Finally a light was dawning somewhere deep in Hunter's brain. He was having a hard time keeping his eyes off of her.

"And you know one from the other?" he asked her.

She seemed delighted. "You might be shocked to hear this, but I am here to make up for any amount of boredom my family has caused you today. You ran such a magnificent race, you deserve more than a ride on that very tacky *Vegasus* or a trip to stare at a big black box in the wilderness."

Hunter sipped his wine. His hand was shaking. "What are you suggesting exactly?"

"I'm suggesting you let me take you to *my* favorite place . . . the place I think is interesting. . . ."

"You? Take me?"

"That's right. . . ."

"Where?"

"Venus," she said with a laugh.

"Venus? The planet Venus?"

"Yes, the planet Venus . . ."

Hunter tried to sip his wine again. But it was a no-go. He could barely bring the cup to his lips.

"When?"

She stood up. "Well, right now, of course."

He looked up at her—she was absolutely gorgeous, in that regal sort of way. And he suspected her bodyguards were lurking just once dimension away. And it was probably not prudent to refuse the Emperor's wife anything.

"How can I say no?" he finally replied.

She smiled again.

Flash!

17

Venus was the second body in the solar system that the Ancient Engineers had puffed. Only Mars had come first.

The morning planet had taken to its terraforming right away, completely transforming itself in a then amazing five hundred years. These days a planet could be made habitable in hours. Several thousand years ago, a five-hundred-year puff was considered absolutely speedy.

So Venus was no longer enshrouded in thick clouds and raining hydrochloric acid. Like Earth, its cloud cover was 30 percent at any given time. Also like Earth, it had one ocean that spread around the planet, pole to pole. This one surrounded two massive continents and several smaller ones. One of these was the island continent of Zros.

These days Earth's sister planet served as a very exclusive getaway for the extended Imperial Family—even the Very Fortunates weren't allowed here. The planet featured tens of thousands of summer palaces, seaside resorts, vineyards, and spas. Zros was the *número uno* place to be, though. Sitting just north of the equator in the middle of the western part of the ocean, its irregular shape looked not unlike a human heart. With lush forests and thousands of miles of exotic beaches dotted with towering, castlelike resorts, Zros pandered only to the cream of the Specials. It was awash in Holy Blood.

Hunter found himself at the top of a very tall building, looking west onto a beautiful jungle and the sea beyond.

This building was the tallest of a vast complex of luxurious châteaus that spread out over high cliffs for at least twenty miles in each direction. This place was called La-Shangri.

It was a three-tiered palace, bigger than the other châteaus by a factor of ten. They had popped in on a balcony atop the highest spire of the place; a cadre of Imperial bodyguards appeared right after them. The palace roof was already crawling with Imperial soldiers. The airspace surrounding the complex was thick with patrol craft and even some larger, armed *culverins,* corvette-size warships more commonly used in space.

The Empress ignored all this commotion and led Hunter down a passageway and into a huge room. This room was made of sheer superglass and hung out over a cliff nearly half a mile above the ocean.

A huge party of the Specials was in full swing here; indeed, it appeared to have been going non stop for some time. Heads turned when the Empress walked in, Hunter just behind her. Most of the revelers simply nodded in her direction and then went back to their dancing, drinking, and general merriment. Hunter guessed there were more than a thousand people on hand, most of them beautiful young women. Unlike the *Vegasus,* the atmosphere here was subtle, sensuous. Sexual.

"Every person in this room is related to me," the Empress whispered in his ear. "Half of them snobs, the other half are slobs. It makes for an interesting mix, don't you think?"

Before Hunter could answer, she began dancing away from him. He found a goblet of sparkling blue liquid in his hand. The Empress had one, too. She drained hers in one gulp. *My kind of Empress,* Hunter thought. Then her jacket came off. The music got louder; the mixture of pulsating bass and ethereal strings was hypnotic. She floated away, kicking off her boots and allowing the crowd to take her over. She was quickly swallowed up by the mass of arms and legs and lips. Hunter felt a sensation run through him; it was not entirely due to the cool blue liquid he was drinking either. The Empress came back into view, dancing slowly, eyes closed. Hunter took a gulp of his drink. Was it his imagination, or could he see right through her tight black top?

Hunter blinked—and a very strange thought went through his head. Was it possible that he was still in the race? And that this, and everything that had happened before, from reaching the finish line to this moment, was really happening *inside* one of the blue screens?

But how could that be? He'd gone through three screens—just as the race procedures called for. But what if the second screen actually incorporated into its madness a scenario where he *thought* he punched out, and then punched back in again and then, maybe . . .

Stop! he heard a voice cry from somewhere deep inside his head. *You're making yourself crazy.*

He opened his eyes and looked at his hands, and at that moment he knew that all this was happening. This was real.

Wasn't it?

The Empress was coming toward him again. Her eyes were locked onto his. She began dancing even closer. Time seemed to jump ahead several minutes. The other partygoers were suddenly becoming extremely intimate with each other. Many of the women were now topless. Hunter began to sweat. He drained his drink, making the situation worse— or better. His goblet was instantly filled again.

The Empress was dancing so close to him now, she was rubbing against his chest. Hunter closed his eyes. The music began pulsating very slowly.

What was the penalty for cavorting with the Emperor's wife? he wondered.

The music got louder. He felt her body start to grind into his. He'd been stuck on Fools 6 a very long time—but not long enough to forget the necessities of life.

Her hands on him now.

"Well, is this better than the desert?" she asked him.

Oh, yeah, I remember this, he thought.

He reached out for her.

Flash!

• • •

"I said: 'Is this better than the desert?'"

When Hunter opened his eyes again, he was sitting on a flat, moss-covered rock, high atop a soaring cliff, looking out over the ocean. The sun was right in front of him. And it was setting—over the water. This could mean only one thing: He was still on Venus, but most likely on the opposite side of Zros.

The pop-in had been so sudden, his hand was still moist from holding his wine goblet. Someone was sitting beside him—a female, but not the Empress. This person was dressed in a nonprovocative white gown. Her hair was brunette and styled long but conservatively. She was wearing no makeup, she had no glow. There was no aura around her, at least not one that he could see.

Yet despite this, she was much more beautiful than the Empress. Or any of the women he'd just seen at La-Shangri. And she was a lot younger, too.

Hunter recognized her right away.

It was Princess Xara.

She smiled. "You didn't really want to stay there, did you?"

Hunter began fumbling for a suitable reply. "Well, I thought that maybe your mo—"

Xara just shook her head. "My mother was trying to entrap you. And La-Shangri? Please. Half the people are dead in that place."

She spread her arms to indicate the beautiful landscape around them. The flower-covered cliffs, the green seas crashing below. The sun, still bright, going down. The sweet breeze. It was stunning. And natural.

"Isn't this place a lot better?"

Hunter had to agree with her. "It is."

She smiled. He saw lots of teeth.

"But why did you bring me here?" he asked her directly.

"Do I have to have a reason?" she replied. Her gown went up a bit, showing her well-shaped legs.

"Yes, you do, because I don't think anyone in your family does *anything* without a reason."

She placed her hand in his. One thing about the Specials,

Hunter mused, they weren't afraid to get touchy-feely.

"Okay, you're right," she said. "And I confess. Ever since I saw you at the race today, I wanted to talk to you—and I wanted to do it someplace where we could be alone. Really alone."

Hunter looked around. He could see nothing but forests and beaches and sand and water for many miles. No châteaus. No palaces. No enormous bodyguards.

"I think you picked the right place," he told her.

"Of course, I'm not sure you want to discuss what I have in mind," she said.

"And that means?"

She slid a bit closer to him.

"I'll be up front with you: I know the circumstances by which you were found. I know what happened during the attack on the *BonoVox*. I know that you can't remember who you are. Or where you came from. Is that correct?"

Hunter nodded uncertainly. "Well, no one has really asked me about any of those things since I've been here on Earth," he replied. "So I've kept my mouth shut about them."

"Another art that we lost as a race sometime ago," she said. "The art of holding one's tongue."

Hunter looked deep into her eyes. There really was something very different in there.

"I'm embarrassed to tell you that I'm probably the smartest one in my immediate family," she said, her lips hovering somewhere between a smile and a grimace. "I don't know why—it's my burden to bear, I suppose. But I care deeply about things. Things I consider important, and not just 'interesting,' or 'sacred,' or reveling in self-gratification— "

She caught herself, and put her hand to her mouth.

"Oh, my," she said with a gasp. "I must sound like the biggest snoot!"

Hunter squeezed her hand. If possible, she was getting more beautiful by the moment. Her eyes, her mouth, her cheeks—they all seemed just a bit bigger than what would be considered "perfect."

And when she smiled . . .

Suddenly there was no other place in the Galaxy he wanted to be.

"I don't think you're a 'snoot' at all," he told her. "In fact, you're the most interesting person I've run into since landing here. Well, the most interesting female, anyway. . . ."

She tilted her head slightly. "Is there a compliment in there somewhere?"

They laughed. "Well, maybe," he said. "But tell me, what are these things you care so much about?"

She looked very pleased to answer that question.

"I care about history, for one," she declared. "I think it's important to know what went on before—well, before *all this*. . . ."

She waved her hand across the sky. The sun had not set, yet many stars were already twinkling above them.

"I mean, my father is the leader of the Fourth Empire," she went on very earnestly. "There have been three empires before us. And yet what we know about them wouldn't fill a single nanodisk. There are some things left over from the Second Empire, and apparently traces from the Third. But we know just about nothing about the First Empire—or anything that happened before it."

She looked over at him.

"Am I boring you yet?" she asked.

Smile. Teeth.

"Impossible," he replied.

She laughed sweetly and went on. "What bothers me most is that my family, the Specials and the Very Fortunates, they're all so quick to take credit for all of this. But the truth is, they stumbled upon it. They didn't invent any of it—it invented them. Yet they feel it's their duty to exploit it, to take advantage of any chance they get."

"Your father must care about the Empire, though," Hunter told her, wondering which one of the Emperor's three incarnations would actually be considered her father.

"Frankly, I'm not sure anyone can tell," she replied slowly. "Don't get me wrong—my family, the military, the Very Fortunates—they *all* care about the Empire. They care about *keeping* it going. How to make it bigger, better, no matter what the cost. Now, I don't know what's wrong with me, but I just think we should learn as much as we can about the past so—"

"So we can avoid the same mistakes in the future," Hunter finished for her.

She looked up at him. Her face was a mixture of surprise and delight. "So you actually understand what I'm talking about?"

Hunter had to think a moment. "Yes," he said finally. "Yes, I believe I do."

She gave him a very spontaneous hug, then let go and fiddled with her hair a moment. A warm wind blew by them. More stars had come out above.

"I actually envy you in a way," she told him. "You know, you're in a very unique position here. Not being like us . . ."

"How so?"

She looked out at the sea. The sun dipped lower into the water.

"Well, in case you haven't noticed, we are a Galaxy full of obsessive behavior," she said. "Everyone needs whatever they can get, as fast as they can get it. Sure, there is wealth beyond comprehension. But whether you're my first-first cousin, or some space pirate robbing old bag planets out on the Fringe, everyone wants a piece. And they want it now. And if they can't get it, they'll drive themselves nuts *trying* to get it. It's not the best way to be . . . at least I don't think so."

She fiddled with her hair again. Hunter could have sat here and talked to her for days.

"And our biggest obsession, of course, is this thing where *everyone* is an expert on their family ancestry," she went on. "They know their bloodlines, their origins. Who married who, on what planet, and when. Everyone must keep track of who they are, or they just go batty."

"Is knowing where you came from such a bad thing?" he asked her. "I wish *I* knew. . . ."

"Yes, but that's my point: You want to know *who* you are—they want to know *what* they are. . . ."

Hunter shook his head. "And that means?"

She sighed. "No one has told you about the Holy Blood, I suppose?"

"Nope."

She slid even closer to him.

"My family, the Specials, are the descendants of the people who ruled the Galaxy in the Third Empire," she began. "That dynasty collapsed about eight hundred years ago. We know very little about those people. Only that they were called the Specials, too—and that at one time they had control over every planet in the Galaxy. Billions? Trillions? Whatever the number is, every last one of them was under their control.

"For whatever reason, no one is sure why, these people had blood pumping in their veins that allowed them to live for very long periods of time. I'm talking about five, six, even seven hundred years or more. As a direct descendant, that blood is my blood, too. As well as that of thousands and thousands of my relatives. My father is nearly four hundred and fifty years old; my mother admits to two hundred and seventy-five."

Hunter couldn't help screwing up his face at that last fact. *Two hundred and seventy-five* . . .

"Now, most people who are not of Holy Blood live to be about a third of that age," she went on. "But some *will* live longer because they have varying strains of the Holy Blood in them, too."

"How did that happen?" he asked.

Xara frowned. "Because in the past, it was not beneath some of my more enterprising relatives to sell a drop or two—for incredibly huge amounts of coin. They say it still goes on today, which makes this even more disgusting."

She played with her hair for a moment and then went on.

"So you see, the more connected you are, the closer you can get to escaping your own mortality. That's what makes a person a Very Fortunate. They have a little more of the Holy Blood in them than a Fortunate, who has a little more in them than a first-class citizen and so on and so on.

"Now, it's up to you to stay out of the way of a moving air car, or a stray Z-gun blast. But if you live in a safe part of the Galaxy, as many people do, then you probably have a long, long life ahead of you. And that's the problem. Everyone wants it—but no one really appreciates it, because they're so obsessed with how much longer they can live, even by a year, a month, a week, based on how much or how little Holy Blood they have in them. It's *crazy*. It leads to all kinds of prearranged marriages, the pairing up of total strangers, industries to figure how much Holy Blood you have and how many years it's going to buy you. It all leads to a total lack of diversity and misplaced energies. And it's created a class system that is not healthy for us as a race and that I personally find appalling."

She looked over at Hunter. He was staring very intently into her eyes.

"And how old are you, my dear?" he asked her.

Smile. Teeth.

"Just nineteen!" she replied happily. "I'm still a kid. Thank God my parents waited a long time before they started working on their heirs. I'm surprised they even stopped long enough to consider it at all."

She let her voice trail off. The sun was just about gone by now. But she looked even more beautiful in the waning light.

"But you, Mr. Hunter—well, you're like a breath of fresh air. Because for once, *finally,* we find someone who *really doesn't* know where he came from. And look at him: He looks normal. He looks like the rest of us. But that's what makes you unique, in a place where no one is truly *unique.* At least, no one we know about."

Hunter wasn't sure what to say, so he didn't say anything. She turned toward him again.

"So then? Can I see it?" she asked him.

"Sure," he answered right away, adding after a beat: "See what?"

"The clue. I heard that you carry something in your pocket—something that might give a hint as to where you came from."

Hunter's hand unconsciously went to his left breast pocket. The piece of cloth. The faded photograph. He never went anywhere without them.

"There are two things, actually," he confessed. "And I haven't shown them to very many people."

The smile returned. So did her hand on his knee.

"I'd be honored to see them," she said sincerely.

Hunter retrieved the cloth and picture and carefully unfolded them. Xara looked at the picture first.

"She's beautiful," she said in a whisper so low it was lost on the wind. "Do you know who she is?"

Hunter shook his head no. There were some days he couldn't bear to look at the faded picture. The emotion that welled up inside him could be that intense.

"I don't have the slightest idea who she is," he told her.

She studied the cloth. Red stripes, white stripes. A big blue block. Designs like stars. It was uneven, yet still symmetric. In a world where just about everything was built as a triangle, the horizontal lines looked alien. And fascinating.

And familiar.

"I was afraid of this," she said.

"I'm not sure what you mean," Hunter replied.

She squeezed his hand again. "It might not seem so apparent now," she said. "But not knowing where you're from. It's a gift. And it's something that you might not want to give up so quickly."

Hunter just stared back at her.

"What are you talking about?"

She turned very serious.

"While the rest of my clan is out doping it up," she said, "I've taken it upon myself to learn as much as I can about what went on long before my father's Empire went into ascension. I've been able to learn little bits and pieces of ancient history—things that happened even before the First Empire. Even before the people they call the Ancient Engineers inhabited the Earth. I'm talking about four to five thousand years ago."

She looked deeply into his eyes. "If you had a chance to *really* find out where you came from, would you take it? Would you being willing to do anything, go anywhere, to find out?"

Hunter sat straight up on the rock. "Of course . . . that's all I care about. It has to be . . . Why?"

She squeezed his hand a little more and penetrated his soul with her enormous emerald eyes.

"Because I think I know how you can find out. . . ."

Hunter stared back at her. "Really? How?"

Flash!

18

The planet was indeed red and the dirt was indeed made up of tiny diamonds. And yes, there were canals here, too.

Lots of them.

This was Mars. First planet to be puffed by the Ancient Engineers. Apparently in the older texts, what few there were left of them, the Ancients believed that Mars ran best when it was crisscrossed with canals—just like Earth. So they built them, hundreds of them. So many, the planet could look like a red gemstone wrapped in a huge spiderweb if the sun's rays were hitting it just right.

Mars was also considered a sacred place as well, on the same par as the bridges that spanned the triads on Earth. Travel here was restricted to only the Specials and an elite contingent of the Solar Guards. And while it supported its own atmosphere and was enveloped in vast plains and forests running along the *canali,* there was a definitely mysterious air to the red planet. Next to Earth's Moon, where travel was banned for all, even the Specials, Mars was the least-visited body in the solar system.

But Hunter was here now.

He and Xara had popped in near a place called Bogus

Charmas. It was near the southern pole, a region where stunted trees and dull red grass coexisted with bitterly cold winds and frozen-over canals. There were no diamonds on the ground here. It was the most desolate place on an intentionally desolate world—and about as far away from the tropical beauty of Venus as one could get.

There was a small scientific station set up here—just a permahut built next to a big hole in the ground. A string of dim lights faded away into the blackness of this cavity, underlying how deep and dark it really was.

"We're going down there?" Hunter asked Xara once he'd shaken off the effects of the sudden transplanetary pop-in.

She nodded eagerly. Somehow during their transport, Xara had managed a complete wardrobe change. Gone was the long, flowing white gown. She was now dressed for action: tight-fitting black jumpsuit, boots, gloves, and helmet. Hunter was still dressed in his ancient flight suit. Lucky for him he was not a slave to fashion.

"Many answers to your questions might be found down there," she told him now as a brisk icy gale blew across the rugged plain.

Hunter fought off a chill.

"At this point I'll do anything to get out of this wind," he said.

They walked about two hundred feet nearly straight down, to a rickety hoverlift. This brought them down even deeper into the hole; the temperature drop was so drastic, Hunter could soon see his breath.

Finally they reached a chamber that was made entirely of ice. Two dull lamps illuminated this place, casting eerie reflections off the clear, glasslike glacier.

Xara pointed to the far end of the ice chamber. "Down there," she said. "Take a look."

Hunter walked farther into chamber and soon discovered what she was talking about. Imbedded in the thick ice, perfectly preserved, was a very small, very ancient-looking spacecraft.

"Only a handful of people know of this object's existence," Xara told him, moving closer in an effort to keep warm. "We have no idea when it came down here or who sent it here. All we can speculate is that the people on Earth—and I mean in very ancient times—sent it here, maybe to study the polar ice cap. Our scientists believe it was damaged on landing and never really fulfilled its mission."

Hunter studied the spacecraft. It was obviously damaged. Its sides were crumpled, as were what appeared to be its landing struts. A large orange piece of material with many slim pieces of rope was draped over nearly half the object, hiding various attachments from view.

"Does anyone have a guess how old this thing is?" he asked her.

Xara shook her head no.

"The best estimate I've heard was also the most outlandish—approximately five thousand years ago," she said. "As far as we can tell, that's just about the same time the Ancients began spaceflight. But we know nothing about the people who built it."

She shivered a bit—and got a bit closer.

"But what does this have to do with me?" he asked her.

She led him around the block of ice, to a point where they could just see under the orange shroud. One of the spacecraft's panels had partially come loose and was poking out from under the orange covering. Hunter took one look at this panel and felt a chill go through that had nothing to do with the conditions inside the chamber. Painted onto the side of this panel was a series of long red and white stripes, a block of blue, and a collection of white designs within.

Hunter was stunned. He took the piece of cloth from his breast pocket and held it up against the ice. He and Xara both nodded at once. There was no mistaking this.

It was the same design.

"I think that might have been a flag of the Ancients," Xara said. "But just like our flags today indicate what planet someone is from, this flag might have indicated a particular region of the Earth. Apparently the people back then were actually proud of what *part* of the world they lived in. They called them *nations*. Not like these days, when entire planets present themselves as one nation.

"So we are pretty sure we know where this machine came from and what that symbol painted on its side means. The question is, why do you have the same kind of symbol in your pocket?"

Hunter was nearly speechless. He had no idea.

"This only deepens the mystery," he whispered.

Xara smiled. She liked surprising him—and she had one more in store.

She pointed to a slight blemish on the side of the ice case just above the part of the spacecraft that bore the red, white and blue symbol.

"Can you see that? It's the result of a VLR/VSA hit. . . ."

"VL-RV . . . S . . . A?" Hunter stuttered.

"It stands for 'very-long-range visual sensing array,' " she explained. "It's a technology that has not been used for centuries. However, I've been told that it was a way to get a visual reading from just about anyplace in the Galaxy, like a very-long-range camera lens, I guess you could say. Primitive by our standards. But when our scientists returned to Mars after the last Dark Age, they were fascinated with this spacecraft but also this evidence of a long-range sensor scan. They discovered that someone at the other end of the Galaxy had scanned this planet—indeed, had scanned this very piece of ice, possibly looking for that symbol.

"Our scientists theorize that a VLR/VSA, located way out on the Fringe, might have been set on unlimited search—a simple device with a simple mission. Go right across the Galaxy looking for this symbol and beam back the information, no matter where it could be found. Well, they found it here. Many, many years ago . . ."

Hunter was quiet for a very long time. There was something very emotional about a faint light crisscrossing the Galaxy on its lonely mission to find a symbol long-ago forgotten.

"The scanning signal that painted this site aeons ago came from someone way, way out there," Xara went on after a while. "My guess is that they wanted to know the same thing you do. They wanted to know what that design on your piece of cloth means."

She nuzzled up very close to him.

"I think we can deduce that the symbol is from Earth. But

it was from an Earth of many centuries ago, a civilization that could have spanned a millennium, for all we know. So now maybe we know *where* you're from. You're from Earth—eventually just like everyone else. But that still doesn't answer the bigger question: Who are you?"

She paused and looked deep into his eyes.

"I think the best way to find that out," she said, pointing to the scan burn on the ice, "is to find them first. . . ."

Hunter could only nod in agreement.

"But how?" he asked. "There are trillions of planets out there that we know about. And probably a trillion or so we *don't* know about. It would take about that many lifetimes to search them all—even if I could get out to the Fringe."

That's when Xara smiled maybe her widest smile. Then she hugged him, tightly, unexpectedly.

"I was hoping you'd say that," she said.

"Really?" he asked, not letting go of her. "Why?"

"Because," she replied, "I have a plan. . . ."

19

On Earth
The next day

The trip up to the floating palace known as Number One took less than the blink of an eye.

One moment Hunter was in his new living quarters, having just climbed into the white ceremonial uniform that had been left for him, and . . . *flash!* . . . he was standing at one end of an immense hall.

Like much of that associated with the Specials, the predominant color here was green, or more accurately, emerald. The walls of this chamber seemed to shimmer like jewels. The ceiling was so high, Hunter imagined he could see clouds forming at the top, due in part to the fact that they were *riding* on a cloud.

There were as many as ten thousand spectators on hand. Some were on the floor, or more accurately, hovering a bit above it. Others were perched in galleries that lined the sides of the hall. All of them were Specials or high military officers.

In front of Hunter were two long line of soldiers; standing on either side of an aisle, they seemed to stretch on forever. On his left side were ceremonial troops of the Space Forces, unmistakable in their blue uniforms and oversized battle hats. On his right, an almost equal number of Solar Guards, again unmistakable in their black combat suits.

At the end of these two long lines was yet another Imperial throne. The Imperial Family was waiting for him upon it. The Emperor's miter was glowing with an ethereal yellow light; a beam was coming through a well-placed window in the hall. The Emperor himself appeared to be StarScraping, drawing the yellow light from his favorite sun, called Impervious C, located at the center of the South Dog Night system some thirty-three light-years away.

Two words came to Hunter's head on seeing this: *Mood ring*.

He started walking.

Music came up from somewhere. Ethereal strings, not so much bass. He was suddenly aware of his boot heels clicking on the pearl floor. Just as quickly, this noise went away.

He saw the color beaming down on the Emperor change slightly. The yellow became a tinge of orange. Hunter picked up his pace. He was very aware that there were thousands of eyes on him—none of them belonging to the soldiers in this multiservice honor guard, though. True, the soldiers on either side of him were standing eyes straight, but they weren't looking at him. They were looking across the aisle at each other, a long-held game of psyche-out between the rival SF and SG soldiers.

It added an interesting if slightly tense element to the room.

Hunter finally reached the end of this gauntlet to find that the last ten soldiers on his right side were not Solar Guards, but representatives from the third, smaller service, the Exploratory and Expeditionary Corps—the X-Forces.

The last two soldiers in this line were Erx and Berx.

Hunter nodded in their direction, then turned eyes front. He looked up at the Imperial Family. The Emperor as usual looked detached—there but not there, his face vacant as always. The glow on his hat had dulled a bit. The queen looked sexy but stern. She could not bring her eyes to meet Hunter's. The Prince simply looked hung over and bored.

And Xara looked beautiful.

A platform appeared in front of Hunter. A man in thick

ceremonial dress materialized along with it. On the platform were three emblems. The five-star gold badge of the Space Forces, the twin gold lightning bolts of the Solar Guards, and the crossed silver stars of the X-Forces.

"By order of all that is holy," the priest said, "our Emperor has declared that as a reward for the ability you displayed in contest, you will be granted your choice of what service in which you will serve him. . . ."

The man looked Hunter in the eye.

"It is now time to select," he said. "Please choose well. . . ."

Hunter looked over at Erx and Berx; they appeared extraordinarily happy—no doubt because their pockets were thick with winnings from the Earth Race. He looked up at Xara, who was gazing down as him, a regal smile in place, but her eyes sparkling. Yes, she certainly had a plan.

Suddenly the Prince spoke up.

"You will look your best in the uniform of the Space Forces," he said, to some amusement of those gathered.

"*I* prefer that he join of the Inner Defense Forces," the queen barked, suddenly coming to life.

Hunter grinned nervously. The Emperor appeared to be looking down at him, but Hunter felt his stare going right through him. At best, the most powerful being in the Galaxy appeared to be caught in a daydream—one that didn't look pleasant.

Hunter stepped forward to the platform. He'd thought about this decision long and hard ever since returning to Earth from Mars.

Although his face had been flashed across the Galaxy, and his name was indeed on the lips of trillions of citizens, no one had come forward claiming to know who he was. This meant he would have to find out for himself, a task that could quite possibly take a lifetime or two scouring the lost planets of the Fringe.

But then again, maybe it wouldn't take quite that long. If he played his cards right.

So he allowed his hand to hover on the Space Forces badge first. Then the one representing the Solar Guards.

Then he reached down and picked up the silver double stars of the X-Forces.

A gasp went through the crowd. The Empress and the Prince looked especially shocked.

But when Hunter looked up to the throne again, he saw Xara smiling down at him.

20

Big Bright City

The night was filled with color.

StarScrapers were lighting up the sky. Big Bright City seemed brighter than ever. The stars shimmered with increased intensity.

Hunter was sitting on the balcony of his new dwelling, looking out on the night of light and counting down the minutes until his new adventure would begin.

On the table in front of him was a package from Xara. It was waiting for him when he returned from his commissioning ceremony and the brief celebration that followed. During that time he had not been able to talk to her; it was important at this stage to keep their alliance secret.

Inside the package he found an ancient star map. It showed a part of the Galaxy so isolated, so uncharted, Xara's accompanying note indicated that no one was sure of its exact location. It was, however, in the Fifth Arm, one of the most remote parts of the Outer Fringe, a place very, *very* far from Earth. This, Xara's note said, was where the ancient scientists postulated that the VLR/VSA beam that hit the Mars polar lander originated.

Then she dropped a bomb: She had been able to pull some strings and arrange that his first mission would be to this very uncharted part of the Galaxy, Fifth Arm, Outer Fringe.

In other words, she was enabling him to go off in search of who he was while serving his commission with the Empire at the same time. It seemed the best of all worlds.

Also included in the package was a poem dating back to the Second Empire—indeed, it was as old as the map itself. The poem was written in the very archaic language that few people in the Galaxy spoke anymore. However, Xara wrote him, they both knew a man who would be able to translate it. This mutual friend would soon be at Hunter's door.

She had finished her note with some verse of her own. The passage caught him by surprise; its sentiments came right out of the blue.

> *It might take you a million years*
> *to find out what you need.*
> *But that is fine with me. We both have nothing but*
> *time. I'll await your return and your touch.*
> *And even if it be those million years,*
> *I will be waiting still.*

Hunter had read the poem probably a hundred times by now, and it never failed to get him right in the throat. He looked up at the stars now, just coming into view as the sun finally set. The next morning he would leave for the farthest part of the Galaxy, to try to find out who he was. Yet at the same time, the sweet words from Xara made him wonder if *Earth* wasn't the place he should be. Was it wise to leave the person regarded as the most beautiful girl in the Galaxy to search for something that was quite possibly unattainable? At the *opposite end* of that Galaxy?

He didn't know.

A soft beeping at his door broke these thoughts. Hunter instructed the door to open. A slight, graying figure shuffled inside.

It was Calandrx.

They greeted each other warmly. Hunter was delighted to see the elderly pilot, their first meeting since the conclusion of the Earth Race.

As usual, Calandrx was all smiles.

"I got a message from a mutual friend," he said mysteri-

ously. "Said I could be of some help to you—but I think she
had something else in mind as well. I think she knew I would
like to see you before you left. I know well the anticipation
of getting one's first assignment."

Hunter poured them some slow-ship wine, and they
walked out to the balcony. The sky was absolutely filled with
colorful StarScrapers now.

"Beautiful as always," Calandrx said, gazing at the display.
"But in the end these StarScrapers are just playthings of the
rich. Just like the Earth Race, something to keep the Specials
and the Very Fortunates happy while people like you are out
there among the stars doing what's really important."

They did a quick toast and sipped their wine.

"You've been given quite a ship, I hear," Calandrx said.

"It's a J-Class," Hunter told him. "The *AeroVox* . . ."

"Yes, highly regarded," Calandrx said. "It is not only a
fast ship, it also is said to be endowed with tremendous good
luck."

Hunter drank his wine a little quicker. "It better be," he
said.

"Ten thousand special ops troops," Calandrx went on.
"Plus educators, scholars, diplomats. Medical people. You
will be carrying both power *and* knowledge—those two
things combined can outdo any warship in the Space Forces
or the Solar Guards any day."

Hunter drank his wine. "I hope you're right," he said.

They were quiet for a while.

Then Hunter asked: "How many are there? Planets, I
mean?"

Calandrx thought for a moment.

"I don't think anyone really knows," he mused. "Hundreds
of billions, certainly. Maybe even trillions. The number is
changing all the time. They say that on average a planet is
destroyed by some catastrophic event every hour of every
day. Star collisions, collisions with asteroids, volcano orgies.
Luckily most of them are known about way in advance, so
evacuations can be undertaken."

He slurped his drink.

"But beyond that, there still are many planets out there
that are uncharted, unknown, forgotten since the fall of the

last Empire. Indeed, it's a major undertaking by this one to recount them all—and then reclaim them all. Like it or not, that's what you'll be doing out there."

He thought a moment.

"The last Dark Age was relatively brief. Only two hundred years or so. The Specials have been reclaiming everything for the past six hundred years, the fastest rate of recovery ever."

He looked back up at the sky. "But I'm sure a few billion planets up there are still lost in the shuffle."

He swept his arm across the sky, indicating the thousands of Empire ships hovering near Big Bright City in all directions.

"And that's what this is all about. Trying to build it all up once more—just so it can fall again."

The sky began turning vivid orange, then red, then yellow. Thousands of beams of fantastically bright light were shooting up from the city now, aimed at the infinity of the gathering night sky.

They could hear cheering coming from below.

"The Empire is reclaiming what they think belongs to them," Calandrx said. "Though I'm not so sure all of its subjects—on all those planets—quite agree. But the Empire is an unstoppable force. At least today it is."

Calandrx took another sip of wine.

"But politics aside, there is untold wonder out there," he said. "The things I've seen. The things you're about to see . . ."

"But if it's so grand," Hunter asked, "why have three fallen before it?"

"Like everyone else, I can only hazard a guess," Calandrx replied. "That said, I believe I know what happened to the Second Empire—and probably the Third as well. They grew too big too fast, and events simply overtook them. Vast empires run mostly on luck and the weather anyway; each one reaches a point where inevitably things get shaken up, usually about two hundred years in. That's what fascinates me. At the moment, the Fourth Empire is nearing its six hundredth year of growth. That tells me one thing: When the time comes for it to crash, it is going to be a hell of a noise."

They refilled their wine goblets.

"I almost forgot," Calandrx said. "I have a present for you."

He reached into his pocket, came out with a small box, and handed it to him. Hunter recognized it right away. It was a twenty-and-six capsule.

"My flying machine?" he asked the elderly pilot.

"I thought you might want to take it along with you," Calandrx nodded. "It probably will come in handy out there."

Hunter examined the capsule. Even now, after everything he'd gone through, he was still amazed by the technology behind hiding things in the twenty-sixth dimension.

"Can *anything* be put in a twenty and six?" he asked.

"Well, just about *anything,*" Calandrx replied. "I mean, not a whole Starcrasher—there *is* a limit. In fact, I heard once that one of the reasons why Starcrashers are built so big is so they can't be smuggled around in a twenty and six. Imagine the possibilities if they could!"

Hunter studied the capsule. "Interesting . . ." he murmured. "And thanks. I appreciate it. When I left Fools 6 I never thought I'd see my machine again."

Calandrx laughed. "My God—now it's as famous as you," he said, adding with a conspiratorial wink, "And in my opinion it's best that you keep secret what really drives the thing. I mean, someone could shove a truth stick in my navel and I still couldn't explain why you're able to go so damn fast in the thing. But I think it's safe to say that you tapped into something no one else had realized before—or maybe was too ignorant to exploit."

"Even with a truth stick thus inserted, I couldn't tell anyone either what the secret is," Hunter confessed. "I just hooked up those boxes I salvaged. It was a random event. I probably couldn't do it the same way exactly again if I tried."

Calandrx looked up at him. "If there's one thing I've learned, my friend, it's that there's no such thing in the universe as a truly 'random event.' Not in this universe, anyway."

More wine was poured.

"Our mutual friend's request notwithstanding, I actually

came for another reason," Calandrx revealed. "More out of curiosity than anything else."

"Details of the Earth Race?" Hunter asked.

"Do you mind telling me?"

"Not at all," Hunter replied. "At least those I can remember."

He went on to tell Calandrx of his bizarre encounters within the three blue screens, from the giant teeth of the first to the unexplainable events of the second to the absolute astonishment of the third.

Calandrx's eyes seemed to go wider with every word.

"You saw the Blackship?" he asked incredulously. "And it was being followed by a round craft? That's the most fantastic thing I've ever heard."

" 'Followed' or chased," Hunter said. "Such an event is not typical of what a blue screen usually holds, I assume?"

Calandrx was almost too chilled to speak. "You assume right, my brother," he said, rapidly gulping his wine now. "And I think it's prudent that we hush about all this right now. This wonderful place you have here doesn't comes with a hum beam, does it?"

Hunter shrugged. "I don't know," he said.

Calandrx put a finger to his own lips. "Then let's talk more about this when we meet again. And I think it best you keep these visions to yourself. If they persist in your memory, that will mean something. If they fade, that will mean something else. Do you get my drift?"

Hunter quickly poured them some more wine.

"Bingo," he said.

They toasted again. Calandrx half drained his glass, then said: "You made a wise if surprising choice by joining the Exploratory service. The things I'm sure you're about to see, out there. I really envy you."

Hunter took a healthy gulp of his wine as well.

"The truth is, I have my ulterior motives," he said.

The gleam came back to Calandrx's eye. "Really? That's my cup of tea," he said. "Can you share them?"

Hunter recounted his adventures with each of the Imperial Family, with the most elaboration coming from his time spent with Princess Xara on Mars. Calandrx was alternately amazed and amused by Hunter's adventures in the past few days.

"My God," he said. "When I won the damn race all they gave me was a house in the woods! The Empress certainly didn't flirt with me!"

Calandrx spotted Mars just rising above the horizon.

"And I certainly had not heard of this spacecraft stuck in the ice up there," he said. "That's a fascinating bit of history the Specials have managed to keep from the rest of us."

"This is my plan," Hunter said. "If I can find out who sent the VLR/VSA scan down to that frozen wreck, I think I'll be well on my way to finding out who the hell I am."

Calandrx clinked his wine goblet against Hunter's.

"Such a noble quest!" he declared. "And one that's wrapped in your own machinations—as well as those of a beautiful woman. I love it! Is there some way I can help?"

"There certainly is," Hunter replied. "In fact, I think that's why you are here."

Hunter unfurled the ancient map on the table in front of them.

"Does this look at all familiar to you?" he asked Calandrx.

The elderly pilot studied the map closely. After several minutes he began shaking his head.

"Nope," he said. "Nothing on here looks familiar. Why? Where did you get this?"

"From Xara," he said. "Along with this . . ."

He handed Calandrx a copy of the ancient poem.

"She thought you might be able to make sense of it, maybe even translate it," Hunter told him.

Calandrx refilled his own glass, then began reading the poem, half out loud.

"Well, this is a semifamous piece from the Second Empire poet warrior Xylanx," he said. "It's called a 'war poem.' They were quite the rage back then. Apparently many of the age's most prominent warriors wrote about their exploits in verse, as a way of preserving them to an oral tradition that would carry on if and when the Empire collapsed—which it did, of course."

He read some more. "Loosely translated, the title is: 'For Those Who Are Searching . . . or more like, 'The Search for the Lost Souls.' It is widely believed to be Xylanx's retelling of a local legend he came across during a campaign at the other end of the Milky Way."

"A legend?"

Calandrx nodded. "Xylanx often did that," he replied. "He would hear a myth popular among people in very isolated parts of the Empire and convert it into verse. Again, as a means of preserving a history of the times."

Hunter felt his heart sink. What kind of directions could he get from a poem written about something that never happened?

It was as if Calandrx read his mind.

"Now, that doesn't mean none of this is true," he said. "On the contrary, all myths have some basis in reality. But they are usually distorted again and again over the ages."

"Can you tell me what this is about then?"

Calandrx read the entire poem silently. His eyes lit up at several points; at others he seemed on the verge of tears. He finished by wiping his eyes and raising his glass in the air.

"Xylanx was quite a human being," he said. "Really knew how to turn a phrase. . . ."

"But what is it about exactly?" Hunter pressed him.

Calandrx went back to the first stanza.

"It is about a place—a planet, probably—where thousands of years before, a certain race of people was banished. They were an ancient people apparently—it sounds like they had direct ties to Earth that went all the way back to the First Empire, or even earlier.

"For whatever reason—Xylanx claims jealousy on the part of the Empire was the culprit—these people and others like them were relegated to 'the place from which few could go beyond.' They were given their own planet, puffed to their own desires, and left alone. But essentially they were exiled for not seeing things the way everyone else in the Galaxy at that time apparently saw them."

Calandrx slurped his wine again.

"Over the centuries, these people became master warriors—and very intent on gathering together anyone who might be related to them—their brothers lost among the clutter of the Galaxy. So they set up a beacon, again near this 'last place.'

It was a kind of signal that would be recognized by all of their kind and would call them back to this new 'home planet.' This beacon was called—again, loosely translated—'a house made of light or 'the lighthouse.' "

"And this beacon was located on the last place anyone could go?"

"Either there, or relatively close by," Calandrx replied. "There is a phrase or two that might indicate that while the location of this 'house of light' was not kept secret, the place where these ancient people lived was. . . ."

He located a passage from the third stanza. " 'Where does one put a lighthouse but on the most distant part of the most distant shore? But this was a lighthouse that pointed its beam inward. Looking not for lost vessels or scattered ships but lost and scattered souls . . .' "

Hunter sipped his own wine now. Could the beacon in the poem be the VLR/VSA? The same one that seared the ice around the crashed Martian lander?

Calandrx put his finger on a line in the fifth stanza.

"To me, this is the most enigmatic part," he said. "It's talking about just who these lost souls might be and how they will know when they've finally reached their home. 'You will meet the people and they will be like you . . . they will talk like you, they will have your name . . . and in their eyes you will know them immediately.' "

Calandrx paused for a moment, then looked up at Hunter.

"The final line is," he said, " 'Hurry home, for they are expecting you. . . .' "

They just stared at each other for a moment.

"Is this what you wanted to hear, my friend?" Calandrx asked him.

Hunter just shook his head. "I'm not really sure. . . ."

They were silent for a while, Calandrx leaving Hunter alone with his thoughts.

Finally Calandrx broke the silence.

"I hear you're to bring along Erx and Berx along on this adventure as well," he said. "A wise choice . . ."

Hunter shrugged, happy to change the subject.

"They needed another ship . . . plus I think they had to get off Earth before they got into some *real* trouble."

Hunter regretted those words instantly. The momentary look of pain that came across the elderly pilot's face told him he'd struck a nerve. It was clear that Calandrx would have given anything to be able to go with them.

"It's all right," Calandrx said, again reading his thoughts. "I am stuck here because it is the wish of my Emperor. Who am I to dispute it? The excitement you've provided in your short time on Earth will last with me for years to come—and our winnings will ease the burden a bit farther. I've had my adventures. Now it's time for you to have yours."

"You sailed the stars for more than a century," Hunter said to him. "May I ask for your counsel? Do you have any advice you can give me?"

Calandrx thought for a long moment. "Just remember this: Many of the people you will find out there won't know who you are, won't know what the Empire is . . . won't have any knowledge about any of this."

He looked up at Hunter. "But that does not mean that the lives they lead, the cultures they've developed, the land they work are unimportant. Indeed, those things are the *most* important aspects of their lives."

"So respect them," Hunter said.

"Exactly," Calandrx replied. "Show them respect, and it will go a long way in helping you accomplish what you're being sent out there to do—officially, anyway."

Once again they were quiet for a while. Hunter sipped his wine and watched the stars above. Calandrx looked down on the brilliant city below.

"What's the strangest thing you heard about, you know, out there?" Hunter asked him.

Calandrx sipped, thought, and smiled. "That's like asking how many drops there are in the ocean. What isn't strange out there? But I get your point. What's the strangest thing I heard about *besides* you?"

"Exactly," Hunter replied.

A floating city passed by overhead. More StarScrapers bolted up into the night sky.

"I heard a story once," Calandrx began, "about a man stuck out there somewhere who was supposedly immortal. He literally couldn't die. I always thought it to be just another

Fringe legend, of which there are billions, of course. But people I trust swear that it is true."

"Are you saying this person was 'forever young'?"

Calandrx shook his head.

"No, simply immortal," he replied. "He could not die. He aged, his body deteriorated. But he simply could not die. A curse, not a blessing."

"That's ironic," Hunter said. "Especially with the obsession for longer life that seems to drive everyone these days."

"That's what made the story so fascinating," Calandrx replied. "When I first heard it, I asked if this person was simply pumped full of Holy Blood—but that wasn't the case. Apparently he's been around *longer* than the concept of Holy Blood. They say he's as old as spaceflight from Earth itself."

"But that would mean, what? Five, six thousand years old?"

Calandrx laughed and guzzled his wine. "At least!" he declared.

He got up to go. Hunter gave him a mighty handshake.

"Thank you for everything," he told Calandrx.

"Be well, old friend," the elderly pilot replied. "And please, when you return, may I be the one you call on first?"

Hunter hesitated just a moment, but Calandrx caught on and smiled. "The first after our gorgeous 'mutual friend,' that is."

Hunter shook his hand again and walked him to the door.

Calandrx started to depart, then paused a moment. "Can I give you just one more small piece of advice?"

Hunter nodded. "Please, go ahead. . . ."

Calandrx lowered his voice in a very conspiratorial manner.

"No matter what you do, my brother," he said, "avoid any planet that has a pyramid. . . ."

PART THREE

The Defenders of Qez

21

On planet Guam 7
Khatru-Delirious Star System
Six months later

The name of the city was Nails, and it was famous for selling two things: combat weapons and slow-ship wine, both in large quantities.

Downtown was a twenty-square-mile sprawl of gun shops, distilleries, and rocket pads. On a typical day, several billion aluminum coins could change hands here. At night, ray gun fights and random blaster fire were not uncommon. Even for the Fifth Arm, Outer Fringe, this was a very rough place.

There were also thousands of 'cloud bars in Nails, and it was at one of these, the Green Star, that two of the city's most successful arms merchants were enjoying a midmorning cup of slow tea. They were Zym Blitz and Beebee "Three Finger" Rappz. Both men were enormous; they barely fit in the chairs provided with their hovering table. Neither was armed, but standing at discreet distances away, their coteries of bodyguards were nervously eyeing each other.

The center of Nails's weapons bazaar was just a half block away, and as their table was the most prominent in the Green Star's outside café section, just about every person bustling by made sure they tipped their cap to Blitz and Rappz. There were many players operating inside Nails. But these two were probably the most notorious.

The Green Star was especially crowded this morning. Peo-

ple drinking, smoking, wheeling, and dealing. A small army
of holo-girls was hanging on the periphery, chatting with the
hired heat. The slow-ship was flowing and the open-air saloon was getting so raucous, some of the holos were beginning to ply their trade right out in the open.

That's why it was so strange when Blitz and Rappz were
suddenly joined at their table by a priest.

His cassock was dirty, his feet dusty and sore. He'd
walked more than forty miles to get to the city, this after
having used an ancient transporter booth to pop him in from
twenty-two star systems away. Blitz and Rappz just stared at
the holy man for a moment. They'd seen just about everything imaginable in Nails over the years—everything except
a priest.

"I'm very sorry to join you gentlemen unannounced," the
priest told them wearily. "I'm usually not this impolite."

"Not a problem, Padre," Blitz told him. "You look like
you need a drink. . . ." Rappz signaled for a robot waiter.

"Thank you, but no," the priest replied. "I fear if I started
drinking now, I would not want to stop,"

"Well, have you eaten recently, Father?" Rappz asked him.
"We can certainly buy you a meal."

Again the priest shook his head. "I am here not for food
or drink, though I would dearly love both," he said. "What
I am looking for is help—help to save some lost souls."

Blitz and Rappz both laughed.

"Are you sure you're in the right place, Father?" Blitz
asked him. "There are a million or so souls here, but I don't
think any of them wants to be saved."

"These are not the souls I'm referring to," the priest said.
"The souls of my concern really *are* lost—or better said, they
are in a lost cause. And while I can't believe I'm actually
saying this, I'm here seeking weapons. . . ."

Blitz and Rappz looked at each other and shrugged.
They'd sell to anyone, just as long as the coin was good.

"Well, then you *did* come to the right place, Padre," Rappz
said. "What type of weapons are you looking for?"

The priest shrugged. He wasn't really sure.

"Well, *weapons* . . ." he said. "My friends are running out
of just about everything. . . ."

Blitz signaled for two more drinks. The robot waiter hurriedly refilled their teacups. "And get this man a pitcher of ice water," Blitz ordered the robot.

Rappz pulled out his notebook and started with a clean page.

"Okay, Father, we understand that this is your first time buying guns," he said. "So why don't you just tell us the situation your friends have found themselves in and maybe we can figure out what they need."

The pitcher of water arrived; the robot spilled a bit while setting it down on the table. Blitz responded by giving the robot a swift kick in the ass; the clang of boot-on-metal echoed throughout the busy saloon.

The priest brushed some spilled ice from his cassock, then poured himself a mug of water and drank from it greedily.

"My friends are mercenaries," he said between gulps. "But they have found themselves on a mission of mercy. . . ."

"Mercs? On a mercy mission?" Blitz asked. "I'd say that was just about impossible."

"Bingo that," Rappz agreed.

"Believe what you will, gentlemen," the priest said, "but that is the case. They are defending an outpost on a moon named Zazu-Zazu—it orbits the planet Jazz 33."

"Jazz 33?" Rappz said. "Isn't that in the Dead Gulch System?"

The priest nodded.

Rappz just shook his head. "Father, that's the last system in the entire Galaxy. It's the fringe of the Fringe. I mean, after Dead Gulch, you fall off the edge, don't you?"

The priest drained another mug of ice water.

"You do," he replied, wiping his chin. "But the concern would be the same if it were happening one star system over from here—or all the way back to the Ball. My friends have come up against some advanced technology. *Very* advanced. How they've been able to hold on this long is a miracle in itself."

"So you're saying there's a little war going on out there?" Rappz asked.

"A most brutal little war," the priest answered. "My friends are practically the sole defenders of about thirty thousand innocent civilians. The enemy has taken over two-thirds of this satellite—though no one can imagine why. It's just a tiny rock in space. But we now fear he will soon launch a final attack—and then all will be lost. And that's why I am here. There is no one else to help us. The moon's people can't afford any further mercenary groups—they aren't able to pay my friends as it is."

"That *is* a mission of mercy," Blitz said, sipping his slow tea. "I've never met a merc who fought for free."

"You don't know my friends," the priest replied.

Blitz looked at Rappz and just shrugged. "Well, do they need blaster rifles, Padre?" he asked. "Ray guns? Z-beam stuff?"

"All that and more," the priest replied. "As I said, this enemy seems to have all kinds of strange weapons. Certainly things I've never seen or heard of before."

"Really? Like what?" Blitz asked.

The priest drank some more water.

"I have seen the aftereffects of these horrible things," he replied slowly. "A man, hit with some kind of strange beam, turns into an X ray of himself. His bones and innards, visible through a thin veneer of very bloody skin. He can still walk, he can still talk—but he is dead nevertheless. I have witnessed more than one brave heart fade away like this, crying for his wife and children as his body slowly dissolved around him. . . ."

Blitz and Rappz stopped sipping their tea. "I have never heard of such a weapon," Blitz said. Rappz nodded in agreement.

"Another kind of ray seems to make a man's bones grow grotesquely large," the priest went on. "In just seconds, they burst out of the skin—and literally tear him apart."

Again, Blitz and Rappz just shook their heads. "A very painful way to go," Blitz said.

"Words cannot describe it," the priest agreed. "And there are many more of these awful things. It's almost as if the enemy is testing out these weapons—and my friends and the people they are protecting are the test subjects."

"A very strange concept," Blitz murmured, almost to himself. "Who *are* these folks your friends are fighting, Father?"

The priest shrugged uncertainly. "That's another thing," he said. "We don't know."

"Don't know?" Blitz asked. "But how could that be? Everyone knows who they are fighting these days. They might not know *why*. But they always know *who*."

"And why are they making war in such a strange place anyway?" Rappz added. "I mean, no offense, Father, but I can't think of anything in the Dead Gulch worth fighting about."

"That's exactly my point," the priest said. "It's a tiny moon with a tiny population, and all they want to do is farm their lands and be left alone—just as they've been doing for centuries. But just about a year ago, this massive army shows up and attacks these very peaceful people. No reason given. No prior communications, no threats. Nothing. Just a sudden surprise attack, a bolt out of nowhere."

He drank another mug of water.

"Now we know the main enemy force is made up of mercenaries and pirate trash from nearby star systems," he went on. "Real dregs—perhaps even friends of yours. They call themselves the Nakkz. But they are just the foot soldiers. We suspect others are actually orchestrating this war. It is the people supplying the Nakkz to attack us who are very mysterious indeed."

"How so?" Rappz wanted to know.

"Well, we have never seen them, for one," the priest said. "They have occasionally appeared out on the battlefield, observing their army of paid killers from afar. But they wear a very different type of combat gear—all black from head to toe—and they never seem to get into the fight directly. Subsequently, none has ever been taken alive. Nor have any of their bodies ever been recovered."

"This is getting strange," Rappz said.

"*Too* strange," Blitz replied, pushing his tea away from him, a first.

"What do you mean?"

Blitz just shook his head. "I don't know. It's just that I keep hearing such weird things lately."

"Like?"

"Well, there was the rumored Blackship-in-Supertime thing, for instance."

" 'Rumored' being the key word there," Rappz said. "And I still don't believe it for a second. But even if it were true, we live in a huge Galaxy. Strange things are bound to happen once in a while."

"But there is 'strange' and then there is just plain 'weird,' " Blitz said, pulling his chair a bit closer to the table.

"You'll have to explain that, please," Rappz told him.

Blitz lowered his voice. "A friend of mine saw some very unusual lights in the sky the other night," he said in a whisper. "Above his château, out in the mountains. He said they were practically right on top of him."

Rappz just laughed. " 'Lights in the sky?' My brother, the Milky Way is *alive* with lights in the sky. I would be concerned if I *didn't* see any lights in the sky."

"But these weren't *typical* lights," Blitz shot back. "My friend said they were acting in a very unconventional manner. Moving incredibly fast, changing direction much quicker than anything we see flying these days. They also had the ability to blink out, just like that."

"Blink out?" Rappz said. "Not even a Starcrasher can do that. What else?"

"Did you hear what happened on Xers 17, over in the Slow Freeze System?"

Rappz shrugged. "I know the place went belly up. Was it a volcano orgy or a star passing?"

"It burned," Blitz said.

"You mean it 'burned up,' " Rappz replied.

"No, I mean, everything on the surface of the planet was *burned*. Consumed. Immolated. The planet is still there, but everything and everybody on it got turned into cinders."

Rappz pulled his substantial chin in thought. "An entire planet catching fire? Just like that? How?"

"They still don't know," Blitz said. "Only that it happened totally out of the blue—without warning."

Rappz sipped his drink, but the worry lines stayed on his face. "Well, again, we live in big Galaxy—by sheer numbers alone, odd things will appear to happen. But that one—I agree, that is *very* odd. I mean, they can forecast a star passing a hundred years in advance."

"The same with a volcano orgy," Blitz said. "But Xers 17 went up. Just like that. And . . ."

Blitz hesitated for a moment.

"And?" Rappz prompted him.

"And," Blitz said, lowering his voice almost below a whisper, "I heard that when the rescue forces finally got to the planet and went through the ashes, they found . . . a pyramid."

Rappz dropped his glass and covered his ears. "My God, did you have to say *that* word? Isn't it enough that you've ruined my morning with these strange tales? Now this? What am I to do with this blasphemer, Father?"

They turned back to the third chair at their table—but it was empty.

The priest had left a long time ago.

22

The moon Zazu-Zazu
Orbiting planet Jazz 33
Dead Gulch Star System

The recon team had been running all night.

Through the darkened trenches, over and around hundreds of dead bodies, some still crawling, some still breathing, the team made its way east, into enemy territory, moving quickly while they still had darkness in their favor.

The mysterious noises had stopped two days before. For the first time in months, no monstrous sounds echoed through the night, no dull mechanical thuds shook the ground below. The silence became deafening.

As soon as the noises ceased, palls of thick black smoke appeared on both the eastern and northern horizons. Whatever the enemy had been doing all this time, it was clear they had completed their task—and this did not portend well for the people of Zazu-Zazu.

In the year since the tiny moon was invaded, the territory held by its citizens had shrunk, until now only the fortress city of Qez and a handful of nearby villages and farms remained in friendly hands. With the much-feared final attack apparently imminent, all of the civilians from the surrounding countryside had sought refuge inside the high walls of Qez. This had caused the city's population to nearly double in size. Thirty thousand people were now crowded into the city. Together, they awaited their uncertain fate.

But what was coming exactly? That's what the recon team had been dispatched to find out. There had been no time to plan their mission in advance. Zazu-Zazu was just nine hundred miles in circumference. It spun very quickly on its axis and so had extremely short days—just three hours of full daylight, followed by three hours of dull planetshine, followed by another three hours of absolute darkness. On Zazu-Zazu, sunrise lasted but a minute and then the day would rush toward the night, when the process would start all over again.

On this particular day, planet Jazz 33 would rise about three minutes after the quick sunset. This would set up a situation where the vast battlefield separating the warring parties would be dark enough to move through, yet faintly lit from the planetshine to let the recon soldiers see where they were going. Under the circumstances, these were the best conditions they could hope for.

As it was, the recon sortie was as close to a suicide mission as one could get. Heavy fighting all around the small moon had prevented such an undertaking as this before. But, perhaps not so surprisingly, as soon as the mysterious sounds stopped, so did all enemy attacks. That's when finding out just what was going on over the horizon became a major priority.

So the recon *had* to be done—no one disputed that. But of the six mercenary groups left defending the city of Qez, only one offered to send men on this dangerous mission. That group was the Freedom Brigade, the friends of the priest. They were known in this part of the Outer Fringe as skillful, loyal, courageous—in short, the best troops money could buy.

But beyond that, the brigade had a traditional tie to the small moon of Zazu-Zazu. Indeed, they had provided security for its people for centuries, ever since their home planet established a "research station" on Zazu-Zazu sometime during the reign of the Second Empire. When the moon was invaded a year before, the Freedom Brigade had been the first mercenary group to answer the call for help. Even in this isolated corner of the Galaxy, loyalty and honor were still held dear.

The five soldiers selected to go were among only ninety-nine men remaining from the brigade's original contingent of 202. Like the several thousand other mercenaries hired to defend the people of Zazu-Zazu, the strange noises had haunted them, too. Even during some of the heaviest fighting, when tens of thousands of blaster shots filled the air, the mysterious pounding and clanging had rumbled like thunder above the fray. Grim curiosity alone would have been enough reason to send out the recon team.

But finding out why the noises had stopped would not be an easy thing to do. For the patrol to get close enough to enemy lines for a visual scan, they first had to cross the killing fields of the Xomme, nearly twenty miles of no-man's-land that separated their lines from those of their enemy. This thick band of trenches, bomb craters, devastated towns, and mile upon mile of flat desolation was the result of nearly one year of brutal warfare in a very small place.

Once the recon team navigated this nightmarish terrain and reached the enemy lines, they were to scan a place called Holy Hell. It was a three-sided valley anchored by small mountains to the north and south. Holy Hell was a known troop-staging area of the enemy; indeed, most of the attacks by the Nakkz had originated from this place.

As such, just about everybody concerned was sure the mysterious noises were coming from there.

Despite being battered by a fierce storm most of the way, the recon team finally reached their objective six hours later.

Hurricanelike storms were routine on the small moon—some said this was because the satellite's ancient puffing was slowly becoming undone. The recon team had been especially deluged during the final hour of their trek. And while the storm had hid its advance, it also had prevented them from clearly seeing into the pit at Holy Hell. Had they arrived under better climatic conditions, the team could have gathered what it needed and then started the long dash back home in the waning darkness. But this time the weather had screwed them.

Not that it made any difference, for when first light arrived and the recon troops saw what had been built inside Holy

Hell, they knew two things immediately: It made no difference when they spotted this thing, and the people they were here to protect were doomed.

It was gleaming in the red light of the dreary dawn when they got their first good look at it.

They thought at first it was an enormous prop of some sort—maybe a religious symbol, though the Nakkz had hardly showed any signs of spirituality. It was only after the last of the rain and mist cleared and the recon soldiers could do a proper scan of the object that they realized to their great dismay that this thing was real.

It was a xarcus, a tracked armored vehicle that could carry men and weapons across a battlefield. During the year of warfare on Zazu Zazu, hundreds of these armored movers had been used by both sides. But a typical xarcus was only twenty feet long by ten feet wide. *This* xarcus was a colossus. It was at least half a mile wide and a quarter of a mile high! Its dual tracks were enormous. There were thousands of Z guns sticking out of innumerable gun blisters pockmarking its body. An enormous Z-beam tube projected out of its massive turret; its barrel alone was at least a quarter of a mile long. Even worse, the colossus appeared to be constructed of reatomized electron steel. This meant it was virtually indestructible.

It seemed unbelievable at first, but the proof was in the viz-scan. Somehow the Nakkz had come upon an enormous weapon that could undoubtedly move many thousands of men at once, and had enough weapons to level Qez or any defensive position remaining along the defense line.

But there was an even more frightening aspect to discovering the monster. The Nakkz could never have built this colossus on their own. They were made up mostly of retread space pirates—fierce fighters, but definitely not a pool of any great thinkers.

How, then, had such a giant come into their possession?

However it happened, as the recon troops contemplated the gigantic xarcus on this awful morning, they knew there was no way they and their allies could put up a defense against it. Most of the conflict's fighting had taken place in areas like the Xomme. On a few occasions the Nakkz had actually come within sight of the Qez. But these had been small and mostly symbolic victories. No matter where these break-throughs took place, the enemy's lengthy lines of communication and the atrocious conditions of the combat zone itself always forced them to withdraw eventually.

But now, with this huge weapon, all that was a thing of the past. The xarcus was itself a self-contained city. Once it made its way across the battlefield and reached the Zazu-Zazu defense line, there would be no way of stopping it. It could crash through the wall surrounding Qez at any point—that is, if it didn't simply level it with its overwhelming weaponry first.

And once it got beyond Qez and into the countryside, it would just be hours before the rest of the tiny moon was conquered.

This would not be good. The Nakkz were well known for their brutal treatment of anyone living on or fighting for Zazu-Zazu. Soldiers or civilians, young or old, it seemed to be the intent of the Nakkz not only to conquer the small moon, but to wipe out its population as well. With a weapon of this magnitude, that terrible moment now seemed very close at hand.

These were the bad tidings the recon soldiers now had to bring back to Qez.

The recon troops had just completed their depressing survey of Holy Hell when their luck began to run out.

Just as they were getting ready to withdraw, an enemy robot aircraft suddenly appeared overhead. This thing was called a Stinger. It was just ten feet long, six feet at its widest, and shaped, of course, like a triangle. It carried no weapons of its own. However, it could send viz-scan information back to enemy gunners, who could then deliver deadly accurate X-beam fire to just about any point of the battlefield.

The recon soldiers knew well that being hit by an X beam would be an especially cruel way to die. Just how the Nakkz had come into possession of a ray gun so different from the Z beams used by just about everyone else in the Galaxy, no one seemed to know. It was a very strange weapon. An X-beam blast could be as murderously accurate as that of a Z beam—but getting hit with an X beam meant that about 80 percent of the victim's atoms were instantly ripped apart from each other—leaving 20 percent of the human being intact, to die incredibly slowly and incredibly painfully. This and their other exotic weapons provided a good insight into the cruel minds of the Nakkz and their mysterious patrons.

The recon soldiers had seen many of their comrades die the horrible death of partial-atomic disassembly. That the same fate awaited them was a frightening thought indeed.

They began their withdrawal in haste now, but it was already too late. A devastating X-beam barrage rained down upon the soldiers just a few seconds after the Stinger spotted them. One man was hit instantly, and slowly began to fade away.

The survivors quickly jettisoned all unnecessary gear and began an all-out retreat. They had no means of communicating with Qez; no way of telling anyone back there what they had discovered. It was imperative that they get away. But the robot craft would pursue them across the bloody mud of the Xomme for the next three hours.

Coordinating the long-range beam fire from Holy Hell, the Stinger was able to zero in on individual members of the recon unit, and allow the Nakkz gunners to pick them off one at a time.

The sun went down quickly, planetrise occurred, and two more of the recon soldiers died.

The robot plane's pursuit became even more relentless with the darkness. Stripped of all but their basic uniforms, their blaster rifles, and their battle helmets, the recon men were running madly through the maze of trenches, stepping over or sometimes into partially disassembled bodies, the remains of fighting from as long as a year before. The two men who died during the night had each been isolated, trapped, and then slowly blasted to death. When the sun rose again, only two soldiers remained.

Noon came quickly—and that's when the airborne robot stalker suddenly disappeared from the sky. But the respite lasted no more than a few seconds, as a heavily armored aerial scout car just as quickly materialized above the two brigade soldiers. Known as an XA-10 Bolt to the defenders, this machine could carry up to twenty enemy soldiers along with a huge gun in its belly. Its appearance signaled a change in tactics by the Nakkz. They had tired of toying with the survivors of the recon unit.

With them almost halfway across no-man's-land, the Bolt had been sent out to deliver the final blow.

Its appearance was a matter of bad timing for the last two recon men. They were crossing a huge crater field, created by a previous bombardment so concentrated it had obliterated the trenchworks for a quarter mile around. The first soldier made it across in one piece—but the second man was not so lucky. He was about halfway through the field when the Bolt showed up. Its big gun unleashed a mighty blast ray at him right away, in effect slicing him in two. As the bottom half of his body began to dissolve away, his upper half began writhing in agony in the mud. He began crying loudly for his comrade.

The Bolt went into a hover over the mortally wounded man. A dozen or so helmeted soldiers peered out from their portholes, enjoying the sight of the soldier in his death throes. A person wounded such as this could linger for hours, even days, in intense agony before finally succumbing. Yet watching the man die seemed to be a form of entertainment for the soldiers aboard the Bolt.

Their blood lust would not last too long, though. With the man screaming in sheer pain, another ray hit him square in the chest, finally killing him completely and blowing his subatomic remains into the unknown dimensions. It was difficult to tell what had happened at first. But then the thin trail of smoke coming from the far end of the massive bomb crater finally told the tale. The last recon soldier had killed his wounded comrade.

It was the last act of mercy for a friend.

Now the Bolt began moving again. There was one live body still out there that could be cut in two, and there would be no one around to save this man from a long, slow death.

The last recon soldier was quickly running for his life

again. Zigzagging through the trenches, the Bolt was firing indiscriminately at him, most of the blasts landing either right in front of the hapless soldier or right on his heels. Finally the Bolt launched one of its incendiary artillery shells. It blew up a section of trenchworks just in front of the desperate trooper, in effect blocking off his means of escape. The soldier tried reversing course, only to find that another blast had sealed the trench in that direction as well. He tried a side route. Another blast, another dead end.

He was trapped. The Bolt came into a slow hover just above him. The soldier knew what fate awaited him. Even more painful was the knowledge that he had failed in his mission—and that his countrymen back in Qez would remain unaware of the colossal xarcus that would soon be coming their way.

He heard the gun on the Bolt lower in his direction. He considered just bowing his head and allowing the blast to come. If he closed his eyes very tightly and thought of his wife and his three young children, maybe it wouldn't hurt so bad.

But then he realized he had something else to do first. He had to display the colors of his home planet. It was a grim if ancient tradition among the soldiers from his long-lost world. Whenever it seemed like the end was near, their flag would be displayed to show their enemy that they might be beaten but never vanquished. The soldier hastily reached into his pocket to retrieve the small flag he always kept there. And that's when a very strange thing happened: The very thought of showing his flag gave the recon soldier the impetus not to give up. Not just yet.

Maybe this gunfight isn't over, he thought.

The Bolt was right above him now. He could see wide grins and steely eyes looking down at him. The aircraft's pilot moved the Bolt a bit to his right, just so the huge nose gun would have a clear, unimpeded shot at him.

That's when the recon soldier simply raised his blaster rifle and fired off one last burst from his power pack. It was a desperate, one-in-a-million shot—and it worked. His last dying beam had just enough energy to pierce the Bolt's tiny generator core, obliterating it. A huge explosion went off over the soldier's head, tearing his blaster rifle from his hands and the helmet off his head. He dove back down into the trench, flaming pieces of the craft raining down upon him. There was another explosion. The soldier looked up and saw the Bolt start to fall. It went right over his head and slammed into the ground not twenty feet away.

The recon soldier waited for several seconds before he dared to peek out over the trench. He did this just in time to see the Bolt explode one final time. This explosion was so powerful it caused a minor earthquake, which in turn led to some of the trench collapsing on top of him.

By the time the soldier dug his way out, the Bolt and its crew were little more than subatomic dust blowing in the wind.

He climbed out of the trench and stared at the debris for a moment.

How could he have been so lucky?

He had no idea—and he wasn't about to stick around to find out. He whispered a short prayer of thanks and tapped his breast pocket three times.

Then he started running again, back toward Qez.

23

The east wall protecting the city of Qez was a thousand feet high.

It boasted six weapons towers along its two-mile length, with many gun stations pockmarking its upper tiers. The city within was big enough to fit about twenty thousand people. But these days, the number had swelled to nearly twice that figure as frightened citizens from the surrounding countryside had sought refuge behind the walls to escape the fighting.

No one could blame them; Qez was the last outpost on the tiny moon. But this increase in humanity had put additional strain on the low supply of food and power. Anxiety also was rampant throughout the city. The citizens also had suffered through the long months of the relentless pounding coming from over the horizon. Now that the noise had stopped, the city was rife with rumors as to what the enemy was planning. The most oft-repeated rumor was that the Nakkz had built a war machine of frightening size and incredible power and soon would launch it against the city.

Little did the frightened population know just how close to the truth those stories were.

The last surviving member of the recon patrol was spotted just before sunset by a patrol of Qez's Home Guard soldiers.

The man was nearly dead of exhaustion; he was dehydrated and suffering for some shrapnel wounds, too. But he insisted on being brought to the war room inside Qez, a place where the leaders of the five mercenary groups defending the city planned strategy with the commanding officers of the city's Home Guard. The patrol leader checked with his superiors, and the man was immediately brought inside.

The soldier's name was McKay. He found the mood grim inside the tiny command center deep in the city's east wall. A total of six mercenary groups had been providing the city's defense; most were from planets in nearby star systems. They were now sitting around a well-worn hovering table with the leaders of Qez itself. The priest also was on hand.

McKay told his story, from the dash across the Xomme, to spotting the gigantic xarcus through the storm, to the frightful withdrawal back to Qez, a trek that killed four of his comrades. With every mention of the monstrous weapon just over the horizon, he saw the spirits of those charged with defending Qez begin to waver.

"Sometimes there is much wisdom in determining when to give up the fight," the leader of one mercenary group said. "If these reports are true, and there is an army inside that thing, then we will be outnumbered *and* outgunned. . . ."

"We cannot possibly build a defense against such a weapon," another merc leader said. "The Nakkz have nearly broken through our front right here on several occasions as well as many other places along the line. If they have the monster that this man describes, how can we possibly stop it?"

"But we have to try," the commander of Qez's Home Guard said; his name was Markus Poolinex. "We can't give up. There are thousands of innocents inside these walls we must think about. You know what the enemy will do to them if they can, don't you?"

A third merc leader spoke up: "I believe you'll find a 'hopeless cause' clause in our contracts. That's what this seems to be adding up to."

"But we have to make a stand *here*," the Home Guard commander insisted. "Even if it fails, at least we won't go down in history as giving up without a fight."

"But even if you were able to stop this gigantic thing," a

fourth merc said, "they'll undoubtedly follow it up with a ground attack."

The Home Guard commander questioned the recon soldier again as to how many soldiers he thought the rolling monster might hold. McKay gave a gloomy shrug. "According to our quadtrol readings, thirty thousand," he said. "Maybe more."

Another dead silence fell on the room.

"Thirty thousand troops?" one merc leader said with a groan. "That's more than three times the strength of our forces combined. Even with the mercenaries and the militias, they still would have a twenty-thousand-man advantage."

It was true. At that moment the entire defense force of Qez was fewer than ten thousand.

"But by giving up the fight, we are condemning our citizens to death," the Home Guard officer said. "The Nakkz is well known for his brutality. Our surrender is not an option for them. For whatever reason, they are bent on destroying us. Wiping us out. By giving up the fight, we will only make it that much easier for them."

"You must look at it from our point of view," the first mercenary leader said. "It is our business to fight in return for payment. But to fight in what will surely be a losing proposition—well, let's face facts: That will be bad for business."

"This has been a queer enterprise from the start," the second merc commander said. "You are a small city, on a very small moon, in a very isolated star system at the very end of the Galaxy. How this place got puffed in the first place, I will never know. But you have to ask yourself: What are you fighting for?"

Now the priest spoke up: "I hate to agree with these paid killers, but I must also question the wisdom of fighting here."

The Home Guard commander was shocked.

"Father, how so?"

"Over on that dastardly planet called Guam, I heard tales of strange things happening all over the Fringe. Awful things. I fear what we are facing here is just another. . . ."

He recounted the stories he'd heard from the two arms merchants in Nails, plus others he'd heard during his brief stay in the weapons bazaar.

At the end of his report the priest finally broke down.

"Why is it our luck to bear witness to this?" he asked, sobbing. "Why are we here, to feel the first breeze of the apocalypse? If I had recognized these signs before this, I would have strongly urged that we give up this useless endeavor and flee this place immediately—with all the citizens in tow. For what awaits us out there I fear is beyond all means of defense, natural or supernatural."

"You see," the first merc leader said, "even the priest thinks we should go."

The leader of Home Guard lowered his head and stared at the table. He knew what all this was leading up to.

"Even if we had enough transport for every person left on this moon, we do not have the time to evacuate them all," he said softly. "The enemy will surely move now that his dastardly machine is completed. That thing is probably heading for us right now. The only rockets out of this place are the ones that you yourselves own. An evacuation is not an option."

A long silence.

"We are fighting for our freedom, our way of life," the Home Guard officer went on, though his words were barely audible. "Such things *are* still important—whether we are here, in this far-out place, or on Earth itself."

"Valiant words," one of the merc commanders said. "But they are the stuff more readily found in legends and myths. This is reality, man. . . ."

This merc leader stood up. "I hereby ask to be released from my contract."

Before the commander of the Home Guard could respond, four of the remaining mercenary commanders stood up and repeated the same phrase. The Home Guard officer sank lower into his seat. Without looking up, he gave them a weary wave of his hand, granting their wishes. The five men filed out of the room; with that gesture, more than five thousand paid defenders of Qez would be gone in less than an hour.

"Maybe all is lost," the Home Guard commander said to himself. "Maybe civilized behavior will start its final collapse here, on this tiny moon, so far out on the Fringe, we can almost see the other side. Maybe this is how the Cosmos seeks to fool us—the puppets of Man. Maybe it begins here ... when no good and decent men are left to fight for the most basic thing in any life."

With that, the leader of the Home Guard looked up and was surprised to find that one mercenary leader was still sitting at the table.

It was McKay, the recon man, the representative of the Freedom Brigade.

"We will stay with you," McKay told him.

The leader of Qez looked at him strangely. He didn't know whether to laugh or to cry.

"But why?" he asked McKay. "You are our finest fighters by far. And we have been allies longer than time can remember. But you have every reason to walk out, just as the others have. This *is* a hopeless cause—I know it now. And I didn't need to have them tell me that. Why then? Why do you choose to stay?"

McKay just shook his head.

"Truthfully, I don't know," he said, his voice breaking as well. "I guess that's just the way we are. . . ."

With the withdrawal of the five mercenary groups, the defense of Qez now fell to the city's small Home Guard and the remaining members of the Freedom Brigade.

Counting various militias and armed civilians, this amounted to a force of just 5,251. Sending these troops into the trenches where most of the war's fighting had taken place would have been foolish. Poulinex, the Home Guard commander, wisely decided that the last-ditch defense of Qez would be made from the walls of the city itself.

Qez was laid out in a rhomboidal shape; the widest wall faced the battlefield to the east. Even before the rocketships carrying the departing mercenaries had lifted off, the ramparts of this east wall were being reinforced by the remaining defenders. Every available Z gun, cannon, and blaster was brought forward and installed atop the very high walls. Extra gunports were burned through the solid parapets; any reserve ammunition mined from the city's magazines was brought up as well. All noncombatants, close to twenty thousand people, were installed in the basements of buildings located as far away from the east wall as possible. The city's meager food and water supplies were placed there with them.

Still, even as the preparation continued at a rapid pace, it became increasingly clear that when measured by what awaited them over the horizon, the defensive procedures would be little more than delaying tactics against the inevitable. There were at least thirty thousand enemy soldiers out there that the people in Qez knew about—plus the monstrous weapon.

The coming battle against such an overwhelming force might prove to be courageous, but the outcome seemed all but predetermined.

However, the soldiers of the Freedom Brigade did have a plan.

They knew of no weapon that could thwart the huge armored mover. If it was built of reatomized electron steel, then even the most powerful of Z beams would not be able to put a dent in it.

But there was one last option. It involved a technology that was more lost than secret; something that had been passed down through thousands of generations on the Freedom Brigade's home planet. In fact, this technology had been around over such a vast period of time, it had entered the realm of myth.

In the end it was just an idea, a desperate one, that might stop the monster.

But would it work?

The quick night fell again; a thunderstorm passed overhead, then the wind died down.

As the defensive preparations continued within Qez, a contingent of volunteers from the Freedom Brigade stole out of the city and began moving through the trenchworks. Their goal was a point about ten miles away known as Heartbreak Ridge.

This was the location of a fierce battle several months before. The enemy had launched a massive three-wave attack—and the defenders of Qez met them at the shallow ridgeline. The battle lasted three days, during which hand-to-hand fighting claimed hundreds of lives. The bodies of the enemy dead were never retrieved. Their skeletons still dotted the nightmarish landscape, hence the area's nickname.

Ironically, the ridge wasn't much of a ridge at all. Its peak had been bombarded so many times, it was now almost even with the devastated terrain surrounding it. However, it was a place where a large part of the Xomme leading back toward enemy territory could be observed.

It was here that the Freedom Brigade would take the first step in their desperate plan.

The volunteers first installed a long-range visual array atop the highest part remaining on Heartbreak Ridge.

They were hoping to catch a glimpse of the monstrous armored mover as it began its ways toward Qez. As it turned out, the long-range scanner was not necessary; as soon as the first brigade soldiers reached the top of the ridge and peered to the east, they were able to spot the gigantic tank by eye. Indeed, it was fewer than ten miles away!

It was a frightening sight for these men, who had never seen the behemoth before. Even in the darkest part of the quick night, its form dominated the star-filled sky. And it was moving, slowly but surely, right at them, no doubt with a destination of Qez.

The troopers got to work. Using their combat tools and even their bare hands, they began digging a hole in the soft ground just west of the battered ridgeline. One of those on hand was a munitions officer. He determined this hole had to be at least fifty feet deep and half again as wide if it was to help produce the hoped-for effect.

The soldiers dug all night, taking turns between lifting out buckets of dirt and dust and keeping an eye on the slowly advancing tracked vehicle.

By the time the first daylight appeared on the horizon, the hole had been dug. Using pieces of white plastic-cloth, a huge X was stretched on top of it.

Then the troopers returned to Qez.

• • •

The plan revolved around a tiny piece of material that by tradition the commander of the Freedom Brigade carried with him in a twenty and six.

Just what this material was called or why, when manipulated properly by an electron torch, it produced the reaction it did, had been lost in the mists of time. The lost technology had not been tried in centuries, at least not that anyone could remember.

But work began in haste now to prepare the mysterious element after it had been recalled from the twenty-sixth dimension by the Freedom Brigade's commander. When it arrived, the material was found to be cast in the form of a tiny cylinder; it was no bigger than a man's thumb. The ancient procedure called for the material to be placed in a metal container, which was then to be filled with what was known as "unbalanced water"—water in which some of the oxygen had been extracted, leaving an "unbalanced" amount of hydrogen behind.

With the commander watching over their shoulders and intoning the ancient instructions, the Freedom Brigade's munitions officer carefully placed the material inside the container of manipulated water, then sealed the container via an electron torch, leaving an opening wide enough only for a thin piece of wire to poke out.

This, they understood, was a fuse of sorts.

The canister had been prepared—but now the Freedom Brigade had to come up with a way to deliver it.

The brigade's combat engineers searched their databases, looking for a simple device that could be built quickly and still do the job. They finally constructed something they came to call "the throwing machine." It was made mostly of old superwood and metal alloys melded together by two of the six electron torches remaining inside Qez.

When it was finished, the device did look alarmingly simple. It sat up high on four large runners. It had one long arm, at the end of which was a huge wooden basket. Attached to the arm and leading to a massive claw in front was a huge spring. Made of recoiled metal strands, when this arm was pulled back, the spring was stretched almost beyond its limit—so much so that the coiled metal actually "sang," it was so taut.

Though it looked completely alien to the Freedom Brigade troopers and anyone who saw it resting in Qez's main square, its design had actually been around for thousands of years.

It was called a catapult.

24

The huge xarcus broke the horizon east of Qez just as the sun began to rise.

There were actually 42,525 Nakkz mercs stuffed inside the supertank; several hundred more piloted the huge weapon and watched over its controls. These crewmen were housed in an enormous control bubble located directly beneath the supertank's massive cannon barrel. The bulk of the combat soldiers rode in the enormous passenger cabin, in the rear of the mover.

The xarcus was, no doubt, a splendid weapon of gargantuan proportions—yet no one inside the supertank knew how their side had come upon it. When their shadowy allies told the Nakkz that the giant xarcus would be just the weapon to give them a victory in the year-long war, there was no reason to doubt them. Shortly afterward the first components of the supertank suddenly began to materialize. They came out of the sky—literally—one piece at a time, arriving with a crack of thunder and hanging motionless in the air, until a few days or a few hours or even a few minutes later, another piece would arrive the same way and attach itself to the previous section. Then would come the relentless banging, the pounding, the nonstop racket as the huge machine was assembled by unseen hands. Reatomizing rays lit up both the day and the night. Strange, bendable metal could be seen melding together. The Nakkz did little more than sit by and watch.

It took several months, but finally the gigantic xarcus was complete. This came as a relief to the scores of Nakkz soldiers bivouacked around Holy Hell. The pounding and the banging had haunted them, too. From their various scattered camps, they had watched as the pieces appeared, streaking in from a place that didn't seem to be anywhere in the Milky Way Galaxy. The soldiers had gone off to battle every day and returned to see the huge tank that much closer to completion. If it hadn't been for all the noise, it truly would have been an amazing sight to behold.

But as to who actually built the thing, the Nakkz had no idea—because when it really came down to it, the thing had built itself

The xarcus had moved out of Holy Hell shortly after being spotted by the recon team from Qez.

Its deployment was just one aspect of a planned attack on the tiny moon's last remaining stronghold. Big as it was, the xarcus still could move at about five miles an hour, and once it started rolling, it was just about impossible to stop. Leaving behind an imprint that was nearly a hundred feet deep, it had torn its way across the Xomme in less a half an Earth day.

Now, as the sun was rising, it had its target in sight.

The plan against Qez was fairly simple. Rather than use the huge cannon to destroy the city and its people in one long Z-beam blast, the xarcus would instead roll right up to the city gate, knock it down if necessary, and then unload its troops: twenty-five thousand men of a "destroyer division"—shock troops in a different day and age. The rest of the soldiers made up the "execution brigades."

In conquering Qez, the Nakkz had only one order: Take no prisoners of any kind—civilian or military.

Prisoners were witnesses. And there could be no witnesses left after this attack.

Once Qez was in sight, the troops within the supertank suited up and prepared for jump-off.

The tank's massive turret weapon was charged up, its gun

crews called to battle stations in case they were needed. The xarcus was indeed the equivalent of a Starcrasher on treads, and getting its crew into its combat position was a long process because of the vast distances involved. Still, the supertank was declared "ready for battle" just two hours after it had come within sight of its target.

By this time it was fewer than ten miles away from the city's main gates.

Weapons fire from Qez started soon afterward.

Long-range Z-beam blasts and incendiary shells began raining out of the walled city; indeed, the fortress seemed to be on fire, so intense were the muzzle flashes and electrostatic discharges. And while most of the Z-beam blasts fell short, some of the fire shells managed to hit the xarcus, exploding on the massive treads or in front of the primary control bubble itself.

These hits created fires that burned hot and bright and could last a long time, but within the supertank itself, they were of no concern. There was no way fire alone could get through its massively thick skin. The destroyer division and the execution brigades continued preparing for their attack; in fact, few of them even knew the supertank had come under attack.

Inside the control bubble, everything was going smoothly as well. The firing from Qez was getting more intense the closer the xarcus crept toward the fortress city. But just as the incendiary shells were of little concern, even a concentrated Z-beam attack on the xarcus would do only minor damage. The tank had been constructed of 100 percent reatomized electron steel—even the superglass making up the control bubble was imbedded with the stuff.

Few things in nature could put a dent in it.

The xarcus had closed to within seven miles of Qez when the people in the control bubble noticed that their enemy's defensive strategy was changing.

Instead of directing many random blasts at the supertank, the Z-beam fire coming out of Qez was now beginning to be concentrated. No longer trying to simply stop the huge war machine with thousands of individual hits, the defenders were all aiming at the same spot on the xarcus: a point about a hundred feet in front of the control bubble, where its gigantic chassis met the lower part of its superstructure. This switch in tactics was more of a surprise than a shock. There was nothing at that point of the tank's enormous structure that could be fatally damaged, even by ten thousand blaster rifles hitting it at once.

The people in the control bubble even began to laugh at the odd but ultimately fruitless effort.

The xarcus was indeed unstoppable.

Just as their mysterious allies had said.

The walls of Qez were indeed on fire.

There were so many blaster rifles and ray guns going off, the static electricity was running throughout the fortification and searing any wires or hemp or flammable materials attached to or located near the wall.

A squad of Freedom Brigade soldiers was positioned at the highest point on the east rampart, their visual sensors trained on the approaching xarcus. Because of the noise coming from endless fusillades of Z-beam blasts by the city's defenders, it was nearly impossible for these soldiers to communicate with colleagues down in the city square, where the throwing machine was located. So the two groups had worked out a crude language of hand signals in which to speak.

Though the soldiers up top were tracking the xarcus's movements, it was lucky for them that the huge mover did not waver much from its dead-on westerly approach. If the huge machine turned either right or left, it was always a minor fluctuation. Still, whenever that happened, the soldiers up top would signal to their comrades surrounding the throwing machine. Using nothing more than musclepower, these soldiers would then push, pull, and drag the throwing machine into a new configuration.

This went on for nearly an hour, the defenders sending out long-range Z-gun blasts, the xarcus moving across the Xomme, unhindered, its huge army safe inside, ready to be called to the slaughter.

Then, just as the sun reached its highest point in the short day, the xarcus rolled out of a slight depression and began crawling up the slight incline known as Heartbreak Ridge. Upon getting this information from the soldiers up on the wall, the brigade's weapons officer in charge of the throwing machine powered his ray gun down to its "dull fire" setting. Then he aimed its beam at the wire protruding from the little silver shell. It took a few moments but finally the wire began to glow.

Then he placed the magic canister inside the catapult's bucket, which was stuffed with highly flammable materials, and ordered its massive arm drawn back.

It was now ready to fire.

The men inside the xarcus's control bubble saw it first.

Coming out of the flurry of Z-beam blasts streaking out from the east wall of Qez, a ball of fire suddenly appeared.

It went nearly straight up in the air, trailing a long plume of black smoke behind it. It reached its apex about three miles away, and maybe two thousand feet above the battle-field. It seemed to hover in the air for a moment; then it started coming down. As it did, bits of the fireball began breaking away, leaving individual smoke trails behind it. Within seconds, most of the fireball had been separated in this manner, and all that remained was a bright, shiny canister, tumbling end over end.

The canister finally landed not three hundred feet in front of the supertank. It went right through the large plastic X, into the recently dug hole. The canister struck the softened earth with such momentum, it continued another two hundred feet into the mud. Now came gales of laughter from those inside the primary control bubble. What was this pathetic attempt all about? To throw such a tiny weapon at such a massive war machine?

Coincidentally, the final ready-call for the Nakkz troops sounded throughout the xarcus at the exact moment the canister became lodged in the mud.

It detonated two seconds later.

•   •   •

No one peering out from the walls of Qez had ever seen a nuclear explosion before.

It was awesome—both in its strangeness and its size. In a world where Z beams essentially disintegrated things, and high-explosive fire simply burned its intended to a crisp, the magnitude of this blast was frightening. The mushroom cloud rising above the bloody mud of the Xomme, the smoke, dust, and debris obscuring all view on the eastern horizon—it all seemed unreal and dreamlike.

Not so the shock wave that hit the city's walls seconds later, though. It was so intense, the walls began to shake and crack; the roofs on houses and buildings began to collapse. The ground literally began rolling. For one terrifying moment it seemed as if the bomb would destroy all of Qez as well.

But the wind finally died down and the dust finally settled and the defenders of Qez were able to look out on the no-man's-land and see just what the tiny canister had done.

The xarcus was so huge and constructed of such strengthened materials even a direct hit by a low-yield nuclear bomb might not have caused mortal damage. That's why the Freedom Brigade had hurled the makeshift weapon not at the tank itself, but directly in front of it.

The explosion had created an enormously deep hole in the ground just a few feet ahead of the xarcus. Like a Starcrasher or a huge oceangoing vessel, it was impossible for the supertank to stop in short order. Momentum alone carried it almost a quarter mile farther once the brakes were applied. With no way to stop in time, the huge mover began to plunge into the enormous crater left by the underground nuclear explosion. The right-side track was the first to go. It seemed to move in slow motion as it began grabbing nothing but air and smoke. The astonished Nakkz drivers inside the control bubble began pushing buttons and madly throwing levers, trying to prevent the supertank from toppling over—but the enormous tracks refused to stop moving. Its forward motion thus uncontrollable, the huge tank finally toppled into the gigantic bomb crater. The gun sticking out of its huge turret hit the ground first; it immediately split in two. The noise of this alone cracked around the moon like a massive rumble of thunder. With the barrel gone, the crumpling of the turret came next. Then the rest of the xarcus simply slammed down upon itself.

Now came another enormous explosion—the shock wave from this was as powerful as the initial nuclear blast itself. Chain reactions and short-circuiting began igniting anything remotely flammable inside the huge armored mover. There was another tremendous explosion. Then another. And another. The ground beneath Qez began shaking violently again as the gigantic tank went up in a huge ball of flame.

The fire was so quick and so intense, there was no way anyone inside could have gotten out alive.

A great cheer went up from the people of Qez. With little more than their ancient magic pellet, the Freedom Brigade had saved them from certain disaster.

Or so it seemed.

For no sooner had the dust settled from the xarcus's explosion than a Home Guard soldier manning an outpost on the far corner of the city's wall saw a glint of light off to the north.

Something is coming, he thought.

He turned his long-range viz-scanner in that direction—and saw something that his eyes did not want to believe.

Out on the horizon, just breaking its way through smoke and dust, was another xarcus.

And it was heading right for Qez.

25

Jubilation quickly turned to panic as word spread throughout Qez that a second xarcus was approaching.

The defenders of the embattled city rushed to positions along the north-facing wall. From here, the view of the second xarcus was all too clear. It was about a dozen miles away and tearing up the no-man's-land at a slow but relentless pace.

And at first it appeared that this xarcus was spewing a thick cloud of black smoke in front of it as it made its way toward Qez. It was only after the defenders were able to get their long-range viz-scanners keyed in that they realized the awful truth: This dense "mist" was actually an army of Nakkz soldiers marching in front of the huge tank.

There had to be at least forty thousand of them, probably more. Some were on foot, others were riding in Bolts, dozens of them, flying about five feet off the surface. The foot soldiers were heavily armed with blaster rifles and electric swords and moving steadily in loose formations across the heavily cratered battlefield.

This xarcus was also of a slightly different, if no less dastardly design. Instead of a huge gun sticking out of its massive turret, this supertank was carrying an enormous semi-circular assembly held in place by two arms extending up on either side of the chassis. This assembly was studded with huge steel teeth so sharp, they were gleaming in the quick-moving sun.

It was a saw—a gigantic cutting device obviously conceived as a means to slash through even the highest, thickest walls. Like those surrounding Qez.

Once again, every person looking out at this second monster was astonished that the motley collection of pirates, mercenaries, and assorted star trash known as the Nakkz had the means and the know-how to possess not just one of these absolutely enormous machines but two!

Had the first xarcus been a diversion? Or half of a two-prong attack? It made little difference now. This second gigantic weapon was coming right at Qez—and this time there was no magic pellet on hand to hurl at it. The only defense left would come from the depleted guns of the outnumbered Home Guards and the Freedom Brigade. And while no one doubted the gallantry of these two groups, their numbers appeared puny in face of the huge tank and its forty-thousand-man army.

So Qez and its people had not been spared after all.

Their fate had simply been delayed.

The combat warning sirens began blaring throughout the city. As the Home Guards solidified their positions along the north wall, the troopers from the Freedom Brigade hurriedly loaded up what was left of their power ammo and rushed out of the city toward a massive set of trenchworks a half mile from Qez's north gate, a position the brigade had previously designated Light Number One.

The Freedom Brigade had two captured Bolts at their disposal. This allowed them to lug two medium-power Z-gun artillery batteries out to this forward position. These guns had a range of about ten miles; soon enough they would be able to fire on the vanguard of the approaching army. The brigades' infantry squads dug into positions along this trench, each man setting up his own gun station complete with blaster rifle and double-barreled ray guns. A special operations team from the brigade gathered together some high-incendiary devices and began moving swiftly in the direction of the oncoming army. The big Z guns were put into place. Communications were established with the Home Guards back in Qez. The spirit among the mercenary group was high.

But not one man among them, or among the home defenders inside Qez, had any illusions about what would soon take place. None of these measures would do much good. Forty thousand enemy troops were heading their way. If the Freedom Brigade's Z guns were able to kill even a thousand of them, that alone would be miraculous. And if the Home Guards were able to duplicate this effort, that, too, would be good.

But there was no way they were going to stop the oncoming juggernaut.

For both the brigade and the defenders of Qez, this would be their last stand.

The enemy was now about ten miles away.

Already the massive size of the xarcus was beginning to blot out the midday sun. The huge saw was slowly lifted high above the turret and began turning slowly. This thing was so massive, it would take some time for it to run up to full speed. Still, the noise made by its gigantic teeth began tearing across the smoky battlefield. It began as a low-pitched cry but quickly built up to a frightening high-pitched wail.

On a signal from their officers, the Freedom Brigade soldiers began blasting away in the direction of the onslaught. Even though they were still out of range, the columns of flames caused by each Z bolt kicked up huge amounts of dirt and debris, turning most of it into microscopic subatomic dust.

Still the huge army kept coming.

Now Z-gun fire started up from the walls of Qez itself. Again, most of it fell about half a mile short of the advancing army, but at the very least, it let the enemy know they would be making it as difficult as possible to overrun their city. Like the blasts coming from the Freedom Brigade's position, this blaster fire kicked up enormous amounts of fire and dirt, igniting just about anything in its path. Soon a wall of flame was burning about nine miles out from the city—it temporarily blocked the view of the advancing enemy from the defenders. But then, after just a minute or so, several enemy Bolts popped through the fiery wall. They were followed by the advance guard of the foot soldiers; their bright green battlesuits apparently gave them adequate protection against the inferno.

Indeed, the enemy soldiers appeared to be walking right through the flames.

A gust of apprehension swept across the devastated plains now, blowing right over the heads of the dug-in Freedom Brigade and through the walls of Qez. The first Bolts were now but seven miles away from the brigade's trench lines. Already their massive nose guns were letting loose enormous bursts of X-beam rays. These were so powerful, they actually flew over the mercenary lines and landed in the area behind the brigade and just before the walls of Qez.

The brigade let go another volley from their Z guns. Again a wall of fire was thrown up right on top of the lead elements of the advancing army. And this time the Z blasts found some marks—many soldiers in the first line of Nakkz went up in the distinctive blue flame of a direct Z-gun hit.

But still they kept coming. Those watching the action through their viz-sensors were appalled at the lack of camaraderie being shown by the enemy soldiers for their fallen comrades. Though a Z-gun blast usually resulted in the quick disintegration of its victims, some not hit directly could be severely wounded. Yet the advancing army was marching right over these fallen souls, and in some cases pushing them farther down into the soft and bloody mud.

And this is where most of them would stay, mangled and dying until the gigantic xarcus came along and finished the job.

The advance units of the enemy were now within four miles of the brigade's battle line.

The vanguard was being led by a dozen Bolts, their nose guns firing massive X beams more or less indiscriminately across the wide arc of the battlefield.

Behind them were the survivors of the enemy's first wave, probably two thousand men in all. Between them was a small river, appropriately nicknamed Bloody Water by the defending troops. This river was barely flowing these days, clogged with the detritus of war—machines, expended weapons, bones. What had once been a twenty-two-foot-wide ribbon of sparkling water was now not much more than a ditch with a trickle running through it.

It was an important place nevertheless.

A five-man team of brigade sappers had stolen their way up to the stream and were planting Z charges in its shallow, putrid water. At this distance, the sound of the huge saw atop the xarcus's turret was loud enough to cause the ears of these men to bleed. Still they went about their mission, setting down more than a hundred charge packs in all before quickly heading back toward their fragile lines.

Just moments later, the first wave of Bolts reached the opposite side of the bloody river's bank. Seeing this through his long-range viz, the brigade's gunnery officer gave his left-side artillery battery a signal. This gun opened up with one long, well-placed Z-beam blast. The bolt of artificial lightning tore across the battlefield and hit one of the Z charges placed in the river.

The charge went up—along with fifty pounds of extremely high-explosive superhelium gas. The result was an explosion equal in brightness to a ton of magnesium going off. The first blast detonated the dozens of other Z charges lining the river; the chain reaction brought yet another wall of white-hot flame down upon the lead elements of the advancing army.

A dozen Bolts were vaporized immediately, along with their crews. Several more were caught in the updraft of the inferno; they went screeching straight up into the smoky air, exploding in unison some five hundred feet above the river of fire.

Now the first of the ground troops stumbled into the river itself. These men were immolated by the hundreds; some were falling directly into the fire, others were running in fear, completely engulfed, touching off their comrades' battlesuits with super-white-hot flames. Two more Bolts were disintegrated. An ammunition supply went up somewhere. Enemy soldiers by the thousands were marching blindly into the microholocaust.

The sheer number of dead finally extinguished the flames on Bloody Water. In all the tactic had killed more than a thousand of the enemy. But it had held him up barely five minutes, no more.

The gruesome advance continued.

The brigade's strategy now was grimly simple: Start firing on the enemy troops as soon as they got within range, and keep firing until the power ammo ran out. After that, hand-to-hand fighting would undoubtedly ensue, but no one expected that to last very long. The second xarcus would arrive shortly after the thousands of enemy troops hit the defenders' lines.

After that, it would be only a matter of time before the real slaughter began.

The enemy was soon just three miles from the brigade's lines. The xarcus was about three miles behind them.

The ground was shaking now beneath the mercenaries' boots—with every foot it traveled the xarcus sent out a tremor powerful enough to cause the walls of Qez to sway.

The brigade now brought every weapon it had forward. They were strung out along a main trench about two thousand feet long, again very close to the point they had christened Light Number One. The xarcus was heading directly toward the center of this line—with the main wall of Qez just half a mile beyond. The huge saw was now moving at near-supersonic speed. It sounded much louder than the worst thunderstorms to sweep the tiny moon. The reverberations of blasters going off, explosions coming from the incendiary shells being fired from the walls of Qez, the howls coming from thousands of advancing Nakkz soldiers. These were things nightmares were made of. Real-life nightmares.

The Freedom Brigade had faced dire circumstances before, but none compared to this. There was no panic—no letting up of fire at all. But most of the mercenaries had come to accept this as the end. All that was left was to go down fighting.

"We must hope that future generations will speak well of what we do here!" one officer yelled up and down the trench, "and not forget that we made our last stand here."

The enemy was now just two miles away. There was one last communication between the front line and the defenders inside Qez. The Home Guards realized that the brigade was gallantly providing them with a few more minutes of life—just enough to make peace with themselves before the blood-thirsty army and giant tank crushed their ancient city.

It was the most valiant of gestures imaginable.

"Be proud, brothers, for lives well led," one Home Guard officer communicated out to the mercenaries' line. "The freedom-loving people of Qez thank you."

The enemy was now just a mile away.

It was getting more difficult to see the brigade's lines from the ramparts of Qez. The smoke and dust kicked up from the approach of the huge army was obscuring the visibility more than any storm that had ever swept the tiny moon. Pervasive above it all was the now supersonic screeching of the gigantic saw, priming itself to cut through the battlements of the walled city.

More than four thousand Home Guard soldiers were lined along the top of this vast wall or at firing stations built into its midsection. Even with the constant roar of Z guns and fire shells going off and the sound of the gigantic saw blade, the Home Guard soldiers still could hear the wails coming from the thousands of citizens—women, elderly, children—huddled in the basements of the buildings deep in the center of Qez.

The men on the wall delivered as much fire as they could, aiming over the heads of the valiant mercenaries and cutting deep into the enemy ranks. The fire shells were particularly effective on the approaching troops, but their explosions were so intense, and the debris they caused so thick, they further obscured the battlefield.

The Home Guards still could see the flashes of the brigade's Z-gun muzzles. And now fierce hand-to-hand fighting was taking place. Flashes of light could be seen reflecting off the electric swords of the mercenaries.

"They are displaying their colors!" someone up on the wall yelled. Sure enough, the brigade's multicolored flag could now be seen flying above their position. Everyone knew this was the unit's traditional signal that the end was near.

The Home Guard's commanding officer, the man named Poolinex, was himself on the north wall, watching the grim events unfold.

His wife and children were back with the rest of the civilians, cowering in a basement somewhere, just as afraid of dying without him as he was without them.

He looked out beyond the battlefield, off to the far horizon. The moon was so small, the joke used to go, that if you looked hard enough in one direction, you would see the back of your own head.

"We are so tiny," Poolinex whispered. "And we are at the last end of the Galaxy. Why would anyone want to destroy *us?*

He felt a tug on his arm. He turned to see three young soldiers, one holding the flag of Qez. There were tears in their eyes.

"Shall we run up our own colors, commander?" one of the soldiers asked.

Poolinex looked back on the battlefield—the enemy was less than a mile away and had apparently overrun the Freedom Brigade's lines with ease.

He finally nodded. It was time for them to face their Maker, too.

"Yes," he said, "run it up the pole—for we have lost."

But then, suddenly a bolt of lightning flashed across the sky.

It went right over the walled fortress, lighting up the dense and smoky battlefield. The crack it made was so loud, the crumbling walls of Qez shook yet again.

No sooner had this happened than a sheet of flame shot up from a point on the battlefield just in front of the brigade's line. Gigantic bolts of Z beams cut through the thick smoke billowing above the intense fighting, and a series of massive explosions walked right up to the vanguard of the enemy force, disintegrating them by the hundreds. The noise from these Z-beam blasts was deafening—yet none of them was coming from the walls of Qez.

That's when everyone realized that an aircraft of some kind was tearing through the air *above* the battlefield, firing a Z-beam cannon, and dropping high-explosive incendiary devices at the same time.

What madness was this?

On a world where nothing flew more than twenty feet off the ground, or any faster than five miles an hour, this airborne hellion was a frightening thing to behold. It was moving so fast and turning so sharply, soldiers on both sides stopped firing to stare up at it. The aircraft was sleek, sharp, all crazy angles with a brilliant color scheme. Its nose was lit up brilliantly—even in the confusion, the Home Guard soldiers could see six separate beams shooting out from the snout of this strange craft. It was traveling so fast it would have been impossible for the Nakkz troops to take a shot at it, never mind hit it.

And there was no question about whose side it was on— the Home Guard soldiers on the wall could see that the enemy advance had been suddenly stopped dead in its tracks. Some of the Nakkz were even retreating—quickly—back to their main lines, leaving dozens of dead and wounded comrades in their path.

Still the strange aircraft kept firing, killing many of the retreating soldiers and frightening those it spared. And it was only by a fluke of the wind that, as this flying machine went over the brigade's line yet again, those behind the walls of Qez got a quick, clear look at it.

That's when they realized that the flying machine was painted red, white, and blue.

At the precise moment this was happening, another strange thing was occurring, in Qez's main square.

This part of the city was a study in chaos at the moment— soldiers either running to firing positions on the wall, or laying wounded beneath it. Gigantic Z-beam blasts were flying overhead. The noise and confusion were incredible.

In the middle of all this, two spacemen suddenly popped in.

They appeared right next to the now-discarded catapult. They were carrying two halves of a hollow cylinder with them. Even in the middle of the turmoil, a number of Home

Guard soldiers stopped dead in their tracks when the two figures unexpectedly materialized.

One of the spacemen grabbed the soldier nearest to him and bellowed: "Go get your commanding officer . . . *now!*" He was sent off with a hearty shove.

Then the other spaceman grabbed a second soldier and yelled: "Get twenty more guys and help us turn this thing around!"

But the soldiers just stood frozen in shock. Zazu-Zazu was a tiny moon at the very end of the Galaxy—the outer fringe of the Outer Fringe. People didn't just pop in here. Yet here were these two men, with bald heads and very long mustaches, wearing incredibly elaborate battlesuits, scars on their faces and tattoos on the arms, issuing orders as if they owned the place.

No one moved for a long moment. Then, seeing only blank faces staring back at them, the two spacemen started moving the huge catapult themselves.

By this time a senior Home Guard officer arrived on the scene. He was fresh from the battle on the wall and he looked it. He, too, skidded to a stop as soon as he saw the two strange men.

"What . . . *what are you doing?*" he yelled at them.

One of the interlopers turned to him and said: "We must move this contraption so it is pointing north!"

Then the second spaceman was in the officer's face. "We must shoot this thing at that monster out there! Quickly help us!"

But the officer didn't budge—he wasn't sure what to do. So he stated the obvious. Looking down at the two halves of the cylinder the men had carried with them, he said: "But that thing is empty! It's not a superbomb like our friends just lit off!"

The two spacemen looked up at the officer and suddenly smiled.

"That's true, my brother," one said. "But the enemy does not know that!"

It took them all just a minute to turn the catapult the way the two spacemen wanted it. Then another minute or so was spent struggling to pull the huge, tightly sprung arm back.

More Home Guard soldiers jumped in, and the arm was finally locked into place and secured with a length of thick rope. The spacemen put the two halves of the empty cylinder together—it was actually a travel flask for slow-ship wine—and joined them with an electron torch. Then the empty container was dumped into the basket of the catapult and the line was severed.

The arm let go with a deafening *whomp!* The silver canister went flying into the air, quickly disappearing in the haze.

No sooner was the empty flask away when the two spacemen started to run toward an elevator that would bring them up to the top of the wall. But the Home Guard officer suddenly ordered his soldiers to grab them.

"You two stand fast!" the officer bellowed at them. "You *must* tell me who you are and what this is all about!"

That's when one of the spacemen used his massive hand to crush slightly the fingers of the soldier who was holding him. The soldier quickly let go.

"There's no time for that!" the spaceman yelled back at the officer. "We must get to the ramparts to see what is going to happen!"

With that, they sprinted away to the elevator, the officer and twenty confused soldiers following close behind.

The silver canister was just coming down from its extra-steep trajectory when this small party reached the top of the battlements.

They watched as the object rocketed through the murk of battle and landed about a thousand feet in front of the xarcus.

That's when the most ungodly noise of all thundered across the devastated plain. It was the combination of a very loud explosion and an incredibly high-pitched screech. Suddenly the air was thick with the stink of metal grinding against metal. Electrical charges began dotting the smoky sky.

The screeching got louder and louder, for more than two minutes, until it finally exploded into one loud *bang!*

And then suddenly the ground wasn't rumbling anymore. The air was no longer filled with the awful sound of the huge saw turning. In fact, if it was possible, a strange peace came over the battlefield. Soldiers on both sides stopped firing their weapons. For a few precious seconds, something had happened here that had not happened in a very long time: It got quiet.

All eyes turned past the battle in the trenches, back over Bloody Water and across another two miles of the devastated battlefield to the xarcus.

That's when it became apparent what had caused the ungodly noise: Simply put, someone inside the supertank had stepped on the brakes—*hard*—and the gigantic armored mover had slowly screeched to a most violent stop. Fires broke out beneath its enormous tracks. Smoke began billowing from its rear end. The saw was just spinning freely now, slowing down with every turn.

The two spacemen literally jumped for joy. They were shaking hands and congratulating themselves profusely. It came together slowly for the officer, but then it finally dawned on him what had happened.

The xarcus had been stopped.

But how?

"Don't you get it, man?" one of the spacemen yelled at him. "Someone inside saw that canister coming and thought it was another superbomb! They couldn't have stalled that thing quicker if they'd tried. . . ."

The officer just stared back at them. "You mean . . . this was all . . . *a bluff?*"

But the spacemen were ignoring the officer by now and talking to each other. "We've got to figure it will take them at least a half hour to get that bastard up and running again."

"Judging from the sound of all that grinding metal, I'd say more like an hour or more. . . ."

"But that means we haven't a moment to lose!"

That's when the officer finally snapped. He pulled out his ray gun and pointed it the spacemen.

"Now you tell me," he said through clenched teeth, "who the hell *are* you people?"

The spacemen smiled again, and the shorter of the two stepped forward.

"My apologies, sir," he said. "My name is Erx. My friend here is Berx. . . ."

But the officer was still stumped. "What I mean is," he said with no little fluster, *"what the hell are you doing here?"*

At that moment the red, white, and blue flying machine roared over their heads and went into a hover mode above the city square.

Erx pointed up at the aircraft and told the officer: "Ask *him*."

26

It all started with the dream.

On the first night aboard his ship, the *AeroVox,* during the first decent piece of slumber Hunter had had in weeks, a dream came to him vividly and real. He was above a beautiful countryside. Below he could see rivers, trees, golden fields that stretched for miles. Sometimes he would soar over small towns and even smaller villages. He could see people below, moving about, talking, laughing, living their lives, either unaware that he was above them or seeing him but not caring.

In his dream, he flew over this idyllic landscape—flying without his flying machine. No extending of arms as if they were wings. No noise. No means of forward propulsion. Just *flying*. He could see all this, smell it, even *feel* it, as clear as day. These were things like nothing he'd seen on Earth, but not completely different either; they were foreign, yet familiar.

It was a magnificent dream to have, especially while flying in the stark beauty of Supertime, heading for the Outer Fringe. But the dream had a catch: Whenever he was in it, Hunter could not stop flying. The dream did not provide him with a hover mode. He had to keep moving, relishing the vision below, but never being able to stop and touch it. Never able to put his feet on the ground.

He came to realize, after having the strange dream every night for the first month the journey Outward, that this place he was flying over must have been his home.

The more times Hunter had the dream, the more elaborate it became.

Every once and a while he'd spot a flag down below that looked just like the one in his pocket. Sometimes he thought he even saw the girl whose picture he carried with him. Blond, beautiful, she always seemed to be running through a field in slow motion. But again this blessing was a curse. Hunter never could stop long enough to see if the colors and patterns of the flag on the ground were exactly the same as the one in his pocket. He never could stop long enough to see if the girl running in slow motion through the field was the same girl in his faded photograph.

All he could do was look—and fly on.

Still, Hunter came to have a strange appreciation of the dream. Some nights he looked forward to having it. Some nights he went to his quarters early just so he *could* have it. It evolved to a point where he was sometimes able to slow his speed down to a crawl, almost a hover, and get to within a few feet of the surface.

But anytime he would try to touch the ground, he would suddenly find himself awake.

Then one night, the recurring dream took a very strange turn. He was flying as usual when he spotted the flag flying near the top of a pole in a small town square. And this time, when he tried to hover, he found he was actually able to stop. And when he tried to get close to the surface, he found he was actually able to land.

And upon touching his feet to the ground, he felt the same electric jolt as when he first stepped on Earth.

In the dream he ran up to the flagpole to find an elderly man hoisting up a multicolored ensign. This flag was *exactly* like the one Hunter carried in his pocket, exactly like the symbol he'd seen on the side of the failed Mars polar lander. Yet it was stained with blood.

And the man at the pole?

It was Calandrx.

"Am I finally home, my brother?" Hunter asked him.

Calandrx just smiled.

"You are very close," he replied. "But she can tell you more."

Hunter turned to see a blond girl running toward him from a nearby field. He resisted the temptation to run toward her and lift her up in a slow-motion embrace. Instead he studied her closely as she ran toward him. Yes, she had blond hair. Yes, she was beautiful.

But she was *not* the person whose picture he carried in his pocket. In fact, he knew who she was.

It was Xara.

She reached him, looked up at him, smiled, and hugged him tightly. He hugged her back.

Then she whispered in his ear: "The lighthouse is on the last place anyone can be. . . ."

She laughed. Calandrx laughed. But when Hunter started to ask her for more information, she kissed him . . . and then he woke up.

The dream stopped coming to him after that.

Hunter and his crew reached the Fifth Arm of the Outer Fringe and wandered its vast expanse for the next five months.

He went about his mission of reclaiming planets for the Fourth Empire, but always with the ulterior motive of finding the lighthouse not very far from his mind. In that time, the *AeroVox* rediscovered sixteen new star systems and sixty-eight new worlds. With each new planet he popped into, either covertly or like a bolt from the blue, Hunter tried to *feel* the kinship bond with the inhabitants that seemed to be promised in the war poem. But though many of the people he met were gracious, hospitable, and friendly—that is, after they realized they were, in essence, being invaded from outer space—none of them looked like him, talked like him, or was anything at all similar to him. Without the dream to count on, it made for some long nights.

In that time, though, whenever they had a chance, Hunter, Erx, and Berx would pore over the ancient map, sometimes for hours on end, trying to translate more closely the sketchy, two-thousand-year-old data. All three had reread the war poem many times as well, trying to appreciate any subtleties they might have missed. They came to the conclusion that the lighthouse probably wasn't a "house" as would normally be thought of, or some entity that somehow was made entirely of light. According to the best translation they could come up with, the lighthouse seemed to be more of a beacon, something to call "the lost souls" home. It was probably an automated device, constructed hundreds if not thousands of years before it struck the base of the Mars polar lander. There also was a good chance that it was no longer operating; one line in the poem suggested it had been shut down centuries before. This, too, could make Hunter's nights seem endless.

Still his mission went on; he continued doing the job he'd been sent out here to do. They followed the reclamation list drawn up by the X-Forces high command, and for the most part, the *AeroVox* found and visited the planets on this list and more or less stuck to the timetable that went along with it. Sometimes it was easy, sometimes it was not. Many sectors in this part of the Outer Fringe, Fifth Arm, had not seen any Empire presence since the last Dark Age. Some people out here knew of the Empire only by word of mouth or rumors; others accepted it as fact. Still others didn't even know space travel was possible or that the stars above them were inhabited and the Galaxy was teeming with life.

It was a strange time then. Hunter's job during these months was essentially to be the first visitor from outer space some of these planets had seen in thousands of years. What an odd profession, to be the first "alien" to visit a world in several millennia. Sometimes the population reacted positively; sometimes not. The whole Empire-returning thing went so much easier when the populace had an inkling that they were not alone in the universe. Past contact that survived in history, or even crashed ships from previous empires, or even the early part of this one, could all soften the blow when the *AeroVox* suddenly appeared in orbit around their world.

In all, they been forced to intervene in three major wars and a handful of smaller ones. These campaigns rarely lasted more than a day or two after the *AeroVox* arrived, though.

There were ten thousand highly skilled and highly special-ized X-Forces troops on board the starship. Their firepower and combat technology were always vastly superior to that found on the planet in question, plus the troops were as much in the business of helping out populations of reclaimed plan-ets as fighting them. Once it was determined which side was being oppressed in any conflict they came upon, the X-Forces troops would intervene on the side of the underdog, and the war would end soon after that.

They'd ridded half a dozen planets of space pirates and other assorted scum in this manner. Some of the fighting had been bitter, some relatively light. Some populations wel-comed them with open arms, some were fearful, some pan-icked. But the social scientists and the diplomats assigned to Hunter's ship were also top-notch. Through a combination of these efforts, most of the reclamation missions went smoothly.

Until they came to a planet called Guam 7.

This was a place where the Empire was known, a place that was supplying a good part of the Outer Fringe Fifth Arm with weapons to continue the thousands of wars being fought throughout the tens of thousands of star systems in the sector.

The *AeroVox*'s special ops soldiers seized the planet's one and only major city—the place called Nails—without firing a shot. They quickly established martial law, ending the out-of-control weapons trade but allowing the distillation and dis-tribution of slow-ship wine to continue.

In the course of this action, Hunter's troops came upon two of the planet's biggest weapons dealers. During a routine interrogation these two men passed on their story about a strange conversation they'd had with a priest who was look-ing for weapons for a beleaguered band of mercenaries fac-ing long odds in the most isolated point in the Galaxy: the Dead Gulch System. A fierce war was being fought on a tiny moon there, orbiting the last planet.

"The last place anyone could be . . ." was their direct quote.

Hunter immediately tried to locate the Dead Gulch star system, not an easy task in this part of the Galaxy. Even the people in Nails weren't exactly sure where it was. Finally Hunter's men tracked down some other individuals who had spoken with the priest that day. They indicated the priest had traveled twenty-two star systems to get to Guam 7. Hunter went to the ancient maps again, started doing calculations, and eventually found it, the last place anyone could go before plunging into the forbidden depths of intergalactic space: the Dead Gulch system.

And here he found the last moon spinning around the last planet and discovered that the name of this place was Zazu-Zazu.

And *that's* why he was here on this fateful day.

But just as in his dream, there was a catch. . . .

By the time Hunter's aircraft settled into a hover over the main square of Qez, a large crowd of astonished civilians had gathered below.

He lowered himself into the center of the square, inducing gasps from the crowd and sending some fleeing in panic. They had never seen a machine such as his before. Wings, wheels, a tail section, the long, sleek body bulked up by Z weapons and bomb racks—*this* was an alien craft to them.

Hunter touched the ground, felt only a slight electric jolt, then popped his canopy and climbed out. The crowd took a collective step backward. They had seen visitors from space before, both welcome and unwelcome, but no one who looked like him. In a place where bald was beautiful—at least for the male population—and thin wasn't exactly in, Hunter's overgrown mane and lean physique marked him as different right away. But after bouncing around the Outer Fringe for the past few months, he was used to this reaction by now.

He scanned the faces in the crowd, trying to locate a high-ranking officer or someone in authority. Finally a man in a bright red uniform pushed his way through, followed by several heavily armed soldiers. Hunter saluted the officer, then held his hands out in front of him palms up, the traditional gesture of peace in the Galaxy. The officer looked wary but signaled his men to lower their weapons.

A fierce barrage of X-beam fire hit the north wall not a

second later, sending the rest of the civilians scattering.

"We need to go somewhere and talk!" Hunter yelled to the officer in the midst of the confusion. *"Right now."*

He was rushed to the nearby war room, dodging all kinds of flying debris as the Nakkz started pounding the city's walls again. Their army might have been stalled, along with their supertank, but apparently this was not going to stop their long-range gunners from pummeling the city while their main forces regrouped.

About a dozen Home Guard officers were in the war room praying over a well-worn battle map when Hunter walked in. There were also some very nervous-looking civilians on hand, no doubt part of the city's government. Every head turned and looked up at him as he entered, their eyes a mixture of weariness and surprise.

"This is the man who stopped the enemy's attack," the escorting officer told the group. "He has a fabulous machine parked right outside."

Their faces brightened—he was undoubtedly their hero of the moment. But Hunter already knew that these were not the people he was looking for. Just like every other person he'd met out on the Fringe, they looked different from him. He felt no spark, no immediate sense of kinship with them.

His heart sank.

Another dead end.

Finally Poolinex, the top Home Guard officer, stepped forward. He thanked Hunter profusely for his actions above the battlefield just minutes before, but then asked the question that was on everyone's mind: *"Just who the hell are you?"*

At least Hunter had an answer prepared. After doing this for the past five months, he was used to people asking him who the hell he was. So he launched into his standard reply, even as the walls of the war room began shaking from X-gun blasts, and plaster and dust began falling down around their heads. This moon and its mother planet are part of an Imperial structure run from Earth, blah, blah, blah. . . . Hunter could recite this stuff in his sleep these days. Even under these dire circumstances, the words spewed out of him automatically.

Not that it made any difference. At the moment, the defenders of Qez had bigger problems than someone falling out of the sky and telling them that they were part of a wondrously immense Empire. In a few hours there might not be any Qez or Zazu-Zazu for the Empire to worry about.

So Hunter decided to pass over most of the "we are back" crap and cut right to the bone.

"I represent the Fourth Empire—let's leave the details for later," he said. "I mean, you're obviously in a bind here."

"How true," Poolinex said, looking back at the map. "For even though you stopped those devils in their tracks, it was just a temporary solution. I expect they'll batter us with artillery all night—and at first light, they'll attack again. And once that army starts to move, and the monster tank as well . . . they'll be unstoppable."

All eyes were now locked on Hunter.

"So you're from this Fourth Empire, did you call it?" one officer asked. "Does that mean you can help us?"

Another officer asked excitedly: "You have a warship in orbit? Troops that can come to our aid?"

Hunter felt his heart sink even farther. Yes, he had a ship. The *AeroVox* was parked up in orbit. And true, it was a warship and outfitted to carry a ten-thousand-man division of heavily armed X-Forces special operations soldiers.

But . . .

"Well, I do have a ship," he finally confirmed.

The knot of men tightened around him.

"Yes . . . but?" Poolinex asked him.

Hunter began stuttering his reply when suddenly the door to the war room opened and two familiar faces were marched in. It was Erx and Berx, followed by a very confused Home Guard officer halfheartedly holding a ray gun on them.

For Hunter, they couldn't have shown up at a better time.

"These are my colleagues," he hurriedly told the Home Guard officers. "They're the ones who launched the empty canister at the xarcus, the bluff that got it to stop in its tracks."

The others in the room let out a great cheer. One look from Poolinex and the officer with the ray gun lowered his weapon and skulked out of the room. Hunter's introductions were interrupted as another gigantic barrage of X beams hit the city.

"May I have a word with my men?" Hunter asked Poolinex.

"To set a strategy, you mean?" the Home Guard officer asked hopefully.

Hunter nodded uncertainly. Erx and Berx rolled their eyes.

"Yes, something like that," Hunter mumbled in reply.

The Home Guard commander nodded and went back to his map. Hunter, Erx, and Berx shuffled through a side door and found themselves outside in a darkened corner of the ancient city square. Enemy X-beam blasts were rocking the buildings all around them.

"You guys didn't happen to bring any wine down with you, I suppose?" Hunter asked them.

Erx and Berx shook their heads.

"We were hoping you did," Erx said.

"I certainly could go for a belt right now," Berx said.

"Bingo that," Hunter agreed.

More X beams went over, landing deep inside the city. The resulting noise and pandemonium were tremendous.

"This is a real mess we've walked into!" Erx shouted above the commotion. "I've never seen a place so churned up with bodies and bones as that battlefield out there. Are you sure these people have been fighting for only a year?"

Hunter shrugged. "I'm not sure how long it's been," he replied gloomily. "But it can't last much longer. These people don't have a ghost of a chance, whether we're here or not. . . ."

And *that* was the catch.

Sure, they had a huge warship up in orbit, one that was built to carry a small army of X-Forces special operations troops and tons of sophisticated weapons. But because Hunter knew this flight to Zazu-Zazu would be completely unauthorized, they had left all those troops back on Guam 7, holding down the city of Nails. Nearly 350 light-years away.

For this little side trip, it was just he, Erx, and Berx.

"I don't suppose either one of you wants to tell them that it's just the three of us?" Hunter asked his colleagues. "That we don't have anyone else with us?"

"Not me," Erx replied. "I don't have the heart."

"Nor do I," Berx added.

The three men grew quiet for a moment. They knew well the dangers of being in the wrong place at the wrong time— the banishment of Zap Multx and his men to the Ball being the most glaring illustration. But it wasn't like they could just snap their fingers and make this all go away. Qez was facing an entire corps of soldiers plus the colossal tank. It was a hopeless situation—and now they were caught right in the middle of it.

"This was a mistake from the beginning," Hunter murmured.

"We knew a war was going on here. To show up, so unprepared—and going against orders . . ."

He shook his head. He had let personal goals get ahead of his professional duty—with disastrous results. In another place and another time, this would be known as a royal fuck-up.

Berx put his hand on Hunter's shoulder.

"Don't fret, Hawk," he said. "We would have come to this blessed place eventually . . . I think."

Another barrage of enemy fire went over the city.

"Has anyone properly inquired as to how these Nakkz characters were able to build such a behemoth?" Erx asked. "I would have thought that after an extended period of warfare on such an isolated world as this, the technology of the weaponry would have started to devolve, not get better."

"That's so true," Berx said wearily. "If you leave two people fighting each other on a planet long enough, they'll deteriorate to throwing stones at each other. So how did these mooks get to build such a huge weapon as that supertank?"

Hunter just shrugged. It was a good question—one of many.

"Maybe they had help," he said, in an offhand way. "Like those guys who attacked the *BonoVox* had help."

Both Erx and Berx shivered at the thought.

"But help from whom?" Erx asked. "Who would be handing out this kind of superior technology way out here?"

Neither Hunter nor Berx replied. Neither wanted to go there.

Another barrage of enemy fire went streaking over the wall and came crashing down somewhere deep inside the city.

"Why didn't the Zazus evacuate when they had the chance?"

Hunter shrugged glumly. "I can tell by the faces in there, running away just isn't their style. Even if they had the transport out—which they clearly don't."

"But the women, the children, the old people," Berx said, indicating the chaotic city behind them. "Our ship isn't large enough to take even a third of them."

They ducked as another barrage of X beams went overhead. Hunter turned back to them. "You know, it goes without saying that if you two beamed out right now and avoided this whole mess, I wouldn't care a—"

Erx held his hand up and effectively shut Hunter off.

"And it goes without saying that we would never do that," Erx replied. "We are officers in the service of our Emperor. We are here fighting for his interests—sort of. This is our job . . . not that he could ever stay awake long enough to appreciate it."

Another barrage of X beams hit the north wall. This one was particularly powerful—so much so, the entire city began to shake. Worse yet, the sky above them was starting to lighten.

"But we must do something to help these poor souls," Berx said.

Hunter thought for a long moment, then eyed his flying machine still sitting in the middle of the city square.

"Okay," he finally said. "How about this: I'll go after the xarcus. . . ."

Erx and Berx just stared back at him, eyes wide.

"You'll what?" Erx cried.

"Go after that tank . . . *alone?*" Berx pressed.

Hunter put on his crash helmet. "If I can just get inside the thing, maybe—"

Another furious barrage of X beams cut off his words. When they could speak again, Erx shouted to him: "But what should we be doing while you are off on this mad quest?"

Hunter could almost hear the sound of the huge army stirring with the first rays of the dawn. When the light of the very quick day arrived, there was no doubt the Nakkz would finish their attack. And that meant that even if he managed to affect the xarcus, the bloodthirsty enemy would soon be coming right over the walls.

"Under the circumstances," Hunter finally told them as he started off toward his flying machine, "I think it might be time to call for help."

27

Hunter's biggest challenge now was figuring out how much of a running start he would need.

He lifted off from the city square and went into a hover about fifty feet above the battered north wall. It seemed as if the entire population of the fortress city was watching him now, not just the people around the square. From the streets, from windows, from the tops of buildings. Even though the city was under heavy attack, word had spread fast about the strange visitors from outer space who were here to help them. Hunter spotted a handwritten sign on top of one building just off the square. Incredibly, it was a child who was holding it.

It read: *Save Us Angel.*

So much for no pressure, he thought.

He slowly moved out over the wall until he had nothing facing him but the vast expanse of no-man's-land itself. It was now about ten minutes before sunrise. He could see the huge army starting to move below. The xarcus was alive, too, full of blinking lights and discharges of steam. He took a deep breath. The plan in his mind was so bare bones, he would need all the advantages he could get, and then some, if it had a chance of working.

He started his mental noodling. First he guessed the approximate distance from his present position to that of the stalled xarcus. Then he did a quick time-versus-speed calculation, factoring in the circumference of the tiny moon. Then he put his aircraft into a slow 180-degree turn until his nose was pointing in roughly the opposite direction. Then he tightened his seat belt until it nearly cut off his circulation, and he locked his chin strap.

I'll try, kid, he thought.

Then he pushed his throttles to full power and streaked away from the battlefield.

No time elapsed.

None at all. In the same moment that he was hovering above the walled city, he was also setting down atop the main turret of the colossal xarcus, this after going around the tiny moon in the opposite direction.

Hunter still didn't know exactly how he was able to do this; he'd tried similar things since arriving on the Fringe, though not in situations as desperate as this, and it had worked every time. His best guess what that his flying machine could go so fast, he was literally able to arrive before himself—all that was needed was a good running start; thus his trip around the tiny satellite. He was still flesh and blood on arrival; he wasn't transparent or in some other form, but he knew from past experience that he could not be seen. He was simply here, and there, at the same time. And after he got what he wanted here, he would return very quickly to there and if he did this quickly enough, it would seem as if he hadn't even left at all.

Or so he hoped.

He'd been banking on the Nakkz not posting guards at the top of the xarcus. Although he seemed to be invisible during these strange excursions, he'd never really figured if his flying machine seemed that way, too.

Luckily, his hunch was right. There were no guards atop the monster's huge turret when he arrived. He jumped out of his aircraft, quickly took out his quadtrol, set it on "high/ special," and beamed the flying machine into the twenty and six. He inserted the resulting box into his boot pocket and began his woefully improvised mission in earnest.

He carefully made his way to the edge of the turret, and fighting the fierce winds, looked down onto the body of the xarcus. The thing was so huge its control center looked like a small city in itself. The closest thing he could compare it to was the control bubble on a Starcrasher. On the largest ships, these could support five hundred crewmen or more. On the gigantic xarcus, he estimated that at least as many individuals were occupying the control deck.

But then he spotted a smaller bubble behind the larger one. It, too, appeared to be made of superglass, but its surface was tinted a very dark green, so dark he could not see into it. Why could this thing be? Perhaps the *real* control center for the huge tank?

He made a note to find out.

Hunter moved to the center of the turret. The xarcus was half a mile wide; its girth was nearly half that of an L-Class Starcrasher. It needed every inch of that bulk to support the gigantic saw. The blade alone measured at least a quarter mile in length. Its teeth were easily fifty feet or more and extremely sharp. Hanging out about two hundred feet in front of him now, this thing was frightening just to look at. Hunter couldn't imagine what it would be like on the receiving end of its enormous, razor-sharp blades.

His quadtrol told him the entire assembly was made from reatomized steel—this meant it was practically impossible to disassemble, even with an electron torch. This was not good. Hunter was looking for a weak spot in order to somehow disable the massive war machine. The gigantic saw was not it.

He lowered himself down a long ladder, off the top of the turret to the frame of the xarcus below. He was still about twenty stories up and maybe a thousand feet away from the massive control bubble. Again, there were no guards that he could see anywhere on this level. This was no surprise really. With an enormous machine such as this, there was no reason to guard it.

Or so the Nakkz thought.

After some searching around, Hunter finally located an

unlocked hatchway and stole inside the machine itself. At
first the passageway within looked like a crude version of
one found on a Starcrasher. Long, narrow, seemingly endless.
There were dozens of smaller doors running off of it, with
simple illustrations indicating they all led to the machine's
power complex. This would have been a perfect place to look
for a weak link—but there was a problem. All of these doors
were not only locked, they were also melded shut, again with
reatomized steel. Despite Hunter's ability to pick just about
any lock in the Galaxy, one pass of his quadtrol over the
sealed latches told him that not even a blast from his Z-gun
pistol would make a dent in them.

He moved on. This passageway took him past the machine's war room, its officers' barracks, its weapons maga-
zine. All of them had locks made of reatomized steel; all of
them were impossible to break open. He passed a number of
crew members while walking through the ship; technicians
all of them, they were hurrying this way and that, obviously
focused on getting the huge tank moving again.

They could not see him, because for all intents and pur-
poses, he was still hovering over the walled city of Qez. Still,
by studying their faces, Hunter knew that everything the people in Qez feared about their enemy was probably true. Even
the techs looked like they ate newborns for breakfast. Scrag-
gly beards, unkempt hair, dressed in varying shades of
black—they looked like tough customers. Again, this was not
good. When the eggheads in the crew look like they could
chew superglass, what did the combat troops look like?

He found out not a minute later.

He crept up on a section of the passageway that featured
a huge slab of superglass, extending down one whole length
of the hallway. Peering through this glass carefully—Hunter
wasn't sure if he could cast a reflection—he found himself
looking down on a muster chamber so huge, it rivaled the
one aboard the *BonoVox*.

Hunter felt his stomach hit his toes. He was looking on a
barracks that at the moment held about thirty thousand soldiers. There were at least another forty thousand spread out
on the battlefield between the xarcus and Qez. Seventy thousand troops? Against a little more than five thousand de-

fending Qez? This last-ditch battle was more lopsided than he thought.

The sheer number brought up a question that had probably passed the lips of just about everyone connected with the defense of the tiny moon. *Why?* Why so many troops, why these gigantic war machines? Why the outlandish and intentionally cruel weaponry? Why all this—to take over a little rock spinning at the far end of the Galaxy?

Could it be the fact that Zazu-Zazu *was* the smallest thing on the farthest edge that made it so valuable? Was there any way that idea could ever make sense?

Hunter didn't know—and at the moment he knew it was best that he didn't waste brain cells on the matter.

He moved on.

He continued walking the long passageway of the xarcus, looking for but never finding a vulnerable spot at which a bit of sabotage might have crippled the giant war machine. Any doorway that looked important was sporting a reatomized lock. He was sure that only the top officers had access to these places and that they were off-limits to the majority of Nakkz soldiers on board.

If they couldn't get access to them, how could he?

His goal had been to find an Achilles' heel in the gigantic tank. But from all appearances, the xarcus was invulnerable. It had no weak spots.

That is, until he found the green door.

It was strange because it was the only hatchway that was not sealed by a reatomized lock. Hunter came upon it, almost by accident, at the end of one particularly long passageway.

Unlike the rest of the huge tank, this hallway was dimly lit—so much so that when he reached the green door it was practically pitch black inside.

As soon as he touched the frame he knew there was something different about it. It was definitely metal, but it also gave way to the slightest pressure from his fingers. It was malleable, rubberlike—yet some kind of metal all the same.

He was amazed when he touched the bottom of the door with his boot that it partially swung open. He hesitated a moment, trying to estimate exactly where he was inside the gigantic xarcus. He retraced his route to get here; he'd walked a hell of a long way, but he stayed on the upper levels. Then it hit him. If his calculations were right, he was in the vicinity of the smaller, tinted control bubble he'd spotted when he first arrived.

Interesting . . .

The pliable material actually made it easy for him to fully push open the hatch door. Inside he was faced with another passageway, but instead of the straight hallways he'd been walking, this one curved to the left. It was very dark inside, and the predominant color was an odd coral blue. Even the smell inside here was different.

He raised his blaster rifle, an odd gesture for one reason. If he was in fact stuck in time a few seconds behind everyone else, did that mean his blaster wouldn't work? He'd yet to try out that little experiment, to his regret now.

Still, pulling his weapon up to the fore gave him a shot of confidence. He walked slowly down the curving passageway. Its ceiling was a lot shorter than the rest of the tank. There were no doors or windows in here. Every once in a while he would stop and push his hand against the wall. It responded with the same rubbery sensation. He discovered some hieroglyphics written haphazardly along the wall. They seemed to be made up mostly of geometric shapes, possibly a code of some kind, though he couldn't imagine anyone actually being able to understand it.

He kept walking, slowly, silently, his ears open for even the smallest sound.

Then, suddenly, the floor beneath his feet start to move. An immense vibration began shaking the rubbery walls of the dark passageway. At the same instant, noise began to grow from somewhere down below. It got louder and louder and the vibrations became more intense until they joined into one loud wave of ear-piercing noise and bone-rattling motion. It became so acute, Hunter had to throw himself against the soft metal wall just to stay on his feet.

What the hell is happening now? he thought.

Then it hit him.

The xarcus was moving again.

The Nakkz commenced their attack just as the first rays of the sun lit up the horizon.

During the night, the enemy's equivalent to a sapper unit had managed to infiltrate all the way up to the outskirts of Qez and install several combat field replicaters. When first light broke, these devices were activated, producing hundreds of climbing tubes through which the Nakkz were able to reach the parapets on the north wall.

Within seconds the enemy soldiers began shooting up to the top of the wall and flooding over the battlements. Just about every man who could hold a weapon met them here, including Erx and Berx. They were front and center on the parapet, firing their ray guns point blank in the face of every enemy soldier who tried to get over the wall in their sector.

The remaining Home Guards—about three thousand or so—plus militiamen and armed civilians were doing the same thing along the entire quarter-mile stretch of the north-side fortification. The Nakkz seemed to be startled by the size of the makeshift garrison and the ferocity of their defense. And while the climbing tubes essentially shot the attackers straight up to the thousand-foot height of the immense wall, they did need to use their hands to exit the transparent tube—and that's when they proved most vulnerable. A direct ray blast to the head or shoulders of an attacker would usually disintegrate his entire body, letting the subatomic remains be carried away by the fierce morning wind. However effective this tactic was for the defenders, it also cleared the top of the tube and allowed the next Nakkz soldier to pop up.

It was Berx who realized that by doing this, the defenders were playing right into the enemy's hands. The first wave was just to wear them down and deplete their ray gun power supplies.

"We've got to start stickin' 'em!" he began screaming. "Stick 'em! *Stick 'em!*"

The trouble was, there was so much noise and commotion going on, few of the nearby defenders could hear him bellowing, and those who could, didn't know what he was talking about.

So he showed them by example. Transferring his ray gun to his left hand, he drew his electric sword and began skewering the Nakkz soldiers appearing at the top of the tubes closest to him. By running these soldiers through with his blade, he left a gruesome, bloody body, which in turn blocked access to the next soldier coming up.

It was probably the screams of dying Nakkz that brought attention to Berx's idea, for within seconds defenders up and down the ramparts were stabbing the attackers just as quickly as they were shooting them. Soon there were massive amounts of blood flowing down the outside face of the wall.

But still the Nakkz kept coming.

This went on for what seemed like forever. Berx and Erx were leading the charge in slicing every other Nakkz soldier who appeared at the top of the tube, but the sheer number of attackers was beginning to grind the defenders down. Throughout all this, the ghostly image of Hunter's flying machine, its nose pointing away from the battle, hovered not more than fifty feet above them.

More time passed. The bloody battle continued, and the defenders' strength began to ebb. Soon Erx was running out of power in both his ray gun and his electric sword. Berx and many others in their vicinity were as well. And while a run-down electric sword still could be used to kill and maim with some effectiveness, a ray gun without power was useless. Erx had already thrown his away and was now using just his sword and his fists against the attackers. This, too, became extremely draining very quickly. And still the attackers kept coming.

"Are you still sending out the call for help, my brother?" Erx yelled over to Berx as he dispatched a Nakkz soldier with a mighty slash to the man's unprotected throat.

"Loud and clear!" Berx yelled back. He had his quadtrol set on "all points/need help," which sent out a coded SOS message to any Empire ships in the vicinity. The trouble was, they were so far out on the Fifth Arm, the chance of any friendly ship receiving such a message in time was practically nil.

"We must hold them off just a bit longer!" Berx yelled— but the fire was gone from his voice. The Nakkz soldiers were gaining the wall not far down the battlement from them, overwhelming the defenders in that area with a combination of numbers and the failing power supply in the weapons of the Home Guards.

Suddenly there was a huge explosion right below them. Then another off to the right. Somehow Erx and Berx were able to look back over the ramparts to see that Nakkz sappers had blown two huge holes at the base of the north wall. Streams of enemy soldiers were now pouring through the two openings.

"Not good, brother!" Berx yelled to Erx.

"Bingo that!" Erx yelled back.

Another explosion. The wall shook beneath their feet. The Nakkz had now gained an opening in the east wall as well. They were being met there only by wounded Home Guards. The screams of these helpless men being slaughtered echoed throughout the ancient city square.

In the midst of this chaos a young Home Guard soldier stumbled up to Erx and Berx. He was bleeding in too many places to count. His eyes already looked dead.

His lips could barely move, but he mumbled something very chilling to the two explorers in the midst of the hand-to-hand fighting.

"Is your friend ever coming back?" he asked.

With that, both explorers looked up to see that the image of Hunter's flying machine had finally disappeared.

Another huge explosion—but this one came from several miles out on the battlefield, from the xarcus itself. The slumbering giant was suddenly moving again. And so was its enormous saw.

Berx threw two enemy soldiers over the side of the wall and looked down at the battlefield. The waves of Nakkz soldiers looked like a thick cloud of smoke again. Not only were they blanketing the battlefield, even more were pouring out of the rear of the xarcus even as the huge weapon began to creep forward again.

Suddenly a barrage of ray gun fire exploded on the ramparts just behind Erx and Berx. The explorers turned to see that Nakkz soldiers were now climbing up to the top of the wall from the inside of the city just as thousands of their comrades were doing the same thing from without.

Suddenly, just like that, the three thousand or so defenders still alive on the wall were surrounded.

And the xarcus was getting closer.

The first of the Nakkz to reach the wall from the inside were battling Home Guards not a hundred yards away from Erx and Berx now. The situation was so desperate, the defenders were using the butts of their blaster rifles against the X-beam weapons being fired by the enemy.

The two explorers Erx and Berx just looked at each other—and then shook hands. It was the same ritual they had performed so long ago when their ship was in the process of crashing on Fools 6.

"See you on the other side, my brother," Erx told his long-time friend.

"Bingo . . ." Berx replied.

The Nakkz were now swarming up both sides of the wall. The explorers were scavenging among the dead Home Guards, looking for usable ray guns. A huge X-beam blast went off not ten feet away from them. It threw both men hard against the concrete battlement. Another barrage exploded just above them, showering them with nasty subatomic debris. Still another blast went off just on the other side of the parapet. This, too, covered them with subatomic shrapnel. Off in the distance, the xarcus was now just five miles away.

"If there is another side . . ." Erx mumbled to himself.

Then . . . suddenly, it seemed as if the sky itself exploded, it became very dark, almost pitch black. Both men were sure this was the end of the world—or at least their part in it. But then they looked up to see that a gigantic spaceship had appeared over the battlefield. It was an enormous vessel, at least two miles long.

Before either man could say a word, another monstrous spaceship exploded upon the scene. It, too, was gigantic.

Then at the same moment, a soldier in a very sinister all-black uniform was standing in front of them. He'd just popped in. He raised his visor and said: "Relax, you two. Help is on the way."

No sooner were the words out of his mouth than a sonic

ripple went through everything and everybody within a five-mile radius of Qez.

And then everything . . . just . . . stopped.

The xarcus had ceased moving again.

There was no screeching of brakes this time, no stink of metal-on-metal, no half mile of ground churning until its momentum finally eased up.

No; this time it just . . . stopped. As had everything else.

Hunter was still flat against the curving wall, trying to keep his balance when the vibrations that had been so acute suddenly disappeared. One second, everything was shaking so badly he thought the heels on his boots would come off; the next, everything became frighteningly still.

What happened?

He steeled himself and took a step out from the wall, surprised that he was able to maintain his footing. He stopped and listened—there was not a sound coming from anywhere.

He began walking again. Farther down the hallway, he came upon another green door. He raised the barrel of his blaster rifle, then toed the door open . . . and that's when the real trouble began.

He was staring into a very strange, dark, and . . . well, creepy control room. It was cramped, oval-shaped, and stuffed with very odd, almost unrecognizable metallic gizmos that seemed to be alive as well. They were full of tubes and glands, and everything seemed to be pumping and spurting weird liquids. The smell was overwhelming and awful. Sections of the floor seemed to be covered with an equivalent of human vomit. Hunter felt his stomach turn upside down. In his worst nightmares, he'd never imagined a place as disturbing as this.

The second he broke the threshold, he was hit by a bright yellow beam. It struck him with the force of a full-power Z-gun blast. He dropped to the floor—hard. His body began trembling uncontrollably. His bones felt as if they were about to burst right out of him. The screeching in his ears was deafening. He looked at his hands and was astonished to see his veins and muscles and bones clearly through his skin, which was suddenly transparent. He closed his eyes. The pain was unbearable; it felt like he was being ripped in two from the inside out.

But then, not a moment later, everything returned to normal. Or somewhat normal. The intense pain was gone. The screeching in his ears disappeared. He looked at his hands and—thank God!—could not see his bones.

But then he realized something. He was no longer in his one-second-ahead mode; he could tell because he could feel his heart beating again, a sure giveaway. Whatever the yellow ray was, it had not killed him; rather it had knocked him back into regular time. And that meant that anyone he could see on this ship, could see him.

And at the moment, he was looking at about twenty individuals . . . and they were looking right back at him.

They were all wearing black spacesuits, with visors pulled down so it was impossible to see their faces.

They look familiar, Hawk?

He had no idea who these characters were, but if they were inside the xarcus, they were the enemy. So he raised his blaster and sprayed the room with Z beams. He took out two of the black-suited spacemen before any of them had a chance to react. Another blast from his rifle—two more went down. Now the others began moving in many different directions at once. They didn't seem to be running, exactly— *scurrying* would be a better word for it, their stubby arms flapping wildly. Hunter cut down three more. But then the two closest to him raised their hands and simply pointed at him. He hit the deck just an instant before a fusillade of X beams went over his head.

What the hell was that? These guys didn't need weapons to fire X beams?

He popped up over a console and let loose another spray from his blaster. Four more of them went down—but another group pointed their fingers at him, and the X-beam barrage that came back at him was twice as powerful as the one before.

Hunter rolled again, went to his knees, fired, rolled, fired, and rolled again. He did this several times, hitting targets while avoiding the vomitlike pools. The return fire gradually decreased until finally there was none at all. Everything became quiet again.

Hunter slowly got to his feet, his blaster up and ready. Through the murk he discovered that, quite unexpectedly, he'd cornered what might have been the last four of the mysterious spacemen. They were frozen in place, obviously confused or frightened or both. Their hands were up, but were not pointing at him in a threatening manner.

Hunter raised his weapon—and that's when it hit him. He knew when he'd seen types similar to these characters before: flowing out of the Blackship . . . during the attack on the *BonoVox*.

And, it seemed, no sooner did that thought come to his head than the four spacemen turned to each other, raised their hands—and blasted each other into oblivion . . .

And suddenly Hunter was alone in the strange control room.

Or at least he thought he was.

A voice was suddenly in his ear: *Get out, Hawk!*

He was so startled he spun around, thinking someone was standing behind him. But no one was. He was alone.

Was it normal to be hearing voices in one's head?

He didn't know, but this one sounded a lot like Xara. . . . *Get out Hawk . . . now!*

He needed no further prompting.

He sprinted out of the smelly control room, back down the curved, soft-metal hallway and finally through the original green door. He hit this hatchway running, blaster rifle up, quite aware that if he was now back in his time, he would be *very* visible to anyone who would want to take a shot at him.

But he could hear no soldiers running through passageways below. No footsteps, no noise at all. The big xarcus was still frozen in place. Hunter began moving faster—he felt like he was running through a ticking time bomb.

Which was not too far from the truth.

He finally reached the top of the turret.

The wind was not howling anymore, and the morning sun was not blazing brilliantly over his shoulder. In fact, it was almost as dark as night, even though it was still early morning in the supershort day. That's when Hunter realized that two enormous objects had appeared in the sky while he'd been inside the xarcus. They were two huge spaceships; their combined size was enough to block out the sun.

He pulled out his long-range viz-scanner and swept the battlefield below him. That's when he saw an unforgettable sight.

It seemed unreal at first. Everything appeared frozen, as if all time had stopped, which it had in a sense. All of the Nakkz soldiers on the battlefield, in front of the north wall, and even atop the battlements, were not moving, as if they were stuck in place. Yet he could still hear these people screaming, shouting. *Wailing.*

Then it got very strange, for this still life was not totally still. There was a legion of soldiers making their way through the paralyzed Nakkz troops, killing them wherever they stood, either by ray gun blast or electric sword. The enemy soldiers were completely defenseless against this army of newcomers—and these new soldiers were slaughtering the Nakkz with a kind of indifferent efficiency, which made it all the more gruesome.

What was going on here? Who were these new soldiers, and how were they able to freeze the Nakkz in place so they could kill them all at leisure?

Hunter turned his scanner skyward—and there he found his answer.

The ship hanging in the air directly above Qez he recognized as a Series 7 war cruiser, a vessel roughly on par with a Space Forces M-Class ship. It was triangular in design, of course, but significantly different from the comparable SF ship.

But it was the second vessel that finally solved the disturbing riddle for him. It, too, was triangular in shape, but from its outward appearance it didn't seem to be a military vessel at all. Only the bright red bubble just behind its control deck gave it away. He was able to see a faint crimson glow emanating from this bubble that seemed to be encompassing the surface of the tiny, war-torn moon for an area of five miles or so.

Hunter knew immediately what kind of ship this was; he'd seen one just like it in action before, above a planet called Vines 67.

It was a Kaon Bombardment ship.

That's when it all fell into place. The Kaon ship could *freeze time*—to paralyze any opponent on the ground so its accompanying troops could mow them down with ease. That's what happened on Vines 67, and that's what was happening here. Hunter felt a strange sensation in his throat. Sure, this was war, and certainly the people of Qez were fighting for their very existence.

But there was something inherently wrong about how the Nakkz soldiers were being dispatched without having a chance to fight back or maybe even run away. Wasn't there?

That's when another question popped into his head: If everything around him was frozen, why could he still move? Why was he not affected? He had no idea. Did it have to do with the creeps downstairs knocking him ahead in time? Or maybe whatever was allowing the killing angels to move freely through the battlefield was allowing him to remain unfrozen as well?

Or was he still stuck back in the second blue screen of the Earth Race, meaning nothing at all here was real?

Either way, he knew at last the terrible secret behind the Kaon Bombardment ship.

But who exactly was doing all the killing?

He turned his scanner back toward the battlefield below. He keyed in the telelens and zoomed right up to a group of soldiers who were cutting the throats of frozen Nakkz troops like a farmer would cut hay. Closer still, and Hunter could see the insignia being worn by these ruthlessly efficient soldiers.

Two lightning bolts: the sign of the Solar Guards.

I should have known, he thought grimly.

Get off this thing, Hawk . . . now!

This time Hunter didn't question his sanity or wonder just who the female voice in his ear belonged to. His own inner sense was telling him the urgently whispered advice was right-on, no matter where it came from. He had to get off the xarcus.

He took the small box from his pocket, activated the twenty and six, and his flying machine appeared again. He quickly climbed inside and ran his power plant up to full throttle.

That's when an enormous explosion went off right below his feet.

No time passed. None at all.

When the second sonic ripple went through Qez, it happened at the exact same moment as the first.

And just like that, everything started moving forward again.

"Time shifter!" Erx yelled to Berx as soon as they were able to talk again.

Thousands of soldiers had suddenly appeared around them. "Courtesy of our friends the Solar Guards," Berx said bitterly.

They looked around them and saw the results of the horrifying slaughter. Dead Nakkz soldiers were simply everywhere—on the ramparts, hanging halfway off the wall, filling the city square below, covering the trenches out on the battlefield. Everywhere was the smell of new death.

Erx and Berx were stunned. Their lives had been saved, but they were repulsed by the means of their salvation. Some of the Solar Guards who had participated in the operation were standing nearby, cleaning the gore from their electric swords.

Erx grabbed one. "Who is your commanding officer?" he demanded of the man.

The soldier was at first startled, but then a cruel smile spread across his gnarled features.

"Look behind you," was all he said for a reply.

The two explorers turned around and found a man of short stature in a shimmering Solar Guards officer's uniform standing right behind them.

It was Jak Dazz, the Solar Guards' first commander himself.

"Was all this really necessary, Dazz?" Erx screamed at him.

Dazz never stopped smiling. "What do you mean?" he

asked with fake innocence. "You guys were crying for help, weren't you? Why, I picked up the distress call myself."

"But look at what you've done here!" Berx thundered at him. "Some of these men would have surrendered as soon as they saw the Kaon ship above them. You didn't even give them that chance!"

Dazz just shook his head. "You two are getting a bit too old for this game," he said snidely. "It's war . . . you were losing. We came to your aid. And now you're complaining? You're lucky we were in the neighborhood."

"You're always in the neighborhood!" Berx yelled back.

With that, the explorer reared back and struck Dazz with a massive blow to the jaw. The SG first commander went sprawling backward, nearly falling over the railing of the battlement to the bloody city square below. Berx jumped on him and began pummeling him further before a squad of SG soldiers pulled him off their commander. But then Erx joined the fray and a full-blown fistfight broke out. More Solar Guards intervened, and soon Erx and Berx were being restrained.

Dazz picked himself back up and dusted himself off. He gave the signal to his men to let Erx and Berx go.

"Boy, are you guys excitable," Dazz said, calmly lighting up an atomic cigar. "You're getting to be pansies—soon enough you'll be as bad as your weak-kneed cousins in the SF!"

That's what really angered the two explorers. They knew for a fact that in most instances whenever the Space Forces used a Kaon ship, they would concentrate on one particular area and then ask for the surrender of those not involved. Though not without its bloody moments, this was a tactic that usually worked. The Solar Guards, on the other hand, never let such things as gallantry and being magnanimous get in the way of a good bloodbath. That was the major difference between the two rivals.

Both Erx and Berx lunged at Dazz again . . . but before his bodyguards could react, a tremendous explosion rocked the tiny moon—this was the biggest one yet. It was so powerful it sent just about everyone up on the ramparts sprawling—Erx, Berx, Dazz, SG soldiers, and Home Guard survivors.

The blast came from the stalled xarcus. The huge tank seemed to be in its death throes. It was covered with thick blue and yellow flame—the heat was so intense, those on the wall could feel it several miles away. But then, just as it seemed the huge tank was going to self-destruct, something burst forth from its body, ripping a hole in its superstructure, right behind the main control bubble.

It was extremely bright, glowing. It rose unsteadily at first, but then seemed to gain momentum.

"My God! What the hell is that?" Dazz cried out.

The thing was so bright, they couldn't even look at it.

"It's the end of the world!" one of the Home Guards cried out.

Finally the bright light began to move, making it a bit easier to see. It was obviously a spacecraft of some kind—but it was shaped like nothing else ever seen in the Galaxy, at least not these days.

It was shaped like a disc. A saucer. It was bright white. As just about everyone in Qez stared in astonishment at the thing, the disc began revolving at an incredible speed. Then it began ascending, picking up speed with every nanosecond, until it was about a mile above the battlefield.

And then it blinked out.

It took them several minutes to revive Dazz.

The Solar Guards' first commander had fainted dead away almost at the first sight of the strange spacecraft. Erx and Berx were not that far behind him. They had seen many strange things in their long careers of exploration, but never anything like this.

His men finally got Dazz back to his feet, but the man was still very shaky. He barked a bunch of orders to his lieutenants, who began blowing ceremonial battle horns always carried by the Solar Guards in combat. In seconds the SG troopers began popping out, returning to their ship still hovering right above Qez.

"Listen, you two mooks," Dazz said to Erx and Berx, his voice still trembling, belying his gruff exterior, "if you're both smarter than you look, you don't say anything to anyone about what we just saw here. I don't know who was responsible for all this—or why such weaponry was used to conquer a pisshole moon like this—but some things I don't want to know. And neither do you."

With that, Dazz pushed a button on his battle tunic . . . and quickly popped out himself.

Not a minute later, both the Solar Guards' vessel and the Kaon Bombardment ship were gone, leaving the defenders of Qez alone again and safe, for the time being—but also knee deep in at least fifty thousand corpses that were in desperate need of burial.

28

The last time anyone saw Hunter, he was out on the battlefield going through the dead.

After getting off the xarcus just before it exploded and became transformed, he'd returned to Qez, stunned like the rest of them by the strange turn of events. But as startling as these things were, Hunter had something more important on his mind. He spoke extensively with Erx and Berx, who eventually returned to the *AeroVox*. Then he sought out the surviving Home Guard commanders and made one last attempt at trying to ascertain why he'd felt so compelled to come to this lonely moon that he would go against mission orders and all but ruin his brief career as a Starcrasher commander.

He'd sat with Poolinex and his lieutenants, listening to the rather unexciting history of the Zazu-Zazu, how its puffing was leaking away, and how its principal export was a substance called *oppie,* a main ingredient in slow-ship wine. The recounting was going absolutely nowhere until someone mentioned the estimated death toll of the war, a figure that included the number of mercenaries killed during the year-long conflict. When Hunter asked for details about the mercs, Poolinex showed surprise that he wasn't aware of at least one of the groups.

"The ones who stayed with us to the end, you must have known about them," Poolinex had told him. "When you first appeared above the battlefield, you were bombing positions right in front of their lines. You might even have saved a few of them, at least for a while."

Hunter was more astonished than Poolinex upon hearing this news. When Hunter appeared at the scene, he'd started bombing and strafing under no set plan. Rather he'd gone where instinct and eyesight told him to go.

"What was the name of this merc group?" he asked Poolinex.

"The Freedom Brigade," was the Home Guard commander's reply.

Hunter left for the battlefield shortly after that.

He'd spent two hours going through the dead, searching for any survivors of the valiant mercenary group.

Two Home Guard soldiers were on hand, as was the priest. As a hot breeze blew across the plain, the soldiers were reading the roll of names belonging to their longtime allies, intoning each with a touch of reverence.

"Johnson . . . O'Leary . . . Mazzeti . . . Bryant . . . Noonan . . . Ignakowski . . . Carey . . . Cook . . . Baulis . . . Santoro . . . Mann . . . Bell . . . Jones . . . Wilson . . . Murphy . . . Kimball . . . Crabb . . . Fowler . . . Robinson . . ."

These names sounded odd in this world—not one of them ended with a *z* or an *x*. But to Hunter's ears, they sounded strangely familiar—and more like his own name than any other he'd heard since finding himself on Fools 6.

He climbed out of the trench where the brigade had made its last stand and approached the priest.

"These men, Father," Hunter asked him. "I understand they were not natives of this moon."

The priest nodded gravely.

"They came here from afar to help," he said. "They weren't even getting paid. Rather they came because the people here were being attacked and were about to lose their freedom. They came here to protect this tiny rock because that's what they'd done for centuries. And should there ever been any trouble here again, I have no doubt that more of them will arrive, and make the sacrifice this brave men did."

"Why did they first come here, Father?"

The priest let out a long sigh. "A reason lost in the mists of time, I'm afraid," he said. "A legend, a myth . . ."

"Please, Father, tell me what you can," Hunter implored him.

Again the priest sighed. "Several thousand years ago, as the story goes, the brigade's predecessors came here to set up what they called a 'research station.' It was a beacon of some sort, something that was supposed to call all of their lost brothers home again. . . ."

Hunter felt excitement welling up in his chest. *Could this be the lighthouse?*

"Where is this beacon? Where is its location?"

The priest shook his head. "I'm not sure anyone really knows now—it was built here so long ago, and so much time has passed. But it was somewhere on this hallowed ground. This place where the brigade chose to make their last stand . . ."

The priest wiped his tired eyes.

"No one was like them," he said, his voice cracking. "I have provided comfort for many soldiers from many planets—but none were more valiant than they. I only wish I had some of their blood flowing in my veins. . . ."

At that moment, they heard a shout above the wind.

"Padre! *Over here!*"

Several Home Guard medics were going through the bodies about a hundred feet away from the reading of the names.

"We have found one alive . . . but you must hurry!"

Hunter practically carried the elderly priest over the bloody trench to where the three medics had gathered. Sure enough, they were hovering over a man lying prone on the muddy ground.

He was part of the brigade; his green combat suit was a sure sign of this. He was clutching a bloody cloth to his chest. It was clear that he was close to taking his last breath.

It was McKay, the man who had survived the horrendous yet crucial recon mission to Holy Hell; the man who had promised that the brigade would stay in Qez when the rest of the mercenary groups opted to bug out.

The priest immediately went to one knee and began reciting prayers at breakneck speed. McKay was quickly fading from view, not a painless experience.

The priest touched his forehead with a spot of holy oil. That's when the dying man opened his eyes to see Hunter looking down at him. Hunter's strange uniform gave him away.

"So the Empire finally reached the end of the Galaxy?" McKay asked him weakly.

Hunter nodded, then knelt down beside him.

"The bastards," McKay said with a painful laugh. "There are many people back where I'm from that long to see the day the Empire comes crashing down. . . ."

"Can you tell me why you came here?" Hunter asked him.

McKay's voice was barely audible. Hunter leaned down even closer, trying to hear every last word.

"They used to talk . . . about the signal," McKay said. "The legend . . . back where I was from. The call for the brothers. It had gone unheeded for centuries . . . but we were bound by honor to protect this place and the people who lived here . . . so if any of our brothers answered the call . . . this place would be here, with these people. . . ."

McKay coughed hard. Hunter looked up at the attending medics. One of them slowly shook his head.

"The beacon used to sweep the Galaxy and point to the place where we are all called back to," McKay forged on bravely. "If you are hearing the call, my brother, then you must be one of us, too."

He slowly let his fingers unwrap the bloody cloth. Hunter picked it up and unfurled it—and felt a lightning bolt run through his body. The flag was exactly like the one he kept in his pocket. All stars and stripes.

Then McKay indicated a safe bag attached to his belt. One of the medics retrieved it and handed it to Hunter.

McKay gestured for Hunter to reach inside. He came out with a glass globe just big enough to hold in one hand. It appeared at first to be made of superglass; Hunter could see clear through it.

But then McKay indicated that Hunter should hold the globe closer to him. Hunter placed it in front of the dying man's lips. With just about all the energy he could muster, McKay blew on it slightly.

Suddenly the globe came to life. It began swirling with different colors—first reds, whites, and blues, but then mostly blues, with some yellows and greens. Right before Hunter's eyes the glass globe magically became what appeared to be a shimmering blue planet. It seemed at first to be mostly made of water, but then one large landmass became crystallized. Its terrain was green and brown, and there seemed to be many lakes and rivers running through it.

Hunter stared at the holographic image of the planet. He realized that this image most closely resembled the Earth. But not exactly, for its coastlines were irregular, and there were no triads or ancient bridges. There was something else about it—it actually looked *natural*. No jewel-like shine of the Earth, no gleam like Mars, or the scent of manufactured paradise, as on Venus.

No, this place seemed real.

Hunter looked down at the dying man again.

"Where is this planet?" he asked him.

But it was obvious that McKay didn't have the strength to tell Hunter its location.

"It's hidden beyond some forgotten stars," McKay said with a cough. "Ask the padre . . . he can tell you what I mean . . ."

"But what is it called?" Hunter pressed him. "I must get to this place. Can you at least tell me its name?"

That's when the faintest of smiles came to McKay's face.

"Everyone just calls it 'home,' " he said.

It was a rare rainy day over Big Bright City.

Though they had tried, the weather engineers just weren't able to make it pleasant and sunny.

A gray drizzle was falling instead; the streets of downtown looked dull, runny. Empty. No one was about, on the ground or above it. Most of the floating cities had drifted farther to the south to avoid the inconvenient atmospheric conditions.

However, the imperial city Number One had stayed overhead, casting its dull Holy Shadow across most of the old city, making a gloomy afternoon even gloomier.

An air-chevy approached the main entrance to Number One. A squad of guards lazily waved it through. Covered in bulky, seldom-used rain gear, the soldiers didn't even bother to scan the tiny flying car. They were too busy trying to stay dry.

The air-chevy zipped through the main gate, then negotiated the labyrinth of streets and alleyways, finally arriving at a nondescript building about half a mile away from the Imperial Palace.

A lone figure dressed all in black emerged from the air car and hovered unsteadily in the fog enveloping the floating city. No guards were on hand to greet him.

He glided up the back stairway of the building without an

escort, arriving at a hallway where the light seemed dimmer than usual. Again, there were no guards on duty. He slipped down the hallway and reached the huge oak door. He knocked once. Nothing. He knocked again. Still no reply.

He lowered himself to the floor and opened the door himself. The two guards inside were asleep. He went by them silently, and into the next room, where the Empress was waiting for him.

The room was cold. There was no fire in the fireplace. Nor was there an assortment of liquor to choose from. Just a single bottle of slow-ship wine and an unclean glass.

The spy poured himself a drink anyway. Instead of sitting on the couch next to the Empress, he slid into the chair across from her.

"My queen, are you well?" he asked.

She shook her head no, and without further explanation, sipped her wine.

"More bad news?" she asked him.

"You asked to stay informed," the spy told her.

"You're right, I did—I just didn't realize that seeing your face again so quickly would cause such a feeling of gloom."

The spy sipped his drink. "I must serve you, my lady," he replied acidly. "No matter what dark clouds follow me here."

She looked at him queerly. "Have you ever been an actor?" she asked. "Or have you always been a spy?"

The man did not meet her gaze. "Though I'm sure each job has a little of both," he replied, "I cannot imagine an actor making as good a spy as a spy making a good actor."

She sipped her wine again. "What is your latest bad news, then?"

The spy leaned forward a bit. "A disturbing battle on a moon within the Dead Gulch Star System."

"And where in the heavens might that be?"

"As far out in your realm as one can go, my lady. Outer Fringe, the very end of the Fifth Arm . . ."

"And why was this battle so disturbing?"

"Both the Solar Guards and the X-Forces were involved," he replied.

The Empress's eyes went wide. "They fought each other?" she asked, troubled.

The spy quickly shook his head no. "We are not to that point, my lady—not yet, anyway," he said.

"What happened then?"

"An intervention," the spy told her. "The X-Forces became involved initially—that man, Hunter, the winner of the Earth Race. It was his command. His ship. His intervention—though it was totally unauthorized. Apparently something must have gone wrong because the X-Forces made a rare emergency call for assistance. The Solar Guards showed up. With a Kaon Bombardment ship."

He let those last few words hang in the air for a moment.

"It's always disturbing to hear when one of those things is deployed," the Empress said darkly.

"It was a quick, violent engagement once the Solar Guards became involved," the spy said. "They wound up slaughtering an army of mercenaries in five minutes, after those mercenaries spent a year slaughtering half the population of the satellite in question."

The Empress seemed to react to a slight pain in her chest. "What is the death toll?"

The spy shrugged. "In all, approaching a hundred thousand souls. Mostly a warring group known as the Nakkz. The feeling in the neighborhood is that they had it coming."

"Good or bad, they were still *our* subjects," the Empress said with a harsh whisper. "What were these people fighting about?"

The spy just shrugged again. "Who knows?" he answered. "I don't think they even know themselves. But this man Hunter and his X-Forces vessel arrived over the planet at what was a crucial time in their history. How and why they decided to intervene—well, we're still looking into that. The ship has been recalled, of course—the crew will be interrogated."

"And who was the Solar Guards commander who came to the rescue, so to speak?"

"Jak Dazz."

The Empress showed some surprise.

"The top man? So far out on the Fringe? Why?"

"He says he had a premonition of trouble," the spy replied.

"He was in the area and diverted his flight to the planet in question."

"And he just happened to have a Kaon Bombardment ship close by, too?"

The spy nodded. "That's his story, and apparently he's sticking to it."

The Empress drained her glass and rose to pour another.

"And have they found one on this moon yet?"

"One what, my lady?"

She turned and looked at him sternly. "Why be coy now? You know what I mean."

The spy hesitated. "A pyramid, you mean? Not that I know of."

"Just a matter of time," she whispered.

She refilled her wineglass but did not speak for a long time.

Finally she asked: "And this person, Hunter, what happened to him?"

"He's gone, my lady. He left the field of battle in the company of a priest."

She turned and looked at the spy. "You're saying he deserted?"

The spy drained his glass and refilled it as well. "I haven't seen anything to the contrary," he replied.

The Empress sipped her wine again and stared into the cold fireplace.

"Some hero he turned out to be," she said.

PENGUIN PUTNAM INC.
Online

Your Internet gateway to a virtual environment with
hundreds of entertaining and enlightening books
from Penguin Putnam Inc.

*While you're there, get the latest buzz on
the best authors and books around—*

Tom Clancy, Patricia Cornwell, W.E.B. Griffin,
Nora Roberts, William Gibson, Robin Cook,
Brian Jacques, Catherine Coulter, Stephen King,
Jacquelyn Mitchard, and many more!

**Penguin Putnam Online is located at
http://www.penguinputnam.com**

PENGUIN PUTNAM NEWS

Every month you'll get an inside look at our upcoming books and new features on our site. This is an
ongoing effort to provide you with the most
up-to-date information about
our books and authors.

**Subscribe to Penguin Putnam News at
http://www.penguinputnam.com/ClubPPI**